Dead Cadillac

Mike Roche

Resort Readers Publishing

Copyright © 2023 by Mike Roche

This book is a work of fiction. Names, characters, places and incidents are either products of the author's imagination or used fictionally. Any resemblance to actual events, locals, or persons, living or dead, is entirely coincidental. All rights reserved. No portion of this book may be reproduced in any form without written permission from the publisher or author, except as permitted by U.S. copyright law.

Cover design by Stuart Bache and The Books Covered Team

Print Book ISBN: 9798390855256

For Debbie,

The most resilient and courageous person that I know.

Contents

1. Chapter 1 — 1
2. Chapter 2 — 5
3. Chapter 3 — 8
4. Chapter 4 — 11
5. Chapter 5 — 14
6. Chapter 6 — 17
7. Chapter 7 — 20
8. Chapter 8 — 23
9. Chapter 9 — 26
10. Chapter 10 — 29
11. Chapter 11 — 31
12. Chapter 12 — 35
13. Chapter 13 — 38
14. Chapter 14 — 40
15. Chapter 15 — 42
16. Chapter 16 — 45
17. Chapter 17 — 47
18. Chapter 18 — 49
19. Chapter 19 — 52
20. Chapter 20 — 56
21. Chapter 21 — 58
22. Chapter 22 — 61

23.	Chapter 23	65
24.	Chapter 24	67
25.	Chapter 25	71
26.	Chapter 26	73
27.	Chapter 27	76
28.	Chapter 28	79
29.	Chapter 29	81
30.	Chapter 30	83
31.	Chapter 31	85
32.	Chapter 32	87
33.	Chapter 33	90
34.	Chapter 34	93
35.	Chapter 35	96
36.	Chapter 36	98
37.	Chapter 37	101
38.	Chapter 38	104
39.	Chapter 39	107
40.	Chapter 40	110
41.	Chapter 41	112
42.	Chapter 42	114
43.	Chapter 43	117
44.	Chapter 44	121
45.	Chapter 45	124
46.	Chapter 46	127
47.	Chapter 47	132
48.	Chapter 48	135
49.	Chapter 49	138
50.	Chapter 50	142
51.	Chapter 51	145
52.	Chapter 52	148

53.	Chapter 53	155
54.	Chapter 54	157
55.	Chapter 55	160
56.	Chapter 56	164
57.	Chapter 57	167
58.	Chapter 58	171
59.	Chapter 59	175
60.	Chapter 60	177
61.	Chapter 61	180
62.	Chapter 62	182
63.	Chapter 63	184
64.	Chapter 64	187
65.	Chapter 65	189
66.	Chapter 66	193
67.	Chapter 67	196
68.	Chapter 68	199
69.	Chapter 69	201
70.	Chapter 70	204
71.	Chapter 71	210
72.	Chapter 72	212
73.	Chapter 73	217
74.	Chapter 74	219
75.	Chapter 75	222
76.	Chapter 76	225
77.	Chapter 77	227
78.	Chapter 78	229
79.	Chapter 79	232
80.	Chapter 80	235
81.	Chapter 81	237
82.	Chapter 82	240

83.	Chapter 83	242
84.	Chapter 84	245
85.	Chapter 85	248
86.	Chapter 86	251
87.	Chapter 87	254
	Also By Mike Roche	257
	About the Author	258

Chapter One

In the still of the night, Tampa Police Officer Doug Pasley had no idea he was about to tug on a thread unraveling a perilous murder plot. The sleep monster was tapping him on the shoulder, begging him to come join him in the land of slumber. After an early morning court case, Doug finally arrived home. He eagerly anticipated slipping under the cool sheets and into the comfort of his bed. He had not expected the construction of the next-door neighbor's swimming pool would deprive him of most of his necessary sleep for the day.

The shift had become quiet and Doug backed into a spot in the parking lot of the 7-11 on N. Dale Mabry Highway. He glanced at the yet opened Dunkin Donuts, yearning for a donut but knowing his heart was thankful to skip the temptation. Standing tall in his blue uniform, the bright lights and the conversation with the clerk brightened his mood. As he inhaled the robust aroma of the coffee, his senses became intensified as he sipped from the warm, multicolored cup.

Nodding goodbye to the clerk, he walked out to his marked Ford Explorer. As he approached the driver's door, he heard a car alarm sounding off and piercing the quiet night. He paused, listened and thought the alarm sounded like it was coming from the Walmart or Target parking lots down the street next to I-275.

Jumping into the front seat, Doug started the car, placed the coffee cup in the console, dropped the shift to drive and edged up through the parking lot. He rolled down his driver's window to hear a car accelerating towards his location.

With minimal traffic on the road at 3:00 am, Doug hoped that the speeding vehicle was associated with the auto alarm. This would provide some excitement and entertainment for the early morning hour. Easing through the parking of the adjoining Marathon gas station, he eased the patrol car onto Spruce Street. Keeping his headlights switched off, Doug crept up to the intersection of Dale Mabry Highway. With both windows down, he listened like a silent cat waiting on its prey.

As a bright blue Kia Sportage SUV approached his location, Doug watched the lonely car approach the intersection. The two drivers stared at each other. Doug's eyes narrowed as the driver of the Kia's eyes widened. With a green light, the Kia hit the gas. Off to the races.

Turning on his headlights and overhead LED lights, Doug engaged the siren. He mashed on the gas pedal and felt the Explorer jump to life. Doug could feel the engine respond as he angled across the intersection.

The two cars sped north on Dale Mabry Highway as Doug picked up his microphone. "Edward 3 in pursuit northbound Dale Mabry Highway. A bright blue Kia Sportage possibly involved in an auto burglary in the vicinity of the Walmart parking lot at Dale Mabry and I-275. We just crossed Spruce Street. Approaching Walnut Street."

The dispatcher responded, "10-4 Edward 3. Any unit in the area that can assist?"

"Edward 3, turning eastbound on Walnut Street. Approaching Himes Avenue. Vehicle is slowing, turning northbound on Himes." Doug no longer needed the coffee in the console as both hands gripped the steering wheel tightly. He glanced at the speedometer and saw they were approaching 80 mph. He looked up and was thankful they had a green light as they crossed the major intersection with Columbus Drive.

As the speed now increased to 90 mph, Doug's focus narrowed to the car in front of him. He knew in his mind that no one runs from the police at this speed without being guilty of some criminal act. He hardly noticed Raymond James football stadium to the left as he updated his location.

"Edward 3, slowing down as we are approaching MLK Boulevard. He is turning eastbound on MLK. Eastbound on MLK approaching the Buccaneers' training camp. He is slowing down, turning north into Tampa Bay Corporate Park. He just pulled off the road, he's bailing. In foot pursuit."

Dropping the microphone, he stomped on the brake. Doug jumped out and yelled, "Stop!"

The suspect ignored the command and ran around the car onto the grass. Doug knew he would have trouble keeping up and catching the much younger and athletic-looking young male. The youth slid down the sloping grass and made a splashing entry into a pond choked with a border of lily pads.

Doug watched with surprise as the suspect began swimming. The experienced officer knew better than to go into a murky pond in darkness in a futile attempt to catch the suspect. Loaded down with 30 pounds of equipment, Doug would've struggled to swim 50 feet.

Keying his hand-held mike, the surprised officer said, "Edward 3, the suspect is swimming across the retention pond in this corporate park, heading towards the helipad of St. Joseph's Hospital. Can you alert their security? We also need any additional units to head to that location and another on MLK bordering the lake."

Watching like a disappointed spectator at not being able to give chase, Doug watched the youth stroking across the wide pond. He shined his flashlight across the dark pond and yelled at the fleeing suspect to stop. To no avail. The suspect was not an accomplished swimmer and would never be confused with a stealthy Navy SEAL operator. Doug listened to the slapping and kicking of the water.

The youth gave a sudden scream and yelled, "Help me!"

Doug watched as the swimmer's progress was halted and he continued to hear, "Please help!"

As the swimmer struggled to keep his head above water, Doug heard the youth's last words, "Alligator!"

The swimmer's head disappeared below the surface, as the roiling water was the last evidence of his existence. Doug moved the beam of his flashlight in the direction where the swimmer had been. All he could see was the water disturbance and bubbles. Keying up his microphone again, he said, "Disregard the units going to St. Joe's. Contact Fish and Wildlife Service. I will need a gator trapper out here. The suspect has been attacked by an alligator, and I see no signs of life. Start me a supervisor and notify detectives."

Doug looked to his right as he watched his backup unit pull into the darkened private drive to the corporate park. Their emergency lights, still flashing along with Doug's lights, bounced off the glass buildings like a light show at a concert. The unit pulled up in front of the blue Kia. Officer Eddy Croissant stepped out of his marked vehicle and extended his arms and said, "Doug, what the fuck have you gotten into?"

"An absolute shit storm. I think he probably broke into a car down at Walmart or Target and had no intentions of stopping. But I did not know that he would jump into the pond and try to swim across. He probably should've paid more attention in science class, realizing almost every body of water in this state has a resident alligator. With his terrible swimming technique, he was all but ringing the dinner bell. Poor kid didn't stand a chance. If you don't mind, just keep an eye on the pond. I haven't seen anything since the bubbles. I'm going to check his car."

Walking over to the Kia, Doug lowered his tall frame and stuck his head inside the car. The car reeked of the acrid odor of marijuana. There was a sandwich size baggie in the console with the green leafy material. A woman's purse was on the floorboard of the passenger side. A USB cable was dangling from the where the push to start button once was located. He knew that the Kia and Hyundai cars were popular models targeted by auto thieves.

He walked to the rear of the vehicle and provided the license plate number to the dispatcher. Doug expected the response that he received from the dispatcher. The vehicle had been reported stolen the day before by an Andrew Singleton in South Tampa. This was why he had run. Driving a stolen car will make you do that.

Opening the passenger door, Doug rooted through the black Michael Kors handbag. He found identification to Sylvia Black. Doug knew Sylvia was not the suspect who had become gator bait. His phone rang. It was Sergeant Drabinak, who told Doug that they had found a car with the window smashed in at the Walmart parking lot. The car was registered to Sylvia Black. Doug updated Drabinak on what happened and said that he had no identification on the suspect. He now had to await the gator hunter as he traded war stories with Croissant.

Chapter Two

Looking across the large pond, Doug could see a patrol SUV parked by the helipad of St. Joseph's Hospital. Ed Croissant, his arms folded with a smirk hidden under his mustache, was keeping Doug company. It seemed like half the midnight shift of the police department had swung past like tourists to a museum. The hours before dawn were often quiet and when an exciting call went out on the radio, it was like moths to a lightbulb in the dark. There was nothing to see, only a dark pond.

Headlights from a black Dodge Ram pickup truck pierced the darkness and the sound of the Hemi V-8 engine throttled up the driveway. The boat trailer being towed behind the truck banged across the apron of the driveway. The driver parked the truck behind Doug's car.

Mike "Cajun" Guidry slid out of the cab of the truck. He reached into a pack of red man chewing tobacco with his fingers, taking a pinch and placing the tobacco inside his lip. He gave a quick spit and looked at the two officers and said, "Howdy, someone called for a gator hunter?"

"Yes sir. We had a car thief who became a runner, then a swimmer, and not a successful swimmer. A gator took a hold of him and pulled him under." Doug said.

"Well, alligators don't naturally feast on humans. Being dark and hearing him thrashing about probably raised the alarm. He may have confused it with it being a deer or something similar. Regardless, it's a horrible way to die. With larger prey, the alligator pulls the victim under the water and goes into a death roll, and it's the drowning that kills. He may have taken a chomp or two, but this is like a seven-course meal. So, he will save most of this poor boy to snack on over the next day or two. They are prolific hunters and one study showed that they commonly eat every two hours."

Doug said, "Well, we can't send in the dive team until we get the gator. Can you get him?"

"Oh yeah. I can get him. It's just a question of how hungry he is, and how patient we are. And hopefully it's just the one, and he is alone. One thing I will need is to put an end to all the excitement. We need to kill all these pretty lights and turn down your radios. Gators are bashful in that way."

Doug slapped the mosquito on his arm and said, "No problem. We can get that done."

Guidry pulled out a can of bug spray, offered it to Doug, who declined and then Guidry began spraying it around his neck.

Doug asked, "What kind of bait are you using?"

"Got me some beef lung here. Tends to be bloody, and it floats. It's easier to smell on the surface and the gator can find it. It's attached with a wooden peg with a two-foot leader of 400-pound monofilament line with the swivel."

The officers watched the alligator hunter as he backed the trailer through a curb cut for a crosswalk and onto the grass. Guidry untethered the metal boat and slid the boat into the water. Sliding wellies over his feet, Guidry pushed the boat into the shallow water. He jumped into the small metal boat and pushed away from the bank.

As the boat drifted away from the shoreline, the cops moved closer as eager onlookers of the hunter. Guidry turned on an electronic gator call, hoping to entice a reciprocal grunt from the target gator. There was no response.

Guidry turned on a spotlight and scanned around the bank of the pond, scanning for the protruding snout or eyeballs of the alligator. He re-started the gator call and finally heard the gator bark. Turning towards the sound, Guidry fired up the trolling motor and steered the boat in the general direction of the grunt.

When he got to about fifty feet away, he stopped the trolling motor. Picking up the long fishing pole with the beef lung bait, he thrust with his upper body. The bait sailed through the night air and splashed in the water. Hopefully close enough to entice the gator to investigate. He started the trolling motor once again and backed out as he spooled out the line. He moved about 100 yards away from the floating bait.

After approximately five minutes, the stealthy hunter snapped out of the water, spearing the bait in one gulp. Guidry continued to allow the line to run while the alligator consumed the beef lung. Once Guidry knew the alligator had swallowed the bait, he began winding in the line along with moving the boat in that direction.

The experienced hunter continued to reel in his prey until the reptile was next to the boat. Once he had the alligator next to his boat, he struck the alligator just behind the skull with a bang stick. This pierced the brain with a .44 Magnum bullet and ending the life of the menacing killer. Guidry tossed in a small grappling hook to pull the gator into the boat. Grabbing a roll of electrical tape, he wrapped the snoot closed, and thus eliminating hazard of the sharp teeth.

Guidry fired up the trolling motor and headed back to the shoreline with its waiting audience. As he pulled up to the shoreline, he hopped out of the boat and gave it a last tug on to the grass.

Doug whistled and asked, "What size?"

"Probably ten feet and around 300 pounds. I didn't see any other activity in the pond. I would wait until daylight before you send your divers in. With the bank covered in lily pads, it makes a perfect hidey hole for gators."

"Well, thank you, Mr. Guidry, for the quick response. I appreciate it and we will let our dive team know. Thank you."

"I'll take the gator for necropsy to empty the stomach contents."

They watched as Guidry pulled the boat back up on the trailer, leaving the dead alligator in the boat. Doug was the first, but not the last, officer to have a trophy picture taken alongside the reptile inside the boat. Their social media feeds would be active with the catch.

Guidry picked up his spit cup, gave a wave to the officers and jumped into the cab of his pickup truck. The throaty engine barely yawned as he pulled the trailer and the 300-pound prize in the boat. The officers watched the red taillights disappear into the darkness. Doug turned his overhead lights on again so that others responding, including the on-call homicide detective, could find them more easily.

Chapter Three

Detective Kate Alexander pulled into the drive in her black Toyota Camry. She stepped out of the car and looked back to her right across the pond at the silhouette of St. Joseph's Hospital as the sun was just beginning to greet the day.

She walked towards Doug and said, "What kind of goat rope have you got me into this time, Doug?"

Doug grinned widely. "A massive goat rope. Except this time, it involved an alligator."

Kate shook her head as she listened to the details that had transpired over the previous couple of hours. She leaned in as Doug shared pictures of the alligator laying in Guidry's boat. Kate and Doug turned as the Ford Expedition carrying the dive team arrived and parked behind Kate's Camry.

Kate said, "So, in simple terms, we have an unidentified young male who, while driving a stolen car, broke into an unattended vehicle, stole a purse, and was then killed by an alligator while trying to evade the police?"

"You could've been Sherlock Holmes."

"Douglas, you are extremely perceptive. So, once we have the suspect identified, the D-1 detectives can exceptionally clear the auto theft and an auto burglary by the death of the suspect. So, unless he had an accomplice, which does not appear to be the case, I would say homicide does not have a case. Since I'm already up this early, it's too interesting not to stick around to see what happens. Pass the popcorn."

Doug walked over to the dive team and brief them. Kate watched as the streetlights extinguished and the sun was fully raised above the hospital in the eastern sky.

Confident that they could see into the murky pond during the daylight hours, they began strapping on their equipment.

With keen interest, Kate watched as the two divers waded through the bank of plants into the pond. Kate yelled, "Gator! Watchout!"

The two divers froze for a moment and looked around. One diver, Corporal David D'Agresta dressed in all black, gave a middle finger salute. All the officers had a good laugh. Eventually, as the divers stepped out further through the clearance of lily pads, they submerged, leaving a trail of bubbles on the surface. She could see the divers swimming just below the surface of the water as their fins left a small wake.

The thick chested and fit, Sergeant Dennis Drabinak joined the officers. They all stood intently watching as the divers went about their business searching for the body of the suspect. Kate contemplated that earlier in the evening, the suspect was enjoying life, albeit a thieving life. He did not know that within hours, he would become the victim of a horrendous death. Kate also knew that this unidentified young man was the son of a mother and father and perhaps a sibling. His family would be left grieving his untimely death.

David D'Agresta came to the surface and swam back to the entry point. He removed the regulator from his mouth and said, "We found him. Hey Eddy, could you toss me the underwater camera from the left front seat?"

After Ed Croissant handed off the camera, the diver once again submerged.

After photographing the position of the body under the surface of the water, they then guided the body to the bank of the pond. They pulled the young black male onto the grass. His jeans were torn and bloodied, his face absent of life.

Kate crouched down next to the body with her hands encased in black rubber gloves. Searching his pants, she removed his wallet from his back pocket. Peeling open the wet leather wallet, she removed his driver's license. She read the license and said, "John Nunez."

Croissant spoke. "Johnny Nylon! That's his street name. It traces back to whenever he was doing a criminal act. He would pull a nylon stocking over his face. I think he had watched one too many heist movies. That became his trademark and worked to his disadvantage. So, every time we would hear that the suspect was wearing a stocking, we knew it was that fucker, Johnny Nunez, a.k.a. Johnny Nylon. I arrested him once before for burglary when he was still a juvenile."

"Me too," said Doug. "It's a shame. His mother and sister are good people and have tried to get him to fly straight. But it's in his DNA. His daddy is doing a long stretch in the Starke Penitentiary."

Croissant said, "You know how McGruff the Crime Fighting Dog is taking a bite out of crime? Well, that gator chomped a bite out of crime. Johnny was headed for a tombstone. It was just a matter of time. Sad outcome."

Kate said, "Okay, I've got his address. I'll make the death knock. And you can have the D-1 detectives finish up here. Once the medical examiner shows up, they can take the body for an autopsy. We all know the cause of death was drowning caused by the alligator. It doesn't look like the wound itself in the leg was enough for him to bleed out, but that will be up to the medical examiner to determine. Doug and Eddy, as always, it's great to see you guys. Let me know if anything else comes of this."

Waving goodbye to the officers, she jumped into the driver's seat of her Camry. Kate reached down and took a sip of coffee from her travel mug. She was surprised when she tasted the robust flavor and found it was still warm. The air conditioner was a welcome treat. Despite the sun making a grand entrance into the day, the air was heavy with humidity and warm. Her dashboard read 76 degrees, and she knew they were headed to the low nineties.

Chapter Four

While preparing to make another death notification, Kate sadly thought of the potential contributions that Johnny could've made had he chosen a different path. Instead, he followed in his father's felon footsteps and was destined for failure and his ultimate death.

Experiencing a death notification first hand, Kate showed as much empathy and humility as possible to the surviving family. She knew the family would somehow have to come up with the financial means to pay for the unexpected funeral services of their loved one. Hopefully, they would be comforted with the memories of better times.

Kate parked at the curb in front of the modest home. The patch of green making up the front yard was consumed with weeds. The Dodge in the carport looked abandoned, listing to the left with two flat tires. An older maroon Ford Taurus parked behind the Dodge appeared to be their primary means of transportation.

Smelling bacon, Kate wondered if breakfast would be ruined by her visit. Her own stomach churned, and she contemplated if that was because of the 4 AM protein bar or the nervousness of telling a mother she would never see her son again.

She rang the doorbell and saw a pleasant looking black woman drying her hands with a dish towel walking towards the door. Kate hoped there would not be a language barrier with the Hispanic surname.

Mrs. Nunez answered the door with a mixture of a smile and puzzlement as she tilted her head slightly to the right. Kate identified herself and asked if she could step inside. Mrs. Nunez's face had now changed to concern.

Kate said, "Mrs. Nunez, I'm terribly sorry to have to tell you that your son, Johnny, was found just a short time ago in a retention pond near Raymond James Stadium. It appears that he drowned."

Mrs. Nunez dropped the dishtowel as the hand moved to her neck like she was guarding against an assault. Her other arm embraced her midsection as her head shook from side to side. A keening howl erupted from her mouth. She collapsed to her knees and continued to scream.

Lowering herself to one knee, Kate put her arm around Mrs. Nunez. A female in her twenties with a towel wrapped around her head appeared from the rear of the house with urgency. Her face was engulfed with panic, knowing that bad news had just been delivered. She asked if it was concerning Johnny, as if she already knew the answer. Kate nodded and stood up as Johnny's sister took the position of consoling her mother.

After several minutes, Mrs. Nunez finally regained composure as her daughter guided her to the beige sofa. Kate surveyed the interior of the home, and despite the appearance of the outside, the inside was immaculate.

Kate explained Johnny had been running from the police while driving a stolen car, which contained evidence of goods stolen from another car. After stopping the car across from the Buccaneers' training facility, he jumped out and dove into a pond to swim away from the officer. It appears he tired and drowned in the middle of the pond. Kate felt it was best to leave out the alligator's involvement, figuring Mrs. Nunez was suffering enough trauma. Mrs. Nunez continued to sob as she listened to Kate.

Kate knew what was going through the mind of Mrs. Nunez. A child that she had nurtured in her womb for nine months and watched grow was gone. Life's milestones would remain unachieved. Kate knew firsthand the emptiness and despair that Mrs. Nunez was feeling.

Mrs. Nunez finally spoke and said, "He was a good boy growing up. Kind and helpful. He was smart as a whip and had great potential, like his sister Adriana." She broke eye contact with Kate and looked admiringly at her daughter, and gave a weak smile. "When his father was sent off to the penitentiary, it left a void in him. I think he felt he needed to live up to the image that his father had in this neighborhood. He embraced the felon life. Instead of wanting to feel loved in the neighborhood, he wanted to be feared. I tried. Working two jobs and trying to keep him in church. He stopped going to school, staying out all night with a bad crew and sleeping most of the day. I was afraid this day would come."

"As a single mother, I can relate to your hardships. All we can do is try to be positive influencers and pray they become successful. Johnny made poor decisions and took the wrong path in life. It's obvious that you tried to provide a loving and nurturing home. You should have no regrets. But I know the demons will come to visit. If only I had done this or that, perhaps he would still be alive. You cannot think like that. It's obvious that Adriana followed the path that you set."

Mrs. Nunez nodded and again looked over at Adriana. "She is an honor student, sings in the church choir, while carrying a full load at Hillsborough State College. She is also working at the Dollar Store and helps at the house. I tried my best."

"I know."

Kate explained the process that would take place. The body would be transported to the Hillsborough Medical Examiner's Office for an autopsy and, within a few days, his body would be released. They will have to make arrangements with a funeral home to collect Johnny Nunez. Kate gave her card to Mrs. Nunez and offered her condolences.

Once outside in the bright sun, Kate sighed heavily. She understood the burdens that Mrs. Nunez had experienced. With a father doing a long stretch in the penitentiary, Johnny had indeed embraced the thug's life. He assumed the life of Johnny Nylon, the most feared criminal, in West Tampa. She knew the sense of failure that Mrs. Nunez must be feeling.

Chapter Five

Ali Azar massaged his chin and felt his naked face. His prideful beard was gone. A victim of blending in with the locals. His deep-set brown eyes looked out through the window of the descending aircraft as he looked at the green fields below. It reminded him of a bed quilt sewn of patches. His mind reminisced about his childhood growing up in Galesh Khil, a small rural town of five hundred people in the lowlands of Iran. The town was twenty-five kilometers to the Caspian Sea and over three hundred kilometers to the capital city of Tehran.

As the plane's landing gear grabbed the runway, Ali felt the jolt and the tug of the seatbelt, as he lurched forward. The Airbus jet slowed to a taxiing speed. Ali became more excited as he contemplated the mission goals ahead of him, which he knew would be successful.

As the jet taxied towards the terminal of Guarani Airport, Ciudad del Este, Paraguay, Ali looked over at his two teammates. Bakhtiar wore a scowl on his muscular face. Every pore emanated arrogance and smugness. Ali's lips tightened with contempt. His gaze moved towards the younger Firouz, who showed the eagerness and excitement of a young child going to the parade.

Bakhtiar looked towards Ali, who gave a head nod and averted his gaze outside the window. He knew for the sake of this mission that he would have to dismiss his lack of respect for the team leader. Everyone knew Bakhtiar had only been selected for this mission because of his political connections through his father and uncle. He certainly had not earned his spot through his accomplishments. Despite rising to the rank of major in the Quds Force of the Iranian Islamic Revolutionary Guards Corps, he had spent most of his time sitting behind a desk. He had little time being tested in the field.

Ali thought of his own accomplishments in Syria and Iraq. He should lead this assignment. He would have taken the place of most people like Bakhtiar, who should lack in confidence in their untested abilities. However, Bakhtiar's ego could fill up the cargo hold of this airplane and he felt at ease ordering subordinates to conduct his dirty work. On the other hand, Ali enjoyed the energy and exuberance of Firouz. Despite his inexperience, he was a willing student and an accomplished linguist. He was also a loyal follower of the regime.

The plane came to a stop and the seatbelt light was turned off. All three men stood up and opened up the overhead bins, pulling out their backpacks. They looked to the front of the plane to see Mohammed, their facilitator, give a head gesture to come forward. Wearing a headscarf, the flight attendant opened up the door as the stairs were rolled by the ground crew towards the opening.

The cabin door opened and the pilot and copilot stepped out, giving handshakes to the four passengers on the airplane that normally carried over 100.

The captain said, "Good luck, my brothers. Inshallah."

Nodding in respect, they returned the Islamic greeting of God willing. Descending the stairs, Ali immediately felt the slap of hot, humid air. He came to the understanding that it would be a long time before he would feel the dry heat of the Middle East again.

At the base of the stairs, a white transit van pulled up to the group. A twenty-something year old driver jumped out with the energy of a mountain goat and said, "I am Mahmood. Welcome to Ciudad del Este."

Bakhtiar looked around and then looked at Mahmood with indifference and said, "Where is everyone else?"

"I am here to take you there."

"I'm surprised no one else came to greet us, considering the importance of our arrival."

Ali interrupted and said, "Did you expect a welcoming party with a band? We are here covertly and trying not to draw any attention that hasn't already been brought by this airplane." As Ali pointed to the Mahan Air Airbus with the green decorated tail art.

Bakhtiar gave a dismissal wave and gestured to Mahmood to collect their backpacks and load them into the van. Mahmood, despite his diminutive size, picked up two bags at a time and hoisted them with ease into the cargo area of the van. The four passengers climbed into the rear of the van as Mahmood shifted into drive and sped away from their last connection to Iran.

As they drove out of a gate from the airport, Mahmood guided the van onto the Airport Access Road through an agricultural area. They turned left on Doctor José Gaspar Rodríguez de Francia. The occupants stayed quiet as the van drove past various businesses and farms. The ride from the airport was disappointing.

Looking outside the window of the van, Ali watched as the landscape slowly changed from rural agriculture to an urban shopping area populated with electronic stores, cellphone merchants and clothing shops. The streets became more congested and narrow with both vehicle and pedestrian traffic.

The neatness of the agricultural community was now replaced with the grittiness of an urban shopping destination. The sounds of the commercial area were permeated with the whine of the motorcycles' engines as they zipped between the gridlock of cars and horn honking trucks, ferrying passengers and goods.

Known as a cheap shopping mecca, the border town of Ciudad del Este, Paraguay sat in an area known as the Tri-Border area of Brazil, Paraguay, and Argentina. Most people referred to it as the TBA. If you were looking for counterfeit goods and cheaply made products, Ciudad del Este was your destination.

It was often referred to as the wild west. With very weak banking laws, being a poor region, corruption was engrained and criminal activity often ignored. The economy of the city was fueled by an abundance of criminal inspired commerce.

It was also the melting pot of terrorist groups sharing tradecraft. There was some presence of the Columbian FARC because of drug trafficking. There was also a presence of the Brazilian and Russian Mafias, along with Hong Kong criminal groups retailing pirated software from China. However, it was Iran that was the biggest player, with arms and a hundred million dollars flowing through the area.

Ciudad del Este was a stronghold for Shia Muslims, who were immigrants or descendants of southern Lebanon. Many had strong affiliations with Iran and sympathizers to Hezbollah, the Party of God, and avowing the extermination of Israel. Ten percent of Hezbollah's budget was generated by operations in the TBA.

The van carrying the operatives pulled up to the curb and as the foursome stepped out of the van, Ali could hear the whistle of the nearby traffic cop. Shoppers walked down the middle of the street carrying plastic bags filled with their booty. The sidewalks were consumed with vendor booths selling suitcases, sunglasses, and clothing. The dirty narrow street looked closer to a wide alley littered with garbage near the curb.

Wiping the beads of perspiration forming at his temples, Ali assessed his surroundings as his mind drifted to the historic Grand Bazaar in Tehran. He crinkled his nose in distaste of the trash and cheapness of his current view. They gathered their belongings and followed Mahmood.

Chapter Six

Carrying their backpacks, they entered the Jebai Center, formerly known as Galeria Uniamerica and, oh yeah, was formerly known as Galeria Page Mall. The name changes could never change the illicit reputation of the two-story narrow older mall. With beige tile and a twelve-foot-wide passageway, Ali felt confinement as they passed shops compacted next to each other. If you were looking for fountains and ambiance, this was not your shopping destination. It was built as a no-frills experience for cheap or counterfeit goods.

They entered a store with an Arabic sign next to another sign reading la Electronica. The inside was cluttered with various consumer electronics. The regional command post for the Hezbollah criminal enterprise was operated out of the store.

As the four Iranians were escorted into the store, a young couple was perusing the merchandise. The Lebanese salesclerk, who was as thin as a palm tree and a bushy head, stood and spoke in Spanish, telling the couple the store was closing. Initially confused, the couple did not argue and departed. The salesclerk pulled down the rolltop door.

Another Lebanese salesclerk with thinning hair and a well-fed face to match his round stomach stood up from his stool with an enormous smile of recognition. He greeted Mohammed with a traditional Lebanese embrace of three alternating kisses on the cheeks. The familiar man was introduced as Hassim as he shook the hands of Ali, Bakhtiar and Firouz. He said, "May peace be upon you."

Ali thought this Hassim would never be confused with being a skilled operative. He watched as the man drew hard on a cigarette and expelled a cloud of smoke. He looked like a lamb meatball with feet and winded despite being motionless.

Hassim explained the details of the logistics for their travels from Paraguay. He provided a detailed briefing on the operation. Ali had heard it all before. He was bored. He knew the plan backwards and forwards. They had trained for months. He was ready to be done with these imbeciles. He looked around the store. They couldn't be bothered to dust their product displays. Attention to detail. No pride.

Handing them three cellphones and each a large manila envelope that was sealed, Hassim instructed each man would be responsible for his individual envelope in case they became separated or caught. The envelopes were not to be opened until they reached their contact at their final destination. Each of the three operators slid the envelopes into their especially constructed Yeti Panga waterproof backpacks. Guaranteed to be a 100% waterproof.

At the conclusion of the meeting, Hassim wished them good luck in the blessing of Allah and success on their mission to strike at the infidels. The operators bid farewell and waited for the palm tree looking store clerk to lift the rolltop door. He motioned for them to stay while he stepped out into the shopping mall to survey the surroundings. Ali was told that intelligence agencies monitored the Lebanese stores. Palm tree gave an approving nod that all was clear.

Known to be fundraising for Hezbollah, the Lebanese shopkeepers were aware of periodic monitoring. Prior to 9/11, Hezbollah was responsible for more American deaths than any other terrorist organization. They had been directly involved in large-scale attacks against U.S. Military in Lebanon. In one bombing attack against the U.S. Marine Corps barracks, over four hundred Marines were killed. There had been rumors of training camps being operated by the Hezbollah in the jungles of the TBA. The Lebanese shopkeepers could not be too careful, especially at the risk of such a huge operation being compromised.

Mahmood drove the four operators the short distance to their hotel. The blazing red and white lettered sign announced their overnight lodging. The Hotel Tresde, which was an austere but clean and comfortable hotel. They would rest here for the night and embark on their journey the next morning.

As the group awakened for the last time from a proper bed, darkness still gripped the horizon. They walked a block away to the morning prayers at the Mezquita del Este. The mosque dome was guarded by two prayer towers. The house of worship was surrounded by a fence and the entrance stairs were a pathway to nine archways sitting under the dome.

He watched many of the morning worshippers arriving with their well-groomed beards. His face still felt irritated by the shave this morning. He rubbed his face as if that would make his beard return.

Ali contemplated his life's achievements to this point in time. He was a decorated veteran with a list of accomplishments in classified covert operations. He knew this mission could be the most dangerous he'd undertaken, and he prayed for the strength, endurance, and wisdom necessary for its successful completion.

The fingertips of sunrise were gripping the horizon as the morning prayers concluded. Mahmood escorted the four to his waiting van. He drove through the mostly empty streets as some shopkeepers had begun setting up their booths.

Pulling up to the gate at the Guarani Airport, Mahmood gave a head nod to the guard. The man wearing a disheveled uniform quickly opened the entryway. Mahmood drove the van out onto the tarmac to meet an idling Citation Longitude sleek white jet. Although much smaller than the previous Airbus commercial flight, the Citation was adorned in luxury as they set down in smooth brown leather captain's chairs.

Ali watched out the window as Mahmood drove towards the exit gate and the pilot pulled up the stairs and closed the door. A few minutes later, the Citation catapulted down the runway and screamed into the skies. Cruising at over 600 mph, the jet made its way to Nicaragua for its first and only stopover to replenish their fuel. Everyone remained on board to avoid any prying eyes.

As they once again descended through the clouds towards the Piedras Negras Aeropuerto Airport in Mexico. Ali looked across the cityscape as he felt the landing gear being lowered in anticipation of their landing. From pictures that he had seen, the town could be mistaken for California, but with the tallest building being a church steeple. The plane jarred as it impacted with the ground and the brakes applied to the landing gear.

Stepping off the plane, Mohammed bid them farewell. He provided a final warning that the federal police were housed in a building directly across the street from the airport and to avoid acting suspiciously. The team of three were now on their own and would be for the rest of their trip.

Chapter Seven

Departing on foot, the three soldiers traversed several blocks to the Universidad Politecnica de Piedras Negras. Housed in a white two-story nondescript building with a maroon stripe, most of the students and staff of the university had departed for the day. Ali noticed a few students sitting at a table and appeared to be studying. He wondered what contributions these students might make in this world. Or would their academic success lead them to a less illustrious path or perhaps criminal activity?

As detailed in their logistics, they located three bicycles that had been chained together on the backside of the soccer field. Gray, black and green bikes. Simple discount bikes as to not draw attention and not desirable enough to be stolen. They would not need them long.

Bakhtiar removed a key from his pocket and unlocked the padlock that was attached to the chain, locking the three bicycles together. He pulled out his cell phone and opened up the map to get the guidance to their first stop. The three intelligence agents climbed on the bicycles and began peddling east from the University.

Traversing dirt roads, they rarely passed a person or a car. They were putting distance with the town behind them. Approximately an hour later, they arrived on the outskirts of a cattle ranch that had been identified to them as their rendezvous point. They would abandon the bikes here, knowing they would not be found until the next day, when it would be too late.

Bakhtiar removed his phone and looked at the WhatsApp and went into the private chat of others that were hoping to make the crossing. Looking at Ali and Firouz, he said, "The others in the chat said because of heavy rain from a tropical storm the previous few days, the river is up and the current is too swift, and we should hold off for a couple of days."

Ali said, "It's a shame we did not know this before we just pedaled out here. We could have stayed in town."

Bakhtiar responded, "That warning is for these immigrants who had been walking for days and weeks without proper nutrition. We are physically fit and well-trained elite members of the Quds Force of the Islamic Revolutionary Guard Corps. We are on a mission for The Islamic Republic of Iran and we will not be deterred."

"I understand what you are saying, brother, but why risk the entire operation if we cannot safely cross the river?"

"Brothers, we have practiced crossing the Aras River on the border of Azerbaijan during our training."

"When we crossed that river, it was well after the spring thaw of the mountain runoff and thus was very temperate. If the Rio Grande is as swift as they say it is, it is best we hold off for a couple of days for it to settle to ensure our successful crossing and completion of our mission."

"No. We must hold to our schedule and cross tonight. We do not want to disappoint Tehran."

"Tehran will not know that we are behind schedule. We have no communications with anyone, and it is better to cross in safety and not jeopardize our assignment."

"With the waters being swift and crossings being low, the guards will be lulled into laziness and will not be on alert. We will actually have a better chance of not being spotted."

Ali shook his head in disagreement, knowing that this dangerous mission would become more treacherous. Despite their training and level of physical fitness, no man was a match against a swift moving river current.

Bakhtiar said, "Tehran has already figured this river crossing based upon weather and the moon. If we wait, the light from the moon will provide a greater chance of being caught, not to mention the border guards on both sides of the river will be more attentive."

Ali scanned the WhatsApp chat and said, "Tehran did not plan on a tropical storm. The river should be about three feet deep. The people in the chat are saying it's five to six feet deep right now and running five times faster than normal. I understand that on an almost daily basis, an immigrant who was too weak to cross, drowns, and last year, an American soldier heroically drowned trying to rescue somebody in the rushing Rio Grande in a similar situation that we face."

"You were talking about an American soldier. Their fitness and training are not at our level. Besides, we have our inner devotion and faith on our side. My name in English translates to 'lucky.'" He smiled and then his face became rigid. "I'm the major and in command of this operation and we are going tonight. Eat your protein pack to keep your strength up."

"Yes sir, Major." Ali seethed at the arrogance of Bakhtiar. He knew all he cared about was maintaining his image with Tehran, which clouded his judgment. He wondered if Bakhtiar had ever led an operation outside of the classroom.

Firouz interrupted the tension and said, "I was an excellent swimmer in training. It may be challenging, but we will do it for our country."

Ali shrugged and said, "I am glad you are a strong swimmer, brother. That gives me confidence."

The three men sat in silence under a shade tree, consuming their protein packs and hydration liquids. As they watched the sunset behind them, they turned towards the east and began their evening prayer. Ali prayed a little harder and with more vigor, knowing they would need the blessings of Allah bestowed upon him. He also thought it would be nice to be lucky and, with Bakhtiar's name, luck would be on their side.

Chapter Eight

With a sky full of stars, and only a sliver of moon providing some ambient lighting, Bakhtiar stood and with his thick muscled arms hoisted his backpack onto his broad back. He nodded at the other two and they followed his lead. They trudged across the field. The soil had been tamped down from the rains earlier in the week. As they passed a herd of cows, they heard them shuffling and some mooing.

Ali inhaled deeply through his nose as the scent reminded him of the farm where he was raised. As a young boy, he had no expectations of leaving that life. Now he was an elite soldier. Taking part in an operation that Ali knew would be historic. They would teach about him and their exploits in schools, exalting them as heroes. He smiled.

Walking in silence so as not to draw any attention to themselves, the tension between Ali and Bakhtiar was palatable. The silence and stillness of the night was lost as they approached the river and could hear the rushing Rio Grande.

At the edge of the bank, all three looked in silence, watching the swift current. They slid down the embankment as soil and rocks slid into the fast-moving water and disappeared. Ali plucked a tuft of grass and tossed it into the rushing river. The grass was carried away faster than a downhill skier on the Alborz Mountains. He dipped his hand in the water and was surprised by the warmth.

Ali crinkled his nose, shook his head, and looked at Bakhtiar. "You really don't expect us to cross this river tonight?"

"It is God's will."

"We are destined for failure. Even if we make it across, there won't be many crossings attempted, and we will be more likely to draw attention to ourselves. Our mission will fail and be exposed."

Staring into his eyes, Bakhtiar said, "Captain, we have our orders and you will comply."

"Yes sir, Major." Ali stared into the water, knowing that it was highly unlikely that any of them would survive the crossing.

"Let's go. May all the blessings of God be with you both."

Ali considered the last statement from Bakhtiar and could sense the fear that Bakhtiar was feeling. Ali wondered if Bakhtiar was hoping he would die a hero and perhaps Iran would name a training building in his honor or give a medal to his parents. It was the first time Ali noticed a crack in his arrogance. Despite his own swimming prowess, Ali did not have the assured confidence that he typically embraced on a mission of this type.

As they waded into the warm water carrying their Yeti waterproof backpacks, they could feel the current tugging at their legs. By the time they had submerged to waist deep, the undercurrent pulled their feet from under them and all three lost their footing. They were swiftly pulled to the west.

It was every man for themselves. Each one struggled to hold on to their backpack. They kept their arms and legs frantically moving while trying to keep their head above water. It was almost an impossible task.

Their progress across the river was slower than their travel down the river. All three were struggling to keep their heads above the water while making progress across the narrow river. Their feet had long ago left the safety of the bottom of the river.

Ali felt the tug, almost like someone grabbing his waist and pulling him under. He submerged under the water and felt fear and panic overtaking his calm exterior. He kicked frantically and paddled ferociously through the wet darkness. His head bobbed back to the surface as he expelled water before being pulled under again.

His head pierced the surface again, and he heard Bakhtiar gulping on water and yelling for help. Ali was pulled under once again and this time, having grabbed a mouthful of oxygen, he began swimming under the dark water toward what he believed was the opposite bank.

Ali's muscles weakened, and he could feel desperation had entered his mind. Knowing death was close, he had no choice but to reach down and find that inner strength. It is what separates warriors from men and heroes from warriors. Ali's head broke through the surface once again. He exhaled and inhaled another lungful of air. Instead of fighting to stay above the surface, he submerged like a submariner swimming under the surface of the water. As he kicked and did the breaststroke, he could no longer hold his breath, and he came to the surface again. Ali could see the bank of the United States was very close. Nearly out of breath, he took one deeper inhale and submerged for what he hoped would be his last few strokes.

Popping up like a buoy, Ali once again swam frantically. Motivated by fear and panic, he started to grasp the wet dirt with his hands. The soil gave way, and the current pulled Ali further downstream.

Slowing his progress by grabbing the muddy bank, he could finally get some footing. Pushing off with his feet propelled him up onto the shoreline. Digging his fingernails into the soil, he crawled the rest of the way and collapsed on his side.

His lungs and throat screamed in pain, and he knew that his gasping for air would alert the border guards to his location. His chest heaved. He raised up on his elbows and looked into the water. He felt the loneliness as he thought that perhaps his two partners were gone.

Approximately twenty-five yards down the riverbank, Ali noticed movement. Trying to silence his gasping, he assessed the movement and whether it was an animal, border guard, or one of his friends.

Opening his backpack, he removed his pistol and held it in a ready position. He finally saw the outline of a figure approaching him. His hand tightened around the pistol as his finger lurked on the outside of the trigger guard. He noticed he was having difficulty keeping the weapon steady.

He could see that the figure approaching him was dragging a backpack, and the person was stumbling and shuffling his feet exhaustively. Ali lowered his weapon, realizing that it was one of his two partners.

As the second operator got closer to Ali, he finally recognized the slimmer figure of Firouz. Upon joining Ali, the younger soldier collapsed to his knees and began sobbing with emotion. Ali patted him on the shoulder and offered comfort. "It's so good to see you, brother. I thought we all would die. Did you see Bakhtiar?"

Still trying to catch his breath, he said, "He is gone. I saw him go under and I never saw him again."

Ali said, "You did the best you could. We both did. He should've listened. Any fool could see it was nearly impossible, and he jeopardized this operation. Despite the translation of his name, he was not lucky. We will carry on in his honor and for our country."

Ali would not say out loud to his partner his true thoughts. He was glad to be rid of the major, who would've been a thorn and a weakness in the operation. His thick body build with power was no match against the torrent of the river. He felt confident that the two of them could carry this plan far more efficiently and successfully without the constant needling oversight of their superior. The two men remained slumped on the bank, trying to regain their strength. Neither could fight off the exhausting sleep that overpowered them.

Chapter Nine

Ali was the first to stir as he jolted awake. He was upset at himself for falling asleep, and they both could have been approached by border guards and apprehended. He was madder at Bakhtiar and his insolence making the nearly impossible crossing of the river. Where they should have been able to wade across the river in nothing deeper than their waist, they were in chin deep water instead. They had to fight for survival and avoid drowning.

Where was Bakhtiar? If he had indeed drowned, Ali hoped that his body was swept far down the river and hopefully would never be recovered. If they found his body, it could compromise their operation. Just then, he heard movement on the bank above them.

He once again clutched his pistol and leaned over and jabbed Firouz. As his partner stirred, Ali put his hand over Firouz's mouth and motioned with his finger over his lips to be quiet. Hearing an all-terrain vehicle, he was concerned that they had been found. He knew most immigrants were unarmed and therefore, the border patrol would not be expecting to confront two highly trained members of the elite Iranian Republican Guard. Both of whom were skilled shooters and killers.

Knowing if they shot a border guard, it would sound the alarm and an all-out response from everyone on a quiet night. Local and state police world converge with the Border Patrol. Helicopters with infrared sensors would locate their heat signatures. If not shot, they would be thrown in jail and never be set free.

Firouz acknowledged the concerns of Ali and grabbed his handgun as they both lay motionless, prepared to strike. Ali could hear the ATV growing fainter, but then heard the movement above them once again. Allie raised up slightly to get a better vantage and despite the limited moonlight, he could make out the figure. A coyote was wandering along the brink of the berm. They both let out with an enormous sigh of relief.

Ali knew they had not been asleep for long, as their clothes were still wet. They could not be caught walking through town with wet clothes, which would identify them as having crossed the river. They reached into their waterproof backpacks and removed their change of clothes and new shoes. The wet clothes were placed into a bag and using rocks from the shore, they provided some ballast to the bags. They each tossed their bag into the fast-moving river and watched them quickly disappear in the current.

Firouz asked if they should continue to wait on Bakhtiar. Ali reasoned that if Bakhtiar had, in fact, survived, he would've caught up with his comrades while they were resting. Being the next in rank, Ali would assume command of the operation and move forward.

Knowing they were behind schedule, Ali concluded they had floated approximately a quarter to a half mile further down the river past the target location. They picked up their backpacks, attached their holstered guns to their waistband and covered the weapons with their shirts. They headed along the bank to where they were originally supposed to land.

After trudging along the riverbank, they finally reached the point of the original target arrival area. From the river, they walked through the muddy patch of scrub brush. Normally, this would have been a dusty soil, but with the recent rain, the soil was still damp. Ali could see they were leaving footprints that would expose their path and allow law enforcement to track their route. They needed to push on and get back on schedule. Ali knew they were at the right location as they began walking through a farm field of what appeared to be onions and melons.

The soldiers had been warned to be aware of ranchers and farmers protecting their property. Armed land owners or their employees often alerted the border guards and occasionally confronted the migrants. He had decided that he would not be taken alive and without a gunfight.

The two finally reached the asphalt of a paved road. Ali recognized it from his map as being Reagan Street. They kneeled at the edge of the road and listened. Ali knew that with their delays, they could not blend in with those who were perhaps leaving a late-night festivity. Now, being into the wee hours of the morning, a half-awake police officer would focus their attention on the two Iranians.

Knowing they had to move, Ali only heard some barking dogs in the distance and the sound of crickets. He tapped Firouz, and they began walking briskly on the quarter-mile trek to the small park with a basketball court. Just like at the University, three bicycles were changed together hidden behind some playground equipment.

After unlocking the bicycles, the two Iranians mounted the bicycles and began peddling. The third bicycle was no longer needed. Ali knew they stood a much better chance of explaining to a police officer they belonged in Eagle Pass, Texas, if they were on the bicycles as opposed to walking on foot. His

Spanish, not as good as Firouz, but it was good enough. He had rehearsed that they were members of the midnight janitorial crew at the casino.

Chapter Ten

Cycling a mile and half west towards the Kickapoo Lucky Eagle Casino, they stayed on back roads and pedaled through neighborhoods as much as they could. The final mile ride was primarily on Rosita Valley Road, which provided little protection from a passing patrol officer.

As they got closer to town, they saw a mixture of signs in English and in Spanish. It made Ali recall an advertisement he had seen for Eagle Pass that read, "Where Yeehaw meets Ole." He thought of some of the bootleg western movies he watched growing up. Cowboys on horses chasing train robbers.

When they reached the Kickapoo Tribal Government Center, they turned left and were now heading south towards the river. Ali now felt comfortable that they were making their escape. He knew no one would question two Hispanic men from Paraguay riding bicycles heading south instead of north.

Once they reached the Kickapoo Lucky Eagle Casino RV Park, they dismounted from their bicycles. There were several travel trailers and recreational vehicles parked in slots in the park, but most were empty. The only noise they could hear was the sound of generators supplying power to the various RVs.

They laid the bicycles down on an empty lot and walked towards the casino. They reached into their backpacks and pulled out their matching black hoodies and two baseball hats. Firouz had a blue-and-white Dallas Cowboys hat and Allie had an orange and white Texas Longhorns hat. Camouflage for locals. After putting their hats on their heads, they pulled their hoods up to conceal their appearance and shield themselves from the cameras at the casino.

They stood on the gravel border amongst the crape myrtle trees, looking towards the parking lot of the casino. Ali could see the neon lights of the casino sign illuminating the entrance. Despite the late hour, there were still quite a few cars in the parking lot. Ali thought how many of these cars were occupied by gamblers hoping to hit it big at the Lucky Eagle Casino. He knew he had been lucky that night. Bakhtiar not so much. His family would not hear of his demise for weeks.

Ali scanned the parking lot and could see the vehicle that would transport them far from the border. A silver Chevrolet Equinox sat alone on the outskirts of the parking lot. He wondered how long the SUV had sat in the parking lot. It was dust covered, and the paint was sun bleached. The car would have been noticed if it appeared abandoned. The bumper displayed a Texas license plate. Dust was part of Texas along with cactus, but he didn't see any. All the western movies had cactus and thus, he was disappointed.

They walked towards the car, keeping their heads down. As they approached the car, Ali leaned down as if to tie his shoe. He reached up into the right rear wheel well and felt around for the keys duct taped to the wheel well. With the key fob, he unlocked the car, and they opened up the tailgate. A box was already in the back. He peeked inside and saw it was filled with blank white paper. They tossed the backpacks into the rear end.

After closing the tailgate, they jumped into the passenger compartment and pulled the doors closed. They both sighed heavily, looked at each other, and smiled with approval. Ali started the car as he looked over at his passenger. They nodded to each as Ali shifted the car into drive and hit the gas, steering the SUV towards San Antonio. The SUV was only to get them to their destination. They would change cars after. Ali was leaving the border and Eagle Pass, Texas, in his rearview mirror. They survived.

Chapter Eleven

Inside the West Tampa, Florida print shop, Mr. Inky, Reza Jaber opened the manila envelope and extracted a sheath from inside. He opened the cover, which merely gave extra support to its contents. He extracted four thin aluminum sheets. Each sheet had perforations at each end. He adjusted the glasses on his thick nose and looked down at the images contained on the aluminum sheets.

He nodded and smiled. Walking to the desk, he turned on the desk light and studied the aluminum. Reza rubbed his head, which was suffering from a drought of hair. He nodded, and a smile creased the stoic face. He turned to Ali and Firouz and said, "These images are superb." The two Iranians smiled contentedly as they too walked closer to examine the images.

On one sheet were three images of a U.S. $50 Federal Reserve Note. On a second sheet were three images of the back of a $50 bill. And finally, on the third sheet, were the treasury seal and serial numbers. On the last sheet was an imitation of the USA 50 security thread.

Reza sipped from a Pepsi can and said, "People today don't appreciate quality. Everyone wants it fast and cheap. The quality of these offset printing presses is unmatched by the digital printers. They cost a little more and they are a little slower, but you will see for yourself when we're done. Ninety-nine percent of the people cannot recognize that these are counterfeit bills."

Ali asked, "How about banks?"

"Maybe, maybe not."

"What does that mean?"

"Depending on the skill and interest of the teller. Many tellers are poorly paid and entry-level jobs. They should be caught in the counting machines. By that time the bills are caught, it will be too late to track it back to the source."

The two nodded in their understanding. Ali wondered if the bank employees were as lazy as most Americans he had heard about. The land of plenty made them entitled, soft and had no passion for their trade.

Reza patted the green printing press with pride. Attaching the first aluminum sheet to the roller, he lined up the perforations to small spikes and then tightened the grip bar down, holding the thin sheet in place. Slowly, he then turned the wheel, pulling the sheet around the drum and attaching the lower perforations and tightening the lower grip bar.

Walking over to the box the Iranians brought into the shop, Reza picked up the paper and thumbed through it. Then he took an individual sheet and holding it up to the light. He rubbed his thick thumb and forefinger over the paper. Another contented smile. "Where did you get this? This is high-quality paper with a high rag content. This paper will pass the pen test or the iodine test that many of these retailers are using."

"The Iraqi Dinar notes use similar paper with a low wood content and high fabric content. Our beloved government intercepted the shipment of paper in Iraq and used it for our own purposes. They shipped it to the U.S. labeled as Turkish cigarette paper. This is some of that stockpile, and we can thank our Russian friends for helping to get it delivered here. It was already loaded into our car that had been delivered to Texas. It was waiting on our arrival."

"The banks may not recognize these bills until it gets to the Federal Reserve Bank. Years ago, they had the Super Note. An almost flawless counterfeit that was being printed in North Korea. It was nearly impossible to detect."

"Do you think that these are that good?"

"No. The printing processes will be different, but I can assure you the quality of these will be excellent. Feel your paper with this paper that we use every day."

Reza grabbed a sheet of paper from a bin and handed the two sheets to Ali and Firouz to compare. The two felt the differences with their fingers and looked at each other with admiration of the quality. Ali was surprised at the quality difference. The standard paper was almost glossy and cheap feeling. The Iraqi paper felt like quality. Pulling out a genuine U.S. $20, he compared the feel. He nodded with pride and handed Firouz the twenty. Firouz nodded and then slipped the bill in his pocket.

Ali held out his hand palm up and said, "I think you forgot something."

Firouz laughed and returned the genuine bill back to Ali.

Picking up a cotton cloth, Reza dampened it and wiped the cloth across the plate to moisten it. He then loaded the stack of Iraqi paper into the paper tray and made sure that it was correctly aligned. On the side of the printing press, he turned a hand crank several times to raise the paper tray to the right level. He made some adjustments on dials next to the crank.

Reza said, "I've put the black ink into the dispenser. What will happen is the ink goes on the ink roller and will attach itself to the plates that you brought, which will then be transferred to this rubber mat on the roller below. The paper will then pass between that rubber mat and the impression cylinder, pressing the paper against the blanket and transferring the image to the paper. The paper comes out the other side, viola. Now for this process we will do four passes. One will print the front side of the paper, second, we will turn the paper over and do the backside. Third, we will do the security thread impression and last, we use the green ink to replicate the serial numbers and treasury seal."

The two Iranians nodded and looked on with the interest of apprentices. Reza reached over and flipped the switch to turn the press on. Once he could see the plate had been properly inked up and was transferring the ink to the rubber mat, he flipped another switch and the paper began feeding into the printing press. They eagerly walked to the output tray and looked at the images of a $50 counterfeit bills.

After the four passes, each sheet contained now what appeared to be three $50 dollar bills. Reza picked up the stack of completed bills and looked over like an approving parent on a child's report card. He took another sip of Pepsi and turned to the two Iranians. "These are marvelous. The only weakness I see is that you only have six serial numbers. It would've been better if we had the nine that I was told were coming. This reduces the chances of someone noticing that they have two bills with the same serial number."

Ali shrugged. "We have to improvise. The other three serial numbers are somewhere in the Rio Grande River."

Reza nodded and gave a half shrug as he brought the stack of paper to a heavy-duty paper slicing machine. Aligning the paper, he made the cuts. He then took stacks of freshly cut bills and tossed them into a commercial dryer, like you would see at a laundromat. He then added polished rocks and poker chips. This would help to weather the bills and take away the appearance of being freshly printed. Once turned on, the dryer sounded like a sledgehammer beating on steel and echoed through the print shop. There was nothing quiet about this operation.

After a period of time, Reza turned off the dryer, opened it up and began shoveling the bills into a bin, and handed it to the two Iranians. As they walked over to a stack of bills, Reza reached into the dryer and pulled out a few remaining bills, which he slipped into his pocket.

The Iranians were giddy with excitement as they prepared stacks of 50's and sorting them into $5,000 piles. Each stack was then rubber banded. Ali patted Firouz on the back, both looking exalted. Ali finally felt that their mission was on a forward trajectory, and he and Firouz were working as a cohesive team.

Returning to the printing press, Reza started another run. Ali walked over to Reza and patted him on the shoulder. Shouting over the sound of the offset printing press, Ali said, "Tehran will be pleased with your contributions. They will take care of your family and your son will be released from Evin prison. When we finish here, we will use our Russian friend to help disperse the money."

Reza patted his heart and bowed his head. "Thank you. Peace be upon you."

Ali was excited to at the quality and the next step in the journey. He had also noticed Reza skimming from the dryer. He contemplated how best to deal with this development without jeopardizing the printing operation. Best to hold his tongue for the time, but he had to address this dishonesty.

Chapter Twelve

Firouz and Ali sat next to each other in a booth of the retro West Tampa Diner, eating yellow rice and chicken. Sitting across from them was Demetri, whose broad shoulders and chest nearly consumed his side of the table. In his previous life, Demetri was in the Russian GRU, which was the main intelligence directorate of the Russian military. Looking to escape the harsh winters of Moscow, he had settled in a Russian enclave of Miami Beach.

His associates in the Russian Mafia had dispatched him to Tampa to extend their influence and develop an alliance with the Cuban community in Tampa. Demetri was supplying credit card numbers stolen from customers at strip clubs in Miami to the Cubans. He also owned a couple of cheap t-shirt shops in Key West that also captured the card numbers from unsuspecting tourists. The stolen credit card numbers were embedded in the magnetic strips of used blank gift cards. It was the valuable information on the magnetic strip that was read by the point-of-sale terminals such as cash registers, ATM's and gas pumps.

This scheme focused on using the gift cards to purchase diesel fuel from unsuspecting service stations. They used covert vehicles with hidden fuel bladders that could hold hundreds of gallons of diesel fuel and then resold at a reduced price to truckers. With the high price of gas, they had a long line of customers and a long line of profits.

The credit card numbers provided by Demetri were compromised by out-of-town whales or big spenders. When they returned to their suburban lives, they were reluctant to make much of a fuss that would arouse their spouse's ire. With a high credit limit, the Cubans could buy a lot of diesel before the card holder reported the compromise of the card.

Demetri was not privy to the entire operation of his dining partners. He had been contacted by a former boss, who asked Demetri to assist in a very sensitive and off book operation. Discretion was of paramount importance. He and his contacts were being tasked with keeping a low profile and maintain secrecy.

Expanding his arms out wide, Demetri said, "It's good, no? Like back home?" Without giving them a chance to answer, he continued, "Yellow rice and meat. Filling stomachs worldwide. So, gentlemen, you brought a sample for me?"

Ali looked around and assessed his surroundings. He hated having his back to the customers and not being ready for an ambush. The Russian had grabbed the seat facing the door first. Satisfied, he reached into his pocket and pulled out one of the counterfeit $50 bills. He nodded and slid it across the table. The Russian looked around the restaurant as his criminal instincts had saved him countless times from jeopardy.

After assessing the environment, he picked up the bill, rubbed with his fingers and studied the bill first on the front then on the back. The feel of the paper was of good quality. Demetri then pulled out his own $50 bill, which he had just received from the bank. He laid it down next to the counterfeit and made a comparison study of the two bills. He was impressed, as he had been led to believe by his superiors, that counterfeit was as exquisite as a forged Picasso painting.

The Russian rubbed his square jaw, nodded and looked across the table and said, "Exceptional quality. I have a network within the Cuban community, who I can use as distributors. They can also move packages to truck drivers, so that the distribution will be widespread and not as easily recognized. What is your price? And how much can you supply?"

Ali put his fork down and leaned across the table while lowering his voice and said, "Fifty percent."

Demetri was stunned. He leaned back against the booth, smiled and said, "My friends, this is good, but no funny money is worth that much. Leave enough for my people to make money and make it worth their time. You have to understand, it may look good, but it's still fake. There is still a risk. It will take work to move this. Besides, maybe in Iran cash is king, here it is credit cards." He held up a Platinum American Express. "This is a status symbol, like driving my Escalade or my nice clothes." He ran his fingers across his chest.

"We have used nothing but cash."

"Maybe so. This economy is credit card focused and online banking. Point of sale terminals, electronic payments, where cash has become cumbersome. Last week in Miami, I stayed at a resort that would not accept cash."

He let that percolate. "If you had counterfeit credit cards, I could move those like precious gems. Cash, fake or real, is more challenging."

"Are you going to help?"

"Only because I was asked by mutual friends. It will be a lot more work. How much quantity?"

Firouz held up one long slender finger.

Demetri mouthed the word million. Ali and Firouz nodded in agreement. Demetri said, "Considering the quality and quantity normally, we don't pay any more than 10 to 15%. Because I've been told to extend courtesies to you, I can go as high as 20%."

Ali and Firouz shook their head in unison. Ali said, "Our bosses said 50%, no less."

Demetri knew Iranians were notorious for driving a hard bargain. He felt like a used car salesperson, but in this case, he had already exposed his final best offer. Now they were insulting him with continued negotiation. He figured they were following orders of ignorant superiors. It was time to turn up the heat on the stove.

He smiled, pushed his plate away from the edge and slid out of the booth and stood up. His large frame stared down at Ali and Firouz and said, "It was nice to meet both of you. Have a nice day." He pointed to his real $50 bill and said, "That's real and will cover the check. Our meeting is over."

He walked towards the exit and waved at the server speaking Spanish to her. "Goodbye gorgeous. Have a day that matches your beauty." Plates clattered on the counter as the server smiled and winked at the handsome stranger. He wondered how far he would get before the Iranians chased him down.

Chapter Thirteen

Ali could not imagine the audacity of the Russian. Just like Demetri's country, it was run by a bunch of bullies and corrupt oligarchs. Having had a few joint exercises with the Russian army, Ali found that their officers acted with a superior brashness. Their tactics, equipment and soldiers were of poor quality. Ukraine was proof. When the Iranians were allowed by their superiors, they easily defeated the Russians in exercises.

The Iranians were motivated by passion and belief. The Russians were motivated by fear. In another situation, he would have let the Russian walk, but sadly, he had little recourse being in a foreign land with no support. The success of the mission was paramount. He would have to be an unwilling partner with Demetri.

Ali and Firouz scrambled to slide out and catch up with Demetri. They walked briskly without acknowledging the server. They pushed through the door and trotted after Demetri, who had already climbed into the driver's seat of his black Escalade. Demetri was wearing a smirk. Ali hated him. He rolled down the driver's window. "Yes? Change your mind?"

"Our negotiations were not complete."

Demetri smiled and said, "Sometimes the mountains are too far apart to cross the valley. You people may have invented arithmetic, but you did not invent fake money. Every drug dealer and kid in high school with a computer can make fake money. No one pushing a large quantity is expecting to make fifty percent."

"This is extremely high-quality and was not made by some high school child. You can walk into a bank with this right now and a bank teller would not be the wiser. My boss said we should split it 50-50."

"Your boss is not here. Call him and explain to him we are not at the shopping bazaar and negotiating over a rug or spices. You have my number." Demetri pushed the ignition and started the SUV.

Ali placed his hand on the windowsill of the Escalade and said, "Okay." Demetri silenced the ignition and looked at Ali, who continued. "I don't have time to call back to my superiors. Because of the urgency of this operation, I will split the difference and sell for twenty-five percent."

Demetri nodded and said, "Twenty percent and we have a deal." He extended his hand through the window and Ali hesitated, grasped his hand, shook it, and nodded in agreement. Ali knew the Russian was going to skim off the proceeds, but he had no choice. Hopefully, he would have time at the end to slice Demetri's throat and watch the blood and life drain out of him. He would never spend his money.

Demetri said, "Text me the address and I will need the one million broken into $25,000 packages for easier distribution. Let me ask, if this moves as well as I think it may, are we able to print more?"

Ali shook his head and said, "That will not be possible."

Demetri shrugged, nodded his head, started the ignition again and rolled up the window as he drove away.

Firouz said, "Tehran told us 50%. That Russian is stealing from us."

"Perhaps my brother. But Tehran is not here in Tampa. We are and I just made a command decision. We are both lucky to be alive. $200,000 will be plenty for us to carry out this operation. Not to mention we will salt in less confidence in the U.S. currency. Once they start to move the counterfeit, merchants and banks will be reluctant to accept $50 bills. We will use their money against them. By the time they realize anything, we will have enough money for our operation and Allah will smile down upon us."

"The grace of Allah is upon us."

"That Russian will get his in the end as The Republic of Iran will wield the power. God willing." Ali smiled at the image of blood spewing from the thick neck of the Russian.

Chapter Fourteen

Drinking a Bang energy drink at his desk, Detective Cody Danko was eagerly sifting through a case file on an aggravated battery investigation. A new lead had been developed. He looked up as Detective Kate Alexander walked in with her workout bag while sipping on a yellow Gatorade.

Kate hiked her thumb towards the closed supervisor's door. "Is our new sergeant in yet?"

Cody shrugged. "Haven't seen him."

Kate said, "What's going on?"

"Before I get to that, you look a little tired. Hard work out?"

"New puppy who won't sleep through the night. He is Brittney's puppy, but mom gets the midnight shift. Brings back memories of midnight feedings with Brittney. Just like a baby, then he wants to play."

"Should have gone with a cat. They almost take care of themselves."

"You don't look so great yourself." Kate said.

"I'm primed and ready to go. My bunny tail is wagging."

"Your bunny tail maybe wagging but your ears are floppy. It looks like you have suitcases under your eyes and a little Visine wouldn't hurt. You might want to take some vitamin D supplements or get outside and soak up some of the beautiful sunshine."

"Ha. Being around you is all the sunshine I need. If you need to know, my mom went out of town for a digital scrapbooking get together."

"Digital scrapbooking?"

"Like the old days of making a physical scrapbook, but they do it with their computers now. To be honest, I think she goes for the socialization. We don't have a lot of happy memory photographs growing up with the drunk bastard."

"I get that. But how does that explain your physical condition? While the farmers away the animals will play? Or were you entertaining some young lady like the one from the smoothie shop?"

"I wish. Too many hours in front of the *Call of Duty* monitor, and perhaps one too many bourbons. When you're in the moment and in that virtual-reality, you kind of lose track of time and place. With mom being gone, I had no guilt."

"When does she return?"

"Tomorrow. I have a big dinner planned for her. Glazed carrots, twice baked sweet potato and marinated sirloin steak."

"You are a real Mama's boy."

"Guilty. She essentially raised me on her own and with her MS, it's my turn to return the favor. She's quite the survivor and thrivor."

"You are right. She is quite a woman to put up with you. Okay, you were going to tell me some great revelation."

"You remember about a month ago I worked a shooting on Thaddeus Carmichael?"

"The one that was kneecapped?"

"Yep, they were two others that were similar. All shot in the knee, but everybody was terrified to identify the shooter. I really shook the tree, talked to everybody that I could, and checked whatever video I could find in the areas. No one was talking. Everyone's lips were sealed."

"Sadly, that has become the way of the world. Homicide clearance rates have plummeted across the country because everyone is scared to cooperate or talk to the police."

"Well, the mother of Thaddeus said that she would like to have a chat with us. So, if you're not too busy, would you mind going with me to speak to her?"

"Well, big boy, let's go."

Chapter Fifteen

Circling out of the parking garage for the Blue Monster, Cody had the radio blaring heavy metal music. Cody was feeling the rhythm of the song. In Afghanistan, the platoon of Wolfhounds loved heavy metal. The louder, the better. Metallica, CCR, Led Zeppelin. He rocked to it during his gaming sessions. The blood pumping was invigorating. Kate reached over from the passenger seat and changed the station to a country.

Kate said, "My eardrums are still vibrating. You really listen to that?"

Cody responded, "A classic! Iron Maiden. It's called The Number of the Beast. When you're not in the car, it puts me in my jam. The juices really get flowing."

"You're confusing brain fluid for creative juices."

"Hey, what happened to the driver picks the music?"

"That only happens when the driver and passenger are the same rank and have the same time on the job. So, since I have more time on the job and more time as a detective, seniority trumps the driver."

"Oh, I see how this is going to go."

"Well, just be glad that I have my selection of country music. You could be stuck listening to Rollins or Duffy in their jazz or easy listening. It made me feel like I was in the dentist's chair and having PTSD associated with a root canal. I felt like I needed to run some laps around the car and do some push-ups just to wake myself up."

Parking next to the curb in front of the modest one-story block-house, Cody was hopeful Mrs. Carmichael could provide some answers. He hoped that would allow him to close some cases and get them off his desk. Knowing it was only a matter of time that the trend of kneecapping would cause someone to be killed. Apparently, the sheriff's office had a homicide that started as a kneecapping. He hoped that a concerned mother would break the veil of silence.

They walked up to the door and a larger woman with a flower-patterned housedress answered the door.

Cody asked, "Mrs. Carmichael?"

"That's Ms. Carmichael. My baby daddy was here long enough to knock me up pregnant. As soon as the first bills came in and that baby arrived, he did a vanishing act faster than Houdini, and I ain't seen his sorry ass since. But he left me with the treasure. That boy of mine is a wonderful child, you hear me?"

She waited, and they both nodded.

"He got mixed up with some bad blood, but I think he has seen the light. That night he got shot, knocked him upside his head, and I told him he was fixing to be fitted with an orange jumpsuit or a coffin and that neither was a good choice."

Cody asked, "Ms. Carmichael, I know what it's like to be raised by a single mother who was abandoned by their father. Mothers can make all the difference in the world and have tremendous influence over their children. My mother worked hard to keep a roof over our head and food in our tummies. It may take some time, but your son will also appreciate your sacrifices."

"Well, thank you, Mr. Cody. I just don't want to see him on visiting days at the penitentiary or his tombstone at the cemetery. So, I'm putting a stop to all this nonsense of not snitching."

"We would certainly appreciate any help that you could provide. Because I've worked hard to find who shot your son in the knee."

"I know you have, and I appreciate everything that you've done. But I also know you ain't no miracle worker. If people are playing three blind mice, you don't know what you don't know."

"That is the truth."

"I can tell that your mama raised you right. So, I'm going to give you the breaking news story. It was that no good Johnny Nylon that shot my Thaddeus. And all the others. Anyone walking with a limp is the victim of Johnny. They say he had a .38 revolver, so that he didn't leave any evidence behind. They also say he always had that gun on him."

"Who are they?"

"They is they. I heard things, but none of it matters. That Johnny Nylon had what was coming to him. That alligator saved this community from a whole lot of heartache. I don't wish any bad will on anyone. We go to church on Sundays, but that man had what was coming to him." She leaned back in the chair and started chuckling and said, "Karma, baby, karma."

"Why was your son shot?"

"Why do most of these shootings happen? Greed, pride, jealousy or, like Cain and Abel in the Bible, simple revenge. That Johnny Nylon thought of himself as some gangsta, and he went down like the thug that he is, in the mouth of an alligator." She clapped her hands together again while laughing.

Cody felt a minor disappointment that a mother was rejoicing at the death of someone the same age as her son. He also knew that one of the most basic motivational desires of people was to exact revenge. Indeed, vengeance had been delivered. He knew no weapons had been recovered from Johnny's body or the stolen car.

Cody and Kate arched their eyebrows at each other and nodded. "Thank you, Ms. Carmichael. I hope Thaddeus recovers quickly and thank you for your help."

"We need to stand up and speak up. Stop these fools from killing each other."

"Amen."

As Kate and Cody walked down the front walk towards the curb, Cody watched a redheaded woodpecker spiral around the rough bark of an oak tree.

Kate looked at her partner and said, "Ms. Carmichael was quite a pistol. I liked her spunk. What do you think?"

"I think it's a trait in all successful single mothers. Like yourself. You will do anything to protect your nest and you have to portray spunk and toughness to let people know that you and your children will not be messed with. Sadly, many times, they circle the wagons of silence and don't want to risk the threat of retaliation. She knows that Johnny Nylon is not coming back from the dead, and none of his companions have any allegiance to him or the legend he was trying to portray."

"True. What now?"

"Let's drive up to the pond where Johnny Nylon met his demise, and have the dive team come out and see if they can find a .38 revolver. As you know, it wasn't on him when they recovered his body, and it was not in the gator's belly or in the stolen car. I heard the County is working a homicide from last month, where a .38 was used. The victim was shot in the leg and bled out from a femoral artery bleed. Maybe Johnny's aim was not so good."

"The FDLE Crime Lab can compare all the bullets and hopefully the dive team can find the gun."

"With Johnny dead, we won't be able to put any meat in the pot with handcuffs, but we can clear some cases and make The Caveman happy."

"The only thing that makes him happy is seeing himself in the mirror."

"Or on Insta and Twitter."

"Truth. Let's go to the final resting spot of Johnny and see what we find."

Chapter Sixteen

Nosing into a parking space near the Jimmy John's, Cody shifted into park. As the two stepped out of the car, Kate's phone rang. It was the Brittney's school. She told Cody to go ahead. "Grab me a number four on wheat. No mayo please."

"Sure. My treat."

She answered the phone. "Hello, this is Kate."

"Hi Mom."

"Sweetie, is everything okay?"

"Yep. Miss Tankersley, gave me permission to call."

"You are sure that nothing is wrong?"

"Nope. Everything is fine. She wanted to know if you could chaperone our field trip to the Tampa History Museum next Thursday?"

"I would love to. Thank you for asking. We can grab a bite at the Columbia Café inside."

"I think we have to brown bag it."

Kate watched three athletic twenty something's disembark from a full-size SUV and walk toward the sandwich shop.

"It will be a fun brown bag lunch with you and the rest of the class."

"And maybe Trent, you and I can come down and take the trolley to the aquarium one weekend."

"That would be awesome."

"I have to run now. I'll talk to you tonight."

"Okay. I love you, mommy."

The three men locked eyes with Kate and she could see them looking at her like she was a rare painting. One with a thick head of hair said, "MILF." As if he were speaking code.

The second one, with a neat beard, answered, "Absolutely. I'd like to take a spin with her."

"I love you too, sweetie." Kate ended the call.

The beard laughed and said, "I love you too, sweetie." They all laughed.

Kate said, "Excuse me?"

"Hey, no offense. Maybe I can buy you a sandwich." He winked at his two co-conspirators.

"Before you crash and burn, you might want to pull the handle between your legs for the ejector seat and land safely by parachute." Kate held his stare.

Beard glared at her while his buddies chuckled. She could see he was contemplating his next action. "Bitch."

"If that's the best you have, instead of taking a spin with me, you better keep your training wheels on. Your line might work in college, but talk to your mom for lessons on impressing girls."

The angry glare resumed. She could see that he so wanted to engage, but she knew he was wondering where this crazy girl was going to take it. Walk away with some dignity and the brunt of jokes from his wingmen, who had remained silent. Or re-engage and risk an escalation. Arching her eyebrows, Kate put her hands on her hips. She shifted her left foot in front to provide a platform to drive a heel strike from her right hand if he came towards her. She was ready.

He scoffed with disdain and muttered his retreating insult, "Ugly bitch."

She sent a sarcastic kiss in his direction and said quietly, "Asshats."

Kate laughed at the departing shot. She might have said nothing until Beard made a direct insult. Especially after speaking with her daughter. It forced her to take off her fuzzy sweater and breakout the warrior princess mindset.

She hoped perhaps she taught all three a valuable lesson. Females were not objects that could be insulted and degraded. Alone, he probably would never have had the guts to say anything, but the threesome was emboldened. They fed off each other, intimidating a lone female. She knew it was three on one, but in reality, it was two on three with Cody a few feet away. They just didn't know she had backup. Their conduct infuriated her, but she had scored a direct hit as all three scurried away with their tail between their legs. Perhaps they would think twice the next time.

Cody pushed through the door and looked at Kate. "What did I miss?"

"An epic takedown. Like a Key West rooster spreading his tail feathers, who had never been rejected by a hen. No mayo, right?"

"No mayo."

"Let's go find you a gun."

Chapter Seventeen

They parked alongside the curb of the pond lined with a border of lily pads and a canopy of oak trees. The two detectives unwrapped their Jimmy John's sandwiches. They knew this would be the last chance to eat. It was going to be a long afternoon of standing around watching the bubbles of the dive team as they searched for a gun that might be covered in mud or not be there at all.

Cody said, "I will say, despite his violent demise. It was a picturesque park, although I don't think he could enjoy the view, especially in the dark."

"Well, I'm just glad this is your case, but look at all them you can exceptionally clear by the death of the suspect."

"Where did he go into the water?"

"So, Doug Pasley chased him in a Kia, which turned out to be stolen, and he abandoned it right here and dove into the water right over there." As she pointed in the general direction where Johnny jumped into the water. "He swam in the helipad's direction across the pond at St. Joseph's Hospital. Somewhere around the middle, the alligator got him and they recovered his body over there towards the right."

They both stepped out of the car and walked over to the edge of the water. As they both stood with hands on their hips surveying the landscape, Kate pointed to a spot in the pond and they both observed the backend of a submerged car.

Curious, they both walked to the edge of the pond a little further and could see the outline of a black Cadillac under the water. Cody said, "Hopefully, it is just a stolen car and there are no bodies inside."

Kate slapped his arm. "Don't jinx us."

"Us? That would be your case, since you are next on the board."

Kate said, "You suck." They both laughed and Kate pulled out her cell phone to ask for a patrol unit to meet them.

Officer Andrea Casale arrived in a marked unit and parked behind Cody's unmarked Toyota. The fit brunette scampered out of the driver's seat and tugged up on her gun belt while tugging down on her ballistic vest. Comfortable in her positioning, she walked towards the two detectives with a broad smile.

Andrea said, "Hey guys, where is the abandoned car?"

The two detectives simultaneously pointed to a spot in the water and Cody said, "I hope you brought your swimsuit."

"And my floatie's. Let me get my snorkel tube out of the unit." She rolled her eyes. "How did you find this?"

Kate said, "The Blonde Boy Wonder here had just wrapped up three shooting assault cases and a homicide for HCSO. So, he just finished sweet talking to the mother of a victim who told him where the potential weapon could be found. Here we are waiting for the dive team to show up to look for the gun, and low and behold, we look into the water and see what looks like a Cadillac that's been dumped. Now, I came out that morning when Doug Pasley chased down Johnny Nylon, who then jumped in the water to become gator bait, and the car was not there."

Andrea said, "You know they say nothing good comes after midnight, but you know nothing good comes after jumping into a pond after dark anywhere in Florida."

She looked over at Cody and said, "Have you been working out? I don't remember your guns looking as well defined?" She squeezed his bicep like she was checking the freshness of melons in the produce aisle of Whole Foods. They all laughed as he pulled his arm away.

"Just trying to keep my edge."

"Kate, I do like the Boy Wonder nickname better than Good Night Danko. It's a more celebratory name instead of a nickname associated with tragedy. Despite its happy ending saving that baby. In the Academy, he won the fitness award, although I gave him a run for his money in the mile and a half."

Cody looked down at the ground and stirred the grass with his foot.

Kate said, "He is definitely a gym rat. Not too bad of an investigator, either. Back to business, Andrea, if you don't mind standing by and writing whatever report we have associated with this car. Once the dive team arrives, they can make their assessment and have the wrecker pull it out of the water. Hopefully, it is just a stolen car and nothing more."

"No worries. This will be like watching them recover a treasure chest from a shipwreck and the excitement of seeing what's inside. I haven't been this excited since I opened my first box of Cracker Jack's and found the surprise."

Chapter Eighteen

They all turned as the dive team's Ford Expedition pulled up behind Andrea's car. Chip DeBlock was shaking his head. "Kick ass, what have you stirred up this time? Another alligator chomping. I can see the car in the water."

"Chip, your powers of observation never cease to amaze me. We thought you scuba boys could find a gun. Then we found the car, which, as you guys know, was not out here when Johnny Nylon sank to the bottom."

"Okay, Dave and I will blow some bubbles and have a look. What kind of gun are we looking for?"

Cody spoke up and said, "A revolver, probably a .38. We don't know what size, but it's connected to three shootings and one homicide."

"Okey dokey."

Cody and Kate stood with their hands on their hips. Andrea had her hands resting inside the opening of her ballistic vest. The three officers watched as the two divers submerged in the pond through the border of lily pads. They watched their path as their bubbles tracked their movements.

It was only a few minutes later that the two divers surfaced and Dave D'Agresta removed his mask from his face and the regulator from the mouth. He said, "Well, this is not what you wanted to hear, but there is a body in the front seat."

Kate folded her arms across her chest and said, "I hope you're saying perhaps a natural death with a sudden medical onset that caused him to erroneously drive across the curb through the lily pods and into the water?"

"I might not be James Bond 007 like you folks, but I would say there appears to be a hole in the back of his head. Now I can't say if it's a bullet hole, but I would say he probably had a sudden and violent ending to his life. Here are some pictures for you."

Everyone huddled around the display of the camera. As D'Agresta scrolled through the various pictures, it was obvious the driver was slumped over towards the console. There was a hole at the base of the skull with a much larger one on his forehead. Kate knew from her experience that this was obviously a gunshot wound, and the gun was fired from behind.

As the bright sun moved past a cloud, Kate slid her sunglasses onto her face and turned toward Andrea. "So much for an abandoned vehicle report. You now get to write a homicide report. You must feel like the joy of getting the last date to the prom."

"I was never much interested in dancing, I was more interested in science and seeing cause-and-effect."

"Yeah, that makes two of us. I was more into psychology and wanting to know the mindset and what drives the evil that causes the murder of another human being."

Cody said, "If you must know, I was a college dropout, but I had an inquiring mind, and I am thrilled to be surrounded by both of you and your intellectual brilliance."

They chuckled and Andrea said, "There you go Kate, the Boy Wonder schmoozing and sucking up the vapors of two bad ass cops." Kate and Andrea fist bumped.

Kate said, "Yes, we are. If you don't mind Andrea, call for a wrecker so we can pull this out and run the license plate of the Cadillac."

"10-4."

Kate asked D'Agresta if the two divers could check around the area of the car for any potential evidence. Once they were satisfied the area was clear, they could resume their original search for the revolver. D'Agresta acknowledged the instructions, and the two divers waded back off into the water and descended under the surface.

Kate sat there, contemplating the sudden change of events. Here she was thinking they were looking for a potential weapon that was carried by an individual who met his demise in this pond. Only to find what was originally suspected as an abandoned probably stolen vehicle but contained the victim of a homicide. All this began with good policing and chasing Johnny Nylon. His nylon stocking was unraveling and revealing a surprise. What had once been a scenic pond was now a toxic pond that had claimed the lives of two men.

Andrea hung up the microphone and stepped out of a patrol unit, and walked to Kate. She told Kate that the tow truck was on the way, her sergeant had been notified, and then handed Kate a sheet of paper with the registered owner of the Cadillac.

Kate had also notified her new Sergeant Benny Thompson, the state attorney's office on-call homicide prosecutor, as well as the medical examiner. Although Kate felt a pang of hunger and thinking about her half-eaten sandwich, she had lost her appetite.

Kate turned to Cody and said, "I've made all the notifications. Our new sergeant is on the way."

"He will be quite a change from Alfonso. In some ways, he is the alter ego of Alfonso, but he has no agenda. So, I think he will look out for us and will not be afraid to battle with The Caveman. But you can say goodbye to the tranquil setting that Alfonso had in his office with the aquarium and the orchids."

"Do tell."

"I only know Benny was on the opposite shift and patrol from me. Let's just say appearance was not high on his attributes. But I never heard his troops badmouthing him."

"That's encouraging. I heard he wasn't given a choice about taking over homicide."

"I don't know about that but, I think he has some friends upstairs."

"Hopefully, Benny will act as a buffer or gatekeeper between us and The Caveman."

Andrea asked, "Who is The Caveman?"

Kate said, "Lieutenant Jack Willard. Frank Duffy gave him that nickname because Willard never leaves his office, as if he is scared. Hence, The Caveman stays in his cave where it is safe and to avoid the scary world outside."

Cody jumped in and said, "He will come out if he hears the click of cameras in which case, you don't want to stand between him and the photographers. It might be a lethal encounter. He is all about sounding like General Douglas MacArthur during World War II, returning to the Philippines. Everyone, look at me, look at me. I am the greatest. He is all about being on the department's Twitter feed and Instagram photos."

All three officers shook their head in acknowledgment and understanding that most nicknames were earned through accomplishments or misdeeds. Now they waited like excited kids at Halloween to see what treat the dive team may find.

Chapter Nineteen

Once again, Chip DeBlock surfaced from the water. He waded ashore and removed his fins as he walked towards the Ford Excursion. He lifted his mask and removed the regulator from his mouth once again and said, "We found it."

Cody said, "The gun?"

"Sure did. Just as you said. A .38 revolver. A Taurus."

Cody and Kate fist bumped into each other and beamed. Chip gathered a waterproof evidence container and once again put his equipment on and swam out into the pond. A few minutes later, the two divers popped up out of the water. D'Agresta was carrying the container. They handed it to Cody, who smiled like a kid who had just blown out the candles on his birthday cake.

Kate thought that while she should be happy that Cody would clear several open cases, she knew that their treasure find would be just the beginning of a whodunit for her.

Sergeant Benny Thompson drove up and stepped out of his vehicle. He was wearing a sports coat that looked like he dug out of the bottom of his closet. His baggy khakis dragged the pavement behind his dull shoes. Benny gave an oversized tug to pull his pants up and the cuffs off the pavement. He adjusted his black-rimmed glasses and said, "This looks like a colossal shit storm. For crying out loud. My first day watching over you misfits. What kind of calamity have your dragged me into?"

Not sure what to make of her new supervisor's entrance, Kate began explaining the scenario from Johnny Nylon's death to the missing gun and finally to the Cadillac and the body. Benny shook his head and combed his fingers through his abundant brown hair. He let out with a long sigh that he blew through his lips.

Kate laughed. "Welcome to the squad."

"I haven't even warmed up Alfonso's chair to my big ass. Well, it doesn't look like you need me sitting in the bleacher section barking out orders. You have this fiasco under control. I'll tell you one thing. That Cadillac will never start again. It's as dead as its driver." There were chuckles at the gallows humor. "If you need any more support, give me a jingle."

"Sure, no problem. What about the lieutenant?"

"What about him?"

"He gets a little... ah..."

"Neurotic? Scared of his own shadow? A hemorrhoid in my ass?"

"Precisely. I couldn't have said it any better."

"I'll handle him. If he calls you, ignore him and let me know."

"10-4."

"Just keep me up to date. You can just text me if that is easier."

"Thanks. What about the media?"

As he shuffled off, he said, "I'll call the PIO. Keep the news leeches as far away as possible."

"Yes, sir."

"I'm Benny, not sir." As he waved goodbye.

After Benny drove off, Kate turned to Cody and fist bumped him. She was ecstatic with her first meeting with her new sergeant. She loved Alfonso and his steadiness. He had always looked out for the squad. The job wore him down, and the current state of anti-police rhetoric did not help. She had been concerned about his replacement and adjusting to the eccentric traits of Benny. Her anxieties had been resolved.

The tow truck pulled up and Andrea guided him into backing up against the curb. She'd called for another unit to assist on corralling the curious onlookers. The truck operator unwound a length of cable and handed it to David, who stepped back into the water until he was about chest deep. He dropped under the water as his fins broke the surface of the water. After attaching the cable to the undercarriage of the Cadillac, he came to the surface and gave the thumbs up to the operator.

The wrecker driver began operating the levers on the winch and tightened the cable. As the winch wheeled the cable in, the backend of the Cadillac appeared. The CTS model sedan reeled ashore. The exposed rear end of the car cascaded water like a broken dam. As the rest of the car was dragged onto the grass, the passenger and engine compartments also spilled water.

The crime scene unit had been photographing the events both with video and still photography. Once they had successfully chronicled the condition of the vehicle, D'Agresta removed his fins and walked up to the bank. He opened the driver's door and more water poured out onto the soggy turf.

The medical examiner, Minnie Zaquera, walked up alongside the crime scene photographers as they both clicked cameras like a couple of paparazzi. Satisfied with their photographic documentary, Zaquera took a closer examination of the body. Once she was satisfied, she turned towards Kate and motioned that it was her turn.

In passing, Zaquera said, "Definitely dead. And definitely a gunshot from behind."

Kate rolled her eyes. "You are so insightful."

Zaquera giggled. "Big surprise, right? See you at the autopsy."

"Thank you, Minnie. You're the best"

Not having expected to go to a crime scene, she had to rely on borrowing Cody's wellies to keep her feet dry. She clomped through the saturated grass and reached in to inspect the body of the driver.

Having examined far too many murder scenes, this was a "no riddle homicide" for the experienced detective. She knew the fatal shot was fired from behind and probably a passenger in the back seat. After entering the skull, the bullet blew out the skull and brain matter from his forehead towards the windshield. Although most of the blood and matter would've littered the dashboard in the windshield, the pond water acted as a cleansing agent and washed most of it away.

The bullet struck the windshield, and it caused cracks, which would have harbored some evidence. The bullet had escaped through the windshield and the likelihood of being able to recover it was virtually nonexistent with the pond. If he had been shot, while submerged, the search area would have been much smaller because the water would have inhibited the bullet from traveling far.

With her gloved hand, she felt his pockets. The front two pockets she could feel its contents, and the back pocket felt like a wallet. She extracted the wet billfold and opened to see the driver's license displayed. She studied the driver's photo and then scrutinized the face of the victim. Despite the swollen face, she felt comfortable that the victim was Mr. Reza Jaber, who was also the registered owner of the Cadillac. She returned the billfold to his back pocket.

She held up his left wrist and looked at his watch. The analog watch was no longer ticking. She wiped the moisture off the watch crystal. The time was 1:12. The murder could not have happened in the PM, as half of Tampa would have seen the car submerged. The time the car rolled into the pond was approximately 1:12 am. Give or take a few minutes to fill up the driver's compartment and stop the watch. She would assume that somewhere close to that time was the time of death. He was killed from behind in the driver's seat. Then Reza and the car were pushed into the pond. Perhaps what day he was murdered could be better determined by visiting the family. She turned and motioned to the Minnie that she was done with her assessment.

The attendants from the Medical Examiner's Office slowly removed the victim from the driver's seat. He would be placed in an empty body bag lying next to the car. They zipped the container close and hoisted Mr. Jabbar onto the gurney and pushed it towards their vehicle.

The crime scene unit would now begin their meticulous examination of the interior of the Cadillac. Kate clumped up towards Cody and said, "You have feet bigger than Sasquatch." As she slipped her feet out of the wellies.

"You would think you would be more grateful and say, Cody, thank you so much for lending me your wellies. Just remember, those are big boots to fill, and I don't know if you're up to the task."

"Keep it up Bigfoot." As she sat down in the passenger side of his car and put her flats back on her feet.

Cody said, "As stylish as you are, I never see you in stilettos."

"Frank Duffy and I had a similar conversation once. Stilettos are for strippers and federal agents. Real cops wear gangsta chasing shoes."

Cody nodded. "Make sense. I've seen you chase fleeing felons. You wear felony flyers."

"Not to mention what heels do to your back carrying a gun, handcuffs, and a radio. Okay, let's go do our death-knock and see what the family has to say."

"Sounds like a plan."

Kate stepped out of the car and scanned the area in a full 360-degree motion. Looking for surveillance cameras, she could not see any external mounted cameras on the buildings at the corporate park. She was disappointed that the lack of cameras that would've captured the crime scene area. She looked across the street to where the Buccaneer's training center was located and thought perhaps, they might have some cameras that could have captured at least the intersection on MLK Boulevard.

Chapter Twenty

Driving across the street, they approached the guard booth to Number One Buccaneer Place. Kate explained to the guard that she needed to speak with the director of security. The guard was more than eager to call his boss. He then opened the gate to allow entry.

Parking outside along the curb, they walked through the front entrance that was under the skeleton structure of a football surrounded by Buccaneer pirate flags. Inside, they were greeted with a nautical theme and lots of red and pewter accents. Standing in front of the desk with the Buccaneers logo was the Director of Security Travis Longstreet. He smiled widely and said, "Kate, I haven't seen you in years."

"It's been a long time since I was wearing blue polyester on a traffic post and dealing with unruly fans outside the stadium. I was hoping you could tell us if you have a video that would cover the intersection of MLK or, better yet, into the corporate park across the street? We are working a homicide across the street in the corporate park. Someone dumped a car with a body."

He shook his head. "Really? Wow! No, our camera coverage only goes out as far as the guard booth. But I'll be glad to check with the night guard to see if he saw or heard anything."

"That would be helpful. What do you think the chances are that he would have seen anything?" She arched her eyebrows as if to say that she was not hopeful.

He half shrugged. "I won't know until I ask."

"Thank you for your help, Travis."

"Anything for you, Kate. Let's do lunch sometime."

"Thanks. I'll give you a shout."

As they walked outside, she turned to Cody and said, "At best, the midnight guard was binging Netflix, and at worst, he was sleeping. We have to hope that it was a student who was wide awake studying for exams or possibly a real G.I. Joe type that was actually awake and paying attention. They probably get the occasional drunk that pulls and wanting to talk to Tom Brady, like he lives here."

"Mr. Security seemed awful friendly toward you."

"Yeah, Travis was in the training division when I first got hired. Then he started ascending up the promotional ladder. When he was coming up on retirement, this job became available and he jumped on it faster than a fumbled football. I'm sure it was a knife fight with lots of competition. It took someone who had a good reputation and was just as good of a politician."

"If I didn't know better, I'd say he wants more than lunch."

"I have no plans to be wife number three. That's why lunch won't happen and besides, I am off the market."

"Trent?"

"He is good for me. We are spending a lot of time together."

"Good for you. Hey, didn't you and Blake Hamilton have something going?"

"Blake? That lazy piece of shit man-whore. Never! We had a mutual hatred of each other. Like Russia and Ukraine. When I first became a detective, I was in missing persons and I caught a case of a missing teenager. From the crime scene, it appeared there had been violence. He started blowing a bunch of shit my way. He is a condescending prick. I was right and turned into an enormous case involving a judge and her family. That case got him bounced from homicide. Before that, when Jake was killed, he was one of those wanting to offer condolences while I was grieving. I put out the closed for the season and forever sign and it's probably the first time he was rejected. He started the rumor that we were a thing. Never happened. In fact, never happened with anyone wearing blue."

"I didn't mean to strike a nerve."

"As girls, we have to have a thick skin on this job. Blake's name is like petting a porcupine to me."

"Peace offering, can I offer you a half of a sandwich? No mayo."

"We are good."

She waved the sandwich off like it had a toxic odor. Death had a way of doing that. Most homicide detectives experienced grief for the victims and the untimely death. Loss of appetite was the first symptom; the haunting dreams would come later. It was time to deliver the death knock.

Chapter Twenty-One

Reza Jaber once lived in a simple craftsman style white framed home on Ivey Street, a little over a mile from where his body was recovered. They parked on the brick-paved street. The home had a short driveway with no garage, occupied by a silver Nissan with the fading paint job.

Kate gave an official knock on the wood door and was greeted by the smiling face of a middle-aged woman, who had her black hair pulled in a bun and olive-toned skin. Kate and Cody identified themselves and asked if they could step inside. Inside the small living room, she identified herself as Asa Jabbar. She spoke with a heavy accent.

Kate asked, "Mrs. Jaber, do you know where your husband Reza is?"

Her body language shuffled with anxiety.

Kate continued, "When was the last time you saw your husband?"

"It's been a few days. He called me yesterday morning." Kate now knew that he had been only dead since the night before.

"Was this typical, that you would not see him for days at a time?"

She looked at the floor and said, "Yes. He works hard, and sometimes he sleeps at his shop when he is doing a big job. And sometimes he goes with some of his friends from the mosque and stays with them."

"Where does he work?"

With renewed pride, she answered, "Mr. Inky Printing. We own the business. America has provided great opportunities." She smiled brightly.

"Do you think he was there?" Asa nodded yes. Kate continued. "Do you know anyone that would want to cause him harm?"

Asa again shook her head no. Her eyes glanced at Kate and then focused back on the floor while she asked, "Did the VEVAK send you?"

"VEVAK?"

Cody spoke, "The Iranian Minister of Intelligence and Security."

Asa nodded in agreement. Kate asked, "Why would the VEVAK have sent us?"

Kate could sense the fear and anxiety from Asa. Looking somewhat relieved at Kate's response, Asa said that they had fled Iran because her husband had printed some flyers for a student protest group.

"Is your husband the primary driver of the Cadillac, or does he allow others to use it for deliveries?"

She smiled. "No one drives his car. He loves that car. It represents success and American strength. He has such pride driving that Cadillac."

"How many employees does he have?"

"Just him. That is why he works so hard. He had to let go of one assistant because the business slowed. The previous owner was mad at Reza for the business slowing. It wasn't Reza's fault. The printing business is losing to the internet."

"Who was the previous owner? Why would he be upset if he sold the business to Reza?"

"I don't know. Marwan Ayoub is his name. I think he still had an investment in Mr. Inky."

Kate realized Asa had little knowledge of her husband's comings and goings or his business. "We are sorry to tell you this, but we found your husband's car in a pond and it appears your husband was inside the car and has died."

Asa shook her head rapidly while moving her hand over her mouth. Her eyes looked upward as she wailed in grief. Her knees gave way, and she collapsed to the floor as the pitch of the wail increased and tears trickled across her cheeks.

Lowering herself to one knee, Kate put one arm around Asa while rubbing her arm with the other hand to provide comfort to the grieving widow. Kate's mind flashed back to her own experience of receiving the death knock and being the one that was an inconsolable grieving widow. She knew all the emotions that Asa was feeling, which were exacerbated by financially depending on her husband.

When Asa did finally gain some composure, Kate asked Asa if there had been anything unusual in his behavior over the previous few days or weeks. Asa then provided the information that they had immigrated seven years earlier. They had escaped from Iran and had settled in Lebanon and had claimed asylum to come to the United States. They came to Tampa because of an uncle who lived in nearby Temple Terrace. Reza began working as a printer at Mr. Inky Printing and eventually bought the business.

Asa told the detectives that a couple of weeks earlier, Reza had said that he met a person who might get their son out of jail in Tehran. The son returned to Iran because of a girl and had been arrested for being associated with a dissident group. She did not know the details because Reza had refused to confide, who he was meeting, or how this would happen. She said he had been spending much more time at the print shop, working late nights, and meeting with clients.

"Do you know who the clients were or how he planned to get your son out of jail?"

With downcast eyes, "No."

Kate could only imagine what Asa must be feeling. Knowing that her son was in an Iranian prison for who knows what trumped-up charges, and now her husband was dead. Kate took time to explain the process and that his body would be taken to the Medical Examiner's Office for an autopsy. She also told Asa that it appeared her husband had died from a gunshot wound and that they would investigate this case as a homicide. Kate assisted Asa in calling a friend to explain the dire situation. The friend said they would be on their way over to provide support.

Understanding the despair that Asa was experiencing, Kate thought of how this was a detrimental loss to Asa. She was obviously very dependent on her husband and knew little about his business affairs. In addition to the stress of her son in prison in another country, her husband was dead. Hopefully he provided for her in case of his death. She would now be faced with an incredible loneliness and constant reminders of his existence. His absence would be felt with the empty bed, the favorite coffee cup and the holiday gatherings. Constant reminders of his existence. Kate was determined to hunt the killer.

The two detectives walked outside, and Kate asked Cody what he thought.

Cody said, "This was like building a puzzle and having the outside border completed and just looking to fill in the middle to complete the picture. Now, all the pieces have come unlocked and after talking with Asa, I think there's more questions than we have answers."

"Agreed. Let's go to the print shop. I'm glad she had an extra key. That is about all she knew of the business. What do you make of her comment about the VEVAK?"

"They are like the secret police or CIA."

"Do you think they would be operating here?"

"Sounds like a stretch. With their son in jail as a dissident and Reza escaping the country because of his alliance with anti-government groups, anything is possible. He would seem to be an awful low-level target after living here for seven years."

"Yes, but that whole thing about springing the son from custody is a strange twist. Let's go talk with Marwan Ayoub, the previous owner, and then look at Mr. Inky."

Chapter Twenty-Two

Driving past the coed Tampa Catholic High School, Cody asked Kate, "Did you go to private school?"

"Nope. Public-school all the way until I got to college. That was paid for by scholarships, grants and loans. Whatever loans I had, after Jake's death, I used the insurance to pay off the rest. Brittney right now is in public school, but I would definitely consider private school for her high school years."

"Yeah, I was public-school all the way and then in the Army. I took some online classes from the American Military University and Saint Leo University. Now I am just a student of life and learning criminal investigations from a wise teacher."

Kate raised her hand in a stop speaking motion. "You may have been a caterpillar for the first week, but you quickly turned into a butterfly with wings fluttering about. I am life long student. The day I stop learning is the day I'm looking up from inside of my coffin."

They pulled up in front of the residence of Mr. Ayoub on Minnehaha Street. The tilted mailbox was planted in a mostly dirt yard. The simple older home looked like it was abandoned. No cars in sight, nor much grass. She could see the front door was open. They walked across the dusty yard, stepping over tree roots.

At the glass door, she depressed the doorbell. They watched through the door as an older man in his sixties with a few strands of gray on the scalp and a stubbly beard lumbered to answer the door. His sagging face had a wide nose plopped in the middle and held up by a thick white mustache.

After identifying themselves and confirming the identity of Ayoub, he asked them to step inside the chaotically furnished small living room.

Kate asked, "Are you familiar with Reza Jaber?"

"Yes." He raised up a finger to pause the conversation and gave a deep, wet cough that seemed to come from the very bottom of his lungs. The cough went into a spasm and Kate asked, "Are you okay? Is there anything we can get for you?"

He raised his hand in a calming motion as he collapsed into a well-worn green leather recliner. His shaking hands reached over for an aerosol inhaler on a TV tray. He sucked the metered dosage into his lungs and once again began coughing. He reached over to the end table next to him and grabbed the oxygen mask and reached up and turned the valve on the tank that was next to the chair. Through the mask, he said, "I apologize. Give me just a moment."

The two detectives watched with concern and empathy as they watched his chest heave up and down. Kate thought how often she took for granted the ability to breathe with no encumbrances. Having been a distance runner for most of her life, and fitness being an essential element to her health, the concept of not being able to breathe normally was a terrifying prospect. They stood silently as the coughing and chest heaving began dissipating.

Ayoub said, "As you can see, my lungs are failing me. Too many years of Turkish cigarettes and inhaling ink fumes from the printing business. How can I help you?" He had turned the valve off the oxygen tank and return the mask to the table while now thumbing through his worry beads.

Kate asked, "We understand that you and Reza were in a business relationship together that perhaps did not end well."

"He was an excellent employee. He came to this country like me as an immigrant and trying to put distance between freedom and tyranny. A mutual friend from the mosque introduced us. I had a printing business. He had printing experience from the old country. It was a good match, and he was a hard worker. We were like brothers."

"You sold the business to him?"

He rubbed his fat nose. "When my lungs betrayed me, I had to reduce my hours and turn more of the operations to him. Eventually, I no longer had the energy or desire to go to the shop. We negotiated the sale, which included a cash deposit, a monthly payment towards the rest and a tiny percentage of the monthly profits." He held his fingers a half inch apart.

"How did that work out?"

"Good at first. Then his son was arrested in Iran for being a stupid protester. What did he and the rest of them think they were going to change?"

"What about the success of the Arab spring?"

He gave a half shrug. "Lunacy. You can admire their courage and conviction, but the theologians have ruled with an iron fist since they kicked the Americans out in 1979. They will not be pushed around by a bunch of students chanting with signs."

"How did his son's arrest impact your business sale?"

His fingers continued to massage the worry beads. "He thought, he can raise enough money to pay some corrupt minister to unlock his jail cell. He was a fool. His son was like a boulder tied to his neck. I noticed the revenues slipping, and he was late with the monthly principal on the loan."

"Did you accuse him of cheating on the agreement?"

He gave a dismissive wave. "We are men of honor. In our culture, to accuse a business partner of betrayal is the ultimate insult and dishonor. I accused him of losing focus on the business and that we had a firm agreement. We argued like two passionate Arabs and at the end he apologized, asked for forgiveness and we shook hands. No bad blood."

"Where are you from?"

"America! I am an American citizen. If you are asking where I was born, I was born in Tehran. People in this country don't appreciate what they have. After the revolution, I abandoned my business and much of my family to move to Lebanon. Much of that family I will never see again. I arrived in Lebanon with the clothes on my back and a few rials in my pocket. If not, I would've been like his son and thrown in jail for being a sympathizer of the Shah's government. I merely did business with the Shah's government. It was that or go hungry. I have been in this great country for over thirty years."

"When was the last time you saw Reza?"

"A month ago. When we had our business meeting. If I may be so forward as to ask why all these questions?"

Ignoring the inquiry, Kate asked, "Do you get out much?"

"Only to see my pulmonologist at Memorial Hospital."

"When was the last time you left the house?"

He looked up at the sky and massaged his chin. "Ten days ago. They send a bus to pick me up to take me to my appointment."

"What about shopping?"

"My brothers from the mosque and Meals on Wheels."

"To answer your question, we found him dead this morning. He was a victim of a homicide and had been shot."

His two hands grabbed the arms of the recliner as if he was bracing to go down the downslope of a roller coaster. He released his grip as his fingers squeezed the prayer beads and sigh heavily. "May peace be upon his soul. What about his widow? I will call the mosque to provide support for her grief."

"She will need help. Are you aware of any enemies or anyone that would want to do him harm? Any problematic clients?"

Shaking his head from side to side with vigor, "No. He was a nice guy. Everyone loved him."

"Not everyone. How about you? Did you have anything to do with his murder?"

His head jolted back like it had just been punched. "That is insulting. We were partners and like brothers. I loved him. I would never want harm to come to him."

"Thank you for your time. One more thing. His wife had information he had come up with a plan that could win his son's freedom. Aside from raising profits from the business, are you aware of anything else that he may have been involved in that would've provided him with the hope of gaining his son's release?"

"No. He mentioned bribing a minister, but he was very guarded. I never knew the plans. I wish I could be of more help. Crime is increased all over and I'm sure they were probably robbing him for cash or his Cadillac. He would've been the type to have fought back. I am so sad to hear of my friend's death."

"Could Asa have been involved or planned his death?"

He waved like there was an annoying gnat. "No. Absolutely not. She had nothing to gain and a lot to lose financially. There was no infidelity. They loved each other. She is very timid, and I can assure you that she had nothing to do with his death."

"Again, thank you for your time. Don't get up. We will see ourselves to the door."

As the warm breeze rustled the fronds of the nearby palm trees and the leaves of the oak trees, Cody asked, "Well, lifelong student, what did you think of Ayoub?"

Her lips clenched. "I'm not sure. I think it's too early to tell. He certainly could not have done it himself. That was certainly no show he was putting on with his lungs. But he could've arranged for someone else to have executed him."

"As he said, in the Arab world, honor and pride are of paramount importance. They have no tolerance for betrayal or the perception of it."

"Let's go to Mr. Inky and see what we find there."

Chapter Twenty-Three

Mr. Inky Printing was on Armenia Avenue across the street from the Oliva Tobacco Company, which was the occupant of the historic red brick Bonded Havana Cigar Building built in 1882. The cigar factory once housed the Garcia E Vega Cigar Company and employed many Cubans, who now comprised most of the population in the area known as West Tampa. They became influential members of Tampa society and politics.

Mr. Inky was in a much more modern building but appeared to be older than its historic neighbor. The brown brick building with a dilapidated awning was mostly vacant except for the one storefront occupied by the print shop.

Cody parked behind the building in the vacant parking lot that at one time served as the loading dock for shipping and receiving of the businesses housed in the building. Now, it was mostly tall weeds and broken asphalt. Kate looked over at the historic cigar factory as she watched several white uniformed employees on a smoke break.

Walking up to the rear entrance of the print shop, Kate used the key provided by Asa to open the deadbolt and the door. Kate was relieved that there was no alarm. They stepped into the darkness of the shop and could immediately smell the sweet aroma of printing ink.

Kate used her cell phone as a flashlight to find the light switch. Once the shop was illuminated, they began looking around the inside of the shop. A well-worn brown sofa was set behind the customer counter near the front of the store. A table with multiple soda cans and food wrappers was to the right. Kate noticed the nearby trashcan was also filled to the rim. There was a one-person cot with a crumpled blanket and a lumpy pillow.

As they continued to look around, Cody picked up some paper trimmings next to the paper cutter. He then looked in the trashcan next to the paper cutter and found more of the same. Continuing to dig through the paper in the receptacle, he found one crumpled sheet of paper. He opened it up and showed it to Kate. On the sheet of paper, was three impressions of $50 bills.

Kate's eyes widened as she looked at Cody's findings. Looking over one machine, she saw the image of a $50 bill on the rubber blanket attached to the printing press roller.

Pointing at the blanket, Kate said, "When he told Asa that he met someone that could help get their son out of prison, this is probably the scheme he was talking about. Counterfeiting currency and perhaps using that counterfeit to pay off someone in Iran who could let his son out the back door or lose his paperwork. You know, corruption runs deep in those types of countries."

Cody said, "Definitely. I'll call for the crime scene unit to meet us here."

"I don't see any evidence of violence in here. We have no doubt he was killed in the car. What secrets are here for us to uncover? I'll call the Secret Service. They deal with counterfeit currency."

Kate called the local U.S. Secret Service Field Office in Tampa and asked to speak with someone concerning counterfeit currency. She was connected to the duty agent named Russell Tenpenny, who told her they had experienced a recent surge in counterfeit $50 bills. He told her that what made this different was that most counterfeit was now scanned and printed using computers and digital printers. But this new circulation of bills was high quality and being manufactured on offset printing presses.

Tenpenny told her he would come over and meet them at the print shop. Kate looked at Cody and said, "I'm quite surprised. They said they have had an influx of counterfeit 50s. He's coming over right now, which is surprising, because most feds will tell you they will be out next week and never get in a hurry about anything. I think that's the first time I have called the Secret Service, and I am impressed."

"It is impressive. Crime scene unit is on its way as well. We can just have a big old party right here."

Chapter Twenty-Four

The crime scene unit knocked on the back door and Cody let them in. Donnie Miller, the crime scene technician, held up a plastic evidence bag, and Cody could see there was one shell casing inside. Miller told them they had concluded their initial assessment of the Cadillac. They told them the vehicle minus Jaber's body was being towed to the nearby FDLE crime lab for more in-depth processing. But they recovered the one shell casing from under the passenger seat. The theory being, whoever fired the shot from the back seat, the shell casing ejected to the right and either bounced off the seat or the floorboard, and landed under the front seat.

Miller said, "I've never seen this brand of shell before. Usually we see the standard Remington, Federal, Winchester, brands and so on, but I've never seen this before."

Cody fingered the bag with his hand and manipulated the casing so that he could see the bottom. He read the evidence tag. "AMIG casing found under the front passenger seat." He looked at Miller and Kate and said, "The AMIG is Ammunition Industries Group. It's Iranian ammo."

Miller said, "You don't see that in your everyday gang banging execution."

"Nope. The only explanation would be if a soldier had brought back a pocket full of it or you had an Iranian shooter. But this ties in with Mr. Jaber being Iranian and wanting to get his son out of prison."

Kate said, "So, what do we have here? A double-cross? The printer, who is Iranian, is making fake bills in his print shop and then gets executed in his own car by an Iranian bullet. The plot thickens, and in fact, this is becoming thicker than New England clam chowder. Frank Duffy once told me about small cases, small problems, and big cases, big problems. This feels like it's going to have huge problems."

The crime scene unit began taking their initial photographs of the scene. And then collecting the food wrappings and discarded soda cans.

Kate asked Donald Miller, "How is your cute little dog, Malibu?"

"After the kids left, Malibu is our focus. She loves traveling with us. She has her own YouTube channel, where we share her adventures."

"That's outstanding. We just bought a golden retriever puppy for Brittney."

"Lots of energy?"

"Lots."

The back door opened and a thick chested man walked in wearing a sport coat and federal agent tattooed to his head. Russell Tenpenny introduced himself and began walking around the shop.

Tenpenny pointed to the offset printing press and said, "AB Dick 360. Offset printing presses are primarily found in museums now. AB Dick went bankrupt back some time ago. Most print shops have gone digital. As you can see, the image on this rubber blanket on the roller is the image of a $50 counterfeit Federal Reserve Note. The counterfeiters with an offset have to make three passes. One for the back plate, another for the front plate, and then another for the treasury seal and the serial numbers. The digital process is much more streamlined, but the quality is decreased."

The two detectives and crime scene technicians listened intently, like students in the classroom, as Tenpenny provided an education on counterfeit currency. Tenpenny then walked over to a commercial dryer with its door slightly ajar. Not touching the outside, he pushed it open and looked inside.

He turned to the group and said, "This is how they aged the money. There are poker chips and polished rocks to weather the bills."

He walked back to the printing press and said, "What's interesting is they are printing an older series bill, pre-dating many of the security features added to recent bills."

"What's that mean?" asked Kate.

"U.S. currency never goes out of circulation. We still receive bills from the 1950's. As good as the day they were printed. The newer bills with all the security enhancements are more challenging to reproduce at a high quality."

"Interesting."

"Well, on the behalf of the U.S. Government, we appreciate your help because this is definitely what we would refer to as a counterfeit plant suppression. We will have the press, dryer and paper cutter seized. My question is how you folks found this?"

Kate explained to Tenpenny how they had found the operation after investigating the homicide of Reza Jaber. Tenpenny told her that each bill has unique characteristics and identifiers. When they started getting an influx of fifties from the banks and merchants, it was quickly identified as a new note, not previously seen anywhere else. Initially, they were being passed in Tampa at the big box merchants, that will offset their loss with their high volume. They don't check as close. Then the bills started being passed at truck stops and outlet malls along I-75, I-4, I-10 and I-95.

They nicknamed it the "Trucker Note." He said that with the plant closed down, they would have to wait for the fake money to pass through circulation. Kate asked how much could they have printed.

"Millions."

"Millions?"

"Yep. A few million would not be unusual. We had a case in Canada, where the printer made tens of millions. The Canadiens shipped a couple of million that was destined for Ft. Lauderdale. Our Miami office intercepted and seized the load."

Kate asked Tenpenny, "So what do we now?"

"We assume Jaber was the printer. We do not know if he was acting alone during the printing process. He would've needed additional conspirators to distribute the counterfeit money. We know from the distribution already that it appears the network was significant."

"So, it is distributed like a drug network?"

"Exactly. The original source or printer will break up the currency into smaller packages. Depending upon the amount, sometimes it's $25,000 or a big package of $200,000. Then each person in the distribution chain breaks it up further. The further away the person is from the distributor, the more they pay."

"So just like drugs, when you catch the lowest hanging fruit, you try to flip them to go back up the chain and track it back to its original source?"

"Bingo. We should sign you up for the Secret Service. We have openings. I can give you an application."

"Doesn't every agency have a staffing shortage? I'll take a pass, thank you. You folks travel way too much and you have to move. Being a single parent, I prefer the stability of what I'm doing now."

"That's a shame. You look physically fit and could pass the PT test. You obviously have the experience, and you are a quick learner."

Cody said, "Hey, you can't have her and don't start filling her head with platitudes. Her enormous head won't fit through the door."

"Before we were so rudely interrupted," she looked at Cody and rolled her eyes with a smile. "So how do we find the potential murderers and major distributors of counterfeit currency unless crime scene can develop trace evidence?"

"Every time a counterfeit bill is turned into the bank, they fill out a form which provides details as to the location and any suspect information. The same for merchants. The form and counterfeit are then forwarded to our office and inputted into the system. If there are any promising leads, then that is assigned to an agent to run out. Probably ninety-five percent of the time we come up with a dry hole. But with persistence and enough shoe leather, we can usually develop a potential suspect and promising information."

"Tomorrow, can we come to your office and start culling through these forms and see which ones are the most promising that we can check out?"

"Sure, no problem. We are very shorthanded in the office right now. In fact, I am the only agent in the office, aside from the two bosses. Every September, we have the United Nations General Assembly in New York City and foreign dignitaries from all around the world descend upon New York. It's a bigger gathering than usual, so it will require more resources than normal. So, most of our office is up there now."

"Well, we can provide help." As she looked over at Cody and they both enthusiastically nodded their heads.

"That would be helpful, as most of our folks will not return from the U.N. for at least a week and some possibly two weeks. We also just had Frank Duffy from your department start as a liaison to our financial investigative strike team. I don't know if you know him or not?"

Kate nodded as a soothing smile crept across her face and said, "Most definitely. We used to be partners. We look forward to seeing you tomorrow and Detective Duffy."

Chapter Twenty-Five

Walking outside, she squinted into the bright sun and as she shielded her eyes with her hand; she turned towards the right. She again looked across the street at the three-story brick building that housed the Oliva Tobacco Company. Kate had previously glanced at the small loading dock when she entered Mr. Inky. She had seen several workers in white uniforms huddled together. There was a new crew of white uniforms smoking. She thought it was a little ironic that workers at a tobacco company were standing by the loading dock, smoking cigarettes.

She nudged Cody and pointed across the street as she started walking towards them. The group watched with suspicion as the approaching detectives walked across the street. Two of the workers dropped the partially smoked cigarettes and rubbed them out with their feet and descended back through the door into the warehouse.

Kate wondered why the two were in such a hurry to go back to work. Obviously concerned that they may get in some sort of trouble. Possibly fearing tobacco inspectors, immigration agents, or owners of the company. She could hear the group speaking Spanish.

She yelled to the last three, "Policia!" The three smiled politely back at her as she approached. She asked the group if anyone spoke English. She knew she would be hard-pressed to ask the questions with her limited knowledge of Spanish.

One of the three said with a thick accent, "Yes."

Kate sighed with relief and asked, "We wanted to know if you've seen any cars back there or anyone coming or going?"

The translator of the group began conversing in Spanish with the other two. There were nods and hand gestures pointing to the rear of Mr. Inky. The translator responded and said, "There were two cars back there. One was a black Cadillac. Another was a gray, older SUV. It was smaller, but no one knew who the manufacturer was. Neither of the three had seen any people coming or going. The Cadillac was a constant. The SUV was there for a few days and then a blue Chevrolet sedan. Then they were both gone. Sometimes other cars would come and go. Maybe customers."

Kate asked why the other two had reentered the warehouse. The translator shrugged his shoulders. "I don't know."

"Okay. Thank you."

Kate and Cody walked around to the front entrance of the building and walked up the ten steps to the double wood door entrance to the Oliva Tobacco Company. As soon as she pulled the door open, the scent of tobacco wafted past them as they entered a smartly appointed lobby. After identifying themselves to the receptionist, she summoned the warehouse manager, Carlos Diaz.

Mr. Diaz entered the lobby wearing khakis and an open neck white dress shirt. With a pleasant smile and demeanor, he asked, "How can I help you?"

Kate said, "We are conducting an investigation at the Mr. Inky print shop across the street." As she gestured in the business's direction. "We thought that perhaps some of your employees may have seen people or cars coming and going. We spoke with three by the loading dock and they gave us the description of two cars. There were two other employees who thought it was best to run back inside. Perhaps they were in a hurry to get back to rolling cigars again."

He appeared to be born with a smile on his face as he nodded and said, "They probably were not supposed to be on break. And I can assure you that all of our employees have been vetted and are legal residents. I will reach out and ask the employees if they have seen anything. I can only speak for myself and say that I have not."

"Thank you very much. Here is my business card with my cell phone number and email. If you find out any additional information, I would appreciate it. This is a beautiful building."

"Thank you. As you can see from the peak of the roof, the signage is 1882 and the Oliva Tobacco Company has been around since 1934. We don't make cigars here, but we do import and ship leaf tobacco to the world's premier cigar producers. If you have time, I can give you a quick tour."

"As much as I would be interested in that offer, perhaps we can get a rain check and come back some other time."

He nodded. "Absolutely. I will let you know if I hear anything from any of the employees."

As they descended the steps that were now in the shadow of the three-story building, Kate said, "Let's head back to the office and brief Benny."

Chapter Twenty-Six

Kate and Cody headed back to the homicide office. When they walked into the sergeant's office, Kate was shocked by the transformation of Alfonso's previous sanctuary. The office, once meticulous and decorated with an aquarium filled with marine life and adorned with several beautiful orchids that most florists would be jealous to own, all had changed. The workplace had now gone through an extreme makeover and not in a good way.

Despite just starting in homicide, it already appeared that Benny's desk was in a disarray. Perhaps this was just the normal chaos before becoming organized, but Kate was not optimistic. Her new sergeant was sitting behind his desk, sipping on a big gulp soft drink with an open container of pork rinds sitting in front of him. Benny released the straw from his mouth and motioned for them to come in.

As he pushed the Costco sized bucket of pork rinds to the side, he said. "What have you got?"

Kate's sighed heavily and then filled him in on the wide-ranging investigation. She told him about the plans to meet at the Secret Service the next day. Their conversation was interrupted by Kate's cell phone. Kate held up her finger to pause the conversation and answered the phone. "Yes sir, lieutenant. I'll be there in just a few minutes." She ended the call.

"You're not going anywhere. You can return to your desk and continue working on this case. I'll go down and brief The Caveman, as you folks like to call him."

Kate and Cody snickered and walked back toward their desk as their sergeant displayed an urgency in his stride before heading out the door. Kate motioned for Cody to follow as they walked down the hallway, trailing in the exhaust fumes of their new supervisor. They watched as he walked into the lieutenant's office. They hovered just on the outskirts but within hearing distance.

She smiled at the thought of the disparity between the two bosses. One with a starched, creased shirt and Windsor knotted tie and the other in a wrinkled, ill-fitting shirt with a tie worn as a loose hanging necklace. Their personalities reflected their wardrobe.

Benny said, "Jack, I understand you reached out to Detective Alexander directly. What am I? A potted plant? I am her immediate supervisor, and I would appreciate if you would show respect to the chain of command. She had just provided me with a detailed briefing. Now, after spending that time, you are requesting her to break off her investigation to repeat the same story she had just relayed to me."

The Caveman replied, "Benny, it was no disrespect to you. Because of the PIO's involvement, the tenth floor was inquiring. So, I figured I would get the most direct information straight from the horse's mouth."

"So, once the penthouse jingled your phone and you didn't have the current information, instead of calling me, you inserted yourself into the investigative arc and disrupted the investigative process. You're more nervous than a satanic witch in church. You need to grow some hair on your balls and learn to stand up for your troops. Show them you have their back and have not been manscaped."

Cody and Kate covered their mouths as they doubled over, trying to conceal their laughter.

That struck a nerve. "Sergeant, I don't care for your tone and your insinuations. I am the supervisor over you and your detectives and you will follow my directives."

"Well, Lieutenant, I didn't ask for this assignment. I was happy wearing the uniform in patrol. The Chief called me and told me I had been selected for the position. I did not volunteer to come here. No doubt this relates back to the longevity and trust in my relationship with the Chief. Our friendship goes back to when I was the Chief's field training officer many sunsets ago. So, Lieutenant, if you don't want to be counting pencils in the supply room, I would suggest that you follow the chain of command and show some respect to your homicide team."

Kate and Cody eased away. They could hear a muffled response and Benny launched again.

"Oh, and by the way, I heard you were looking to move one of your suck-asses up here named Wilson Smith."

Cody and Kate traded surprised looks.

"No decisions have been made on that vacancy, Sergeant."

"Well, I heard he is trying to get his wife pregnant. If his swimmers are anything like him, they are too lazy to swim upstream and find the egg. So, I don't want him in my squad."

"Thank you for your input, Sergeant. I'll take it under advisement, but I make the personnel assignments."

The two detectives scurried back down the hallway to put some distance from the office. As Benny returned to his office, he looked at the two and said, "You two need to brush up on your spy skills. If you worked for the CIA, we would all be speaking Chinese by now."

They both shrugged and their body language acknowledged that they had both been caught. Kate felt exuberant and had an overwhelming feeling to pump her fists in celebration. Cody looked over at Kate and said, "I wonder how he knew about the manscaping incident?"

"You know, there are no secrets inside the Blue Monster. Who knows, The Caveman may have told on himself. But this building is like a 24/7 gossip convention. Who is getting promoted, who has relationship woes, and who's banging who."

"True."

"What Benny said in there tells me I would run through a hail of gunfire to come to his rescue. Finding someone that will stand up and fight for his troops in police work anymore is almost as rare as unicorns and mermaids."

"I know unicorns are rare, but are you telling me that mermaids don't exist?"

They both laughed and sat down and discussed their investigative strategy going forward, while they both updated the paperwork for the murder books. Before we call it a day, I'd like to have another chat with Marwan Ayoub about this Iranian angle.

Chapter Twenty-Seven

The two detectives parked in separate cars once again in front of the disheveled home of Ayoub. They rang the doorbell and could hear the TV playing. As Kate looked through the glass door, she could see Ayoub holding up the remote control and muting the TV, while he waved with his arm for them to enter the home.

Ayoub said, "How am I so honored to have two visits on the same day? Are you here to arrest me?" He held up both of his hands as if preparing to be handcuffed and laughed. His chuckle turned into another fit of coughing, followed by another surge of oxygen.

Kate said, "Not hardly. But we had some questions that we were hoping you could help us with."

"By all means." As his breathing was still labored.

"When we went to Mr. Inky, we found some potential evidence showing that he might have been counterfeiting U.S. currency."

"Impossible. He would never jeopardize his freedom, his business or his wife."

"Even to get his son out of prison?"

"There is a saying in the Muslim world that wealth comes as a turtle and runs away like a gazelle. He would have been a fool to embark on such an imprudent path."

"He said nothing to you about exploring alternate revenue streams?"

"It was essentially his business, so he no longer had to share details with me. Perhaps what you found was preparations to use in an advertising campaign. I have had car dealers wanting to use money in their ads showing the potential customers would save cash. There are restrictions on how you can reproduce that. So, he may have been reducing the sizing that would comply with the U.S. Treasury oversight. He would've been an imbecile to jeopardize the business."

"You said that you left Iran in 1979?"

"Yes. I wasn't overly political, but most of my business was derived from the government or those associated with the Shah's government. When the revolution overthrew the government, just as the Shah and his secret police cracked down on dissenters, the same happened to those who were former members of the revolution. The persecuted became the oppressors. I did not want to risk being on the wrong side of justice, and with my business falling faster than a missile out of the sky, I left everything."

"Do you still have contact with any family back in Iran?"

"Sadly, very little. My parents died of broken hearts. I still have some distant family, but I rarely hear from them."

"What about locally or at the mosque?"

"I don't know if you attend a house of worship, but you gather under the prayerful roof of your religion joined in unity. You don't go around asking your fellow worshipers where they come from. We are all Muslims and we come from many parts of the world. We are a proud religion of two billion strong and three a half million in America. I know because of the poisonous acts of a few, we are all labeled as a bunch of terrorists."

Ignoring the attempt by Ayoub to throw the interviewers off stride with a remark insinuating an intolerant slur, Kate asked, "To your knowledge, neither you nor Reza had any connection with any Iranians that would've been up to no good?"

He defiantly shook his head. "No."

Kate wanted to soften the line of inquiry so as not to show her hand that she was even contemplating a terrorist angle. "I didn't think so. But I had to ask the question. He may have been forced to print counterfeit to comply with a business takeover."

"Perhaps."

"I understand that both you and he have been long-time residents of America and contributing members of society. As you said, it's a shame when a small group casts aspersions on the entire population. My apologies if I offended you." She bowed her head.

"I understand that you have a job to do and hopefully you will find the killer of my friend."

"What happens to the business after his death?"

"The business will be sold along with the equipment. That will settle the outstanding debt with me and any vendors. What is left over will be split between me and his wife. I don't imagine there would be much left to split. I had no motive to kill my friend. His death leaves me in a desperate financial situation."

"Thank you for your time, and I apologize for having to bring up such painful thoughts."

Fingering his worry beads, he nodded in acceptance and said, "Thank you. Good luck with your investigation."

Outside, standing in the dirt yard, Kate said, "Let's pull the shade on this for the night. I'll see you in the morning and we will head to the Secret Service. Enjoy your culinary delights with your mom. Get some sleep."

"Who needs a mom when I have you?"

"Keep it up, son."

Chapter Twenty-Eight

Parking next to her Jeep, Kate stepped out of her city issued vehicle. She looked up at the freshly painted wood sign that read "Over the Moon Stables" with a half-moon crescent on one end and a horse's head at the opposite end.

Kate saw Trent still wearing his khakis and casual shirt, leaning against the fence, watching Brittney riding Knight around the corral. Trent turned towards the movement of Kate as they embraced and kissed.

"If you had a hat and boots, I would have confused you with a genuine cowboy." She said.

"Guilty. I look like the professor that I am. Knowing that Brittney was scheduled to ride today, I thought I would give your mom a break and pick her up myself."

"My mom probably appreciated the break. That was so sweet of you."

"My pleasure. I'm glad I could help. How was your day?"

"Very bizarre. Remember that pond with the suspect who was killed by the alligator?"

"Oh, sure."

"Well, we went back to see if we could recover a handgun that may have been used in several shootings and a homicide. Only to find a black Cadillac had been dumped in the same pond and had a body. Now he is Iranian, and they found a bullet casing manufactured in Iran."

"The wife or the butler? It's always one of the two."

"I have not ruled her out yet, but come to find out he was counterfeiting $50 bills. His wife thought he was engaging in some effort to get their son out of prison in Tehran. So, the Secret Service is now involved."

"Well, the way they lock up dissidents in Iran, that is probably true. And with the level of corruption, it could be plausible."

"All true. But the most bizarre aspect, and the best part, was my new sergeant who went into The Caveman's office and yanked his pants to his ankles and proceeded to chew his ass out. It was fabulous."

"I can see a little vigor in your step."

"So much so, I'm going inside to change into jeans and take Duke out for a trail ride with Britney. I'm craving some much-needed mom and daughter time. If you don't mind going home and I'll call you to come pick us up."

"Sure. Being that we are at the end of September, I made a pot of chicken white chili and picked up a sixpack of Sam Adams Oktoberfest."

"You're the best. I think I'm going to keep you around." They both laughed, and she carried her duffel bag into the office of the stables. She said to Patty Moon, "Patty, if you don't mind, I'm going to change and take Duke out for a ride with Britney." She pulled her hair up into a ponytail and snaked it through a blue Tampa Bay Lightning ball cap.

"Girl, you look like you scored a date with a rodeo champ."

"Better. I scored the best date to the prom, who is standing out there, watching my daughter, cooked dinner, and even brought adult beverages."

"He is a keeper. I am thrilled that you corralled him."

"I have you to partially thank."

"Me?"

"You talked sense into me. Let me tell you what, put the cherry on top of the ice cream sundae today. My new sergeant is kind of eccentric, but he ripped The Caveman and put a line in the sand."

"That is sensational. Hey, we can catch up some other time. I don't want to interfere with your energetic high. I'll go out and saddle up Duke for you."

"Thank you for your help and for always having a listening ear for me. You truly are like the Lucy the psychologist from the Peanuts cartoon. I owe you a lot more than a nickel."

"I'll add it to the hay feed charge on this month's billing."

"How about if I just bring over a bushel of carrots for your borders?"

"Done." They both laughed as Kate headed towards the restroom to change.

Chapter Twenty-Nine

After a glorious trail ride alongside Brittney, talking about life, Kate felt that peace had been restored to her life. For a long time, she'd felt an undercurrent of anxiety but could portray an image of calm and control. But in reality, life was closer to the duck gliding across the pond while its feet were frantically paddling to stay afloat and to keep moving.

The foundation of her life had collapsed with the death of her husband Jake in Afghanistan. She was a single mother, and a newly promoted detective in a homicide squad filled with seasoned and grizzled veterans. She was fortunate that her mother moved from North Carolina and moved in with Kate and Brittney. It provided some stability and support.

Although they weren't living under the same roof, Trent brought stability to her chaotic life. Sometimes it was difficult to determine that they were not a married couple. Trent spent most weekends with Kate, while spending most of the work week at his condominium. They were mutually exclusive. Having worked through her personal laundry basket, she got her emotions sorted. She had always been affixed to the memory of Jake. Kate had come to terms with the heartbreak as well as the happy memories together, which brought a smile to her face. She knew for her sake and that of Brittney that she needed to open up her emotional vault to allow for new memories to be created.

When they had returned to the stables and said goodbye to their mounts, they waited for Trent to return to pick up Brittney. The city had a policy of not allowing non-authorized family members to ride in the assigned take-home city car. Kate pulled out her phone and saw a message from Russell Tenpenny of the Secret Service.

As she read the message, her cheerful spirit faded. Tenpenny said that because of additional unanticipated dignitaries coming to New York for the United Nations General Assembly, he was leaving on an early morning flight. Despite being in the middle of a case, he was being called away. Russell said he was as frustrated as no doubt she would be when she read the message. He said his two supervisors were the only ones left in the office and not to count on a lot of help from them.

Tenpenny said he had spoken with the civilian investigative assistant, who would gather up all the information on the passing of the counterfeit $50 Federal Reserve notes. He also said that Frank Duffy would be the Secret Service representative in the ongoing investigation. He apologized and signed off.

Kate thought to herself, how could you be in the middle of a case, apparently a large case connected to a homicide investigation, and be called away to guard some minister of fruits and vegetables from some country that you had to Google to find out where it was located. Duty calls. She understood that soldiers have to follow orders, like when Tampa Police would have to drop everything to provide staffing and support for the Super Bowl or the Gasparilla Parade.

She knew that if Tenpenny's bosses were anything like The Caveman, they were probably too far removed from putting on their Sherlock Holmes hat and remembering how to conduct investigations. They probably kept their guns in their desk and couldn't find their handcuffs with a team of K-9s. She had trust in her old partner Frank Duffy and looked forward to saddling up and riding the trail together again.

This was going to be the new and improved Frank Duffy. Fresh from a stint in rehab, a week of PTSD therapy, he was learning to deal with his trauma from the death of his wife and the wounding of his partner, Lester Rollins. He had gone through some hard times but had clawed his way out of the whiskey bottle. He had been her mentor, and she hoped he was the same tenacious investigator that existed in the past.

Chapter Thirty

As the two operatives stood next to the van, they removed their safety goggles and scrutinized the hole that Firouz had drilled through the side panel. Ali pursed his lips and blew through the hole, displacing the fine shards of metal. Ali looked at his partner and nodded with approval.

Firouz was excited to receive recognition from his superior. He felt great pride at his youthful accomplishments. Popular with the female students, his smile and charm were bright enough to attract moths in the darkness.

His father had once been a tailor working in a fine clothier for wealthy clients. After the revolution, the business closed and his father found work in a commercial laundry. A man who had once caressed fine fabric with his fingers and sewed high quality garments for the aristocracy, he was now reduced to handling soiled uniforms. His back ached from transferring the wet government uniforms from the washing machine to the dryers. With inflation skyrocketing, they could no longer afford the rental prices for their shabby apartment.

In 2007, the family moved into the public housing towers, into one of the isolated satellite cities outside of Tehran. The commute to the city took hours and wore down his father, who grew more depressed and finally lost hope. He succumbed to a malady of health conditions and died a bitter and broken man. Firouz's mother had been forced to become a street vendor selling homemade scarves.

His parents instilled the value of education and compelled him to study hard. His diligence paid dividends when he took the university entrance exam known as the Konkour. He scored well enough to be selected to the Sharif University of Technology, considered the most prestigious university in the country. Having hopes of becoming an engineer, he also drew attention to himself for his natural ability to learn multiple languages, including Spanish and English. Before his graduation, he was recruited into the Quds Force. He would never realize his dreams of becoming an engineer.

He knew being recruited for this mission was his ticket to success, but he also felt a pang of guilt knowing the hardships that his parents had endured.

In his brief time in Tampa, he looked upon the community with jealousy at the abundance of wealth and ease that most people appeared to live under. Everyone appeared to have jobs, cars, and affordable food, which was abundant in stores. Every day, Iranians struggled to make ends meet and keep a roof over their heads under the sanctions imposed by the West. Iran was being strangled. The elites were not hurting as they skimmed off the top for food, gas, and jobs rewarded by favoritism. Meanwhile, common people like his family were struggling.

Seeing Tampa reminded him of the tales from his father, who reveled in the way Iran was before the revolution. The tales were often laced with bitterness as Firouz listened to antigovernment preaching's. Firouz wondered what his father would think of him now, being a part of that same government that he railed against.

Prior to his departure from Tehran for training, he learned of his sister's arrest. She had been protesting after the death of a young woman for showing too much hair beneath her headscarf. She was among the twenty thousand who had been arrested. He was relieved that she was not one of the hundreds killed as the government attempted to crush the movement. He couldn't help but feel somewhat conflicted that he was embarking on one of the boldest foreign operations on behalf of the government, while his own family suffered at the hands of the same government.

Firouz and Ali aligned the beam of light through the hole in the van and took measurements of the stanchion that would provide the stationary platform for the beam.

Chapter Thirty-One

Standing in the austere and cavernous commercial garage, Ali looked upon their handiwork with satisfaction. He was enthralled with the progression of their mission and that the success of the operation would fall squarely on his broad shoulders. Bakhtiar would be hailed as a hero, despite being a contemptible failure and unable to carry through with his own orders of incompetence. The thought brought a smile as he thought how Bakhtiar ignored Ali's wisdom and died following through on his own ignorant and perilous orders.

He looked at the Chevy Equinox with the Texas license plate and thought of that frightful night in the river. The SUV had served its purpose, delivering them to Florida. If Bakhtiar's body was recovered and the Chevy was linked to them, no one would see the getaway car again. With only a quick nap, the two warriors had driven twenty hours from the casino parking lot in Eagle Pass to Tampa, only stopping for gas. Their entry had been undetected.

Ali knew that upon his and Firouz's successful operation, he would be hailed a hero and perhaps given the Order of Faith given to warriors with dramatic victories. Promotions would come easily. He imagined striding through the halls of their headquarters in Ahvaz, as others would point towards him and whisper that he was the commander of the most victorious operation in the West. Vengeance had been delivered at the hands of that warrior. That warrior being Ali.

Growing up in a small farming village of Galesh Khil, he knew his exploits would provide heroic recognition to his family. They would beam with pride, reveling in the exploits of their oldest son.

The U.S. with its arrogance of wealth, deserved retribution for being an active enemy of the Republic of Iran. They had propped up and supported the corrupt and vile Shah. They stood arm in arm in concert with the most atrocious enemies of the Republic. Israel, Iraq, Saudi Arabia, Yemen and other European countries that had isolated Iran with sanctions and brought great discomfort to the population. He would swing the sword of revenge and deliver a crippling blow.

He smiled at Firouz, whose white teeth were as white as snow and on full display with the grin. They adjusted the stanchion holding the beam and aimed it at the hole in the side of the van.

Ali looked at Firouz and said, "Remember when they had the three of us in the general's conference room and telling us we had been selected for a special assignment?"

"Yes, of course. I will always remember that day."

"I felt immense pride that the honor had been bestowed upon us to carry the sword for the Republic. We will be heroes. Our names will be in history books forever as warriors."

He put his arm around Firouz and pulled him into a joyous embrace.

Chapter Thirty-Two

Although Trent had left for the evening, the aroma of the fabulous chicken chili lingered in the air, reminding Kate how fortunate she was to have Trent in her life. Meeting through the hypnosis of a witness on one of her cases, they meshed like two perfectly aligned gears and enjoyed a mutual attraction.

It was Kate that slammed on the brakes. Conflicted on still holding a torch for the memory of her beloved Jake. She and Jake enjoyed a mutual interest in outdoor athletic endeavors. Working out, horse riding, mountain biking, scuba diving, and even tumbling out of a perfectly good airplane and skydiving to the ground. Then it was over. Aside from the horse riding, she'd given up on many of the activities, which it had become too painful, spurring memories of more joyous times.

Emptiness had consumed her after losing Jake. She had progressed through the five stages of grief. She had gone to a therapist. Her passion for life had left her wanting to give up on life. Brittney was her lone inspiration. Her mother moving in helped fill the hollowness. Two widows under one roof and the unconditional love of her horses and Brittney, all helped her to move forward and open up to life again.

As her relationship with Trent heated, she couldn't help but feel the burden of guilt in betraying the memory of Jake. She also felt the guilt of the single parent and the responsibility of assuming the dual role of mother and father to Brittney. Time spent with Trent was time lost with Brittney.

She knew Jake would have encouraged her to find a new companion. It had been a struggle to put her baggage to the side and accept the intimacy with someone who adored, supported, and loved her. This had been her first serious connection and perhaps her only relationship.

After the funeral, there were several attempts amongst the many warriors in blue who offered to provide comfort during her grieving. She all but had to illuminate the no vacancy sign and chase off potential suitors. It was a challenge to meet men outside of the cop world. Most men outside of the public service community were intimidated by her confidence and authority. There were the snide remarks pertaining to being handcuffed or being arrested. She wanted to put each one of those in a chokehold.

Inside, the cop world was off-limits to her, as she did not want to tolerate the resulting gossip. Despite her off limits posture, there were still rumors of various conquests by male counterparts. Pigs. Then others, who she rebuffed, had put the word out that she was stuck up. A man's world. Bitch or whore? She grew a thick skin and allowed her performance to outshine the rumors. She liked the nickname Kick Ass. It was better than others.

She had become reticent to being solely focused on work, Brittney and having the support of her mother who'd moved into the house. She'd come to terms that she would never find the love she had shared with Jake and had stopped the search.

Trent had become a surprise. She'd stumbled upon the gem without looking. He was like the cozy sweater on a cool night that provided the warmth and embrace of comfort. She allowed herself to become happy.

As she finished brushing her wet hair, Kate opened up her laptop and waited for it to come alive. She turned to the sound of paws pattering and watched Louie come trotting in to check on her. His tail wagged softly as she greeted him. He dropped his head on her lap and sat. She began stroking the golden fur and was thankful again for the decision to bring Louie into the family. Despite working through the challenges during the puppy stage, he brought such joy to Brittney and to Kate as well.

She started typing "Iran" into the search field. Over the next two hours, she jumped from one article or post to the next, educating herself as much as she could on the culture within the isolated country. She read about the relationship between the U.S. and Iran and the deep divide between the two countries.

She wanted to be prepared with background knowledge that might illuminate the investigative trail ahead of her. The finding of the Iranian casing kept bringing her back to an Iranian shooter. She knew from Reza's discussion with both Ayoub and his wife, Asa, that there was a plan that would help extricate his son from an Iranian prison. Had this plan gone awry and simply turned into a robbery? Perhaps it had been someone close to Reza who may have had access to a weapon. Conceivably, it was Reza's pistol, and had already been loaded with that ammunition. He may have had the handgun at the shop to ward off robbers and the gun was turned against him. There was no evidence of a crime scene at Mr. Inky. The aperture of her investigative lenses was wide open, as she had to consider all possibilities this early in the investigation.

Louie had previously wandered back off to sleep in his bed at the foot of the slumbering Brittney. Kate's hair was long ago dry from the shower. Closing her laptop, she headed to bed and looking forward to teaming up with her old partner, Frank Duffy.

Kate sent a text message to Frank and said she was looking forward to working with him at the Secret Service and she would see him in the morning. She asked him to meet her and Cody in the homicide office.

Chapter Thirty-Three

After sliding her feet between the cool sheets, Kate reached down and pulled the duvet up to her chest. The extra weight brought the comfort of an embrace that had long been absent. As she wiggled into comfort, her phone rang. Life as a homicide detective.

She reached over and saw the caller ID identified the caller as Ed Croissant. Ed had been the backup unit at the alligator pond with Doug Pasley when Johnny Nylon had drowned.

"Hi Eddie. What's up?"

"I hope I didn't disturb sleeping beauty. It's late for you, but early for me."

"You know the motto of homicide. Our day begins when your day ends. To answer your question, I was still awake and just getting into bed."

"I don't think you have to get out of bed on this one. No steaming bodies to come out for. I was talking to Andrea Casale, and she was telling me about the dead Cadillac in the alligator pond and that there was a counterfeiting angle to it."

"Yes, there is."

"We have detained a homeless guy named Elmo Price because he was trying to pass a fake $50 bill."

"If he only had the one bill, you might have trouble proving intent."

"That would normally be true, but this fucking wizard went to three different convenience stores on three different corners of the same intersection on Kennedy Boulevard. Each time, the clerk would not accept it and told him to beat it and that it's counterfeit. Another mistake was each clerk handing it back to him instead of taking it from him. Finally, the third one held on to it and called 911."

"Well, that would prove intent. It's just whether the state attorney would be bothered with only passing one bill. Can you read me the last four digits of the serial number?"

"Sure, 4538."

"That's definitely one of the serial numbers. Did he say where he received it?"

"Once we got past the Kennedy assassination, the CIA using spy balloons and merely blaming the Chinese. Elmo claims to have found it outside the church."

"Which church?"

"Sacred Heart. The bill is in kind of bad shape. I don't know if that's because of his grimy pockets or from finding it in the bushes in front of the church."

"Eddie, what are your thoughts?"

"I think Elmo is going to get a complementary bed-and-breakfast stay at the Orient Road jail. Part two of the story is the church filed a theft report two days ago. They claimed a homeless person was attending service and sitting in the last pew. When the collection basket arrived, the suspect reached up and grabbed a fistful and squirted out the rear of the church. I don't know if Elmo was the grabber. The possibility exists that whoever the thief was, he was so busy stuffing his pockets as he ran downstairs that perhaps he dropped the $50 and it blew into the garden."

"I don't know what's more disturbing to me, a homeless person grabbing a fistful of dollars out of the collection basket or someone dropping the counterfeit $50 into the collection basket. They should be charged with the theft of spiritual services."

"Amen to that." Croissant said.

"Knowing the church does not have cameras, as I'm sure they look at it as not wanting to be distrustful of their flock. I'm surprised they even filed a theft report. I would think their view is if someone was that desperate, we should embrace them with love and support."

"Well, I will leave it up to the state attorney and for you to follow up to see if there's any connection."

"There's no way we can prove that he did not find it in the garden unless we can find video in the area that covers the church entrance. I'll leave it to Rollins and Felix in the morning to canvas the neighborhood and cameras. The bottom line is, it doesn't bring us any closer to who dropped the $50 in the collection basket."

"I'll leave it to you Princess or should I say Kick Ass to run this to ground. Sleep well."

"Thanks for the call, Eddie. Stay safe."

"Guaranteed."

Now Kate was wound up. Although she was relieved that she didn't have to leave the house, her mind felt like a series of spinning plates. She was almost sure that this was a dead-end with the arrest of Elmo. Regardless of whether he found the bill blowing in the wind or snatched it from the donations, he still would not know the origin of the bill. However, it wouldn't be the first time that criminals took advantage of the homeless and paraded them as a front person in fraudulent schemes, especially forged checks.

As she tussled under the covers and fluffed her pillow to get comfortable again. Her mind raced with thoughts that interrupted the sleep she had so welcomed fifteen minutes earlier. She would have to wait until morning to check the Secret Service to find out if the homeless population was being exploited in the passing of this fake money.

Chapter Thirty-Four

While shoveling down some oatmeal, Kate looked up the mass schedule for Sacred Heart Church. The first service was at 7 am. She looked at her watch and figured she could catch the priest after the first mass.

After parking in the garage at the Blue Monster, she walked over to the landmark church. Built in 1905, the picturesque house of worship was constructed with white and gray veined granite and marble. The crucifix topped arch was adorned with a spectacularly grand circular stained glass.

Walking up the stairs, she passed a few parishioners from the early mass, who were loitering out front, along with a few panhandlers. A statue of Jesus cast a gaze downward. She thought briefly if it was an approving gaze of her life's work. She made a difference. That should be enough.

As her shoes echoed inside the enormous sanctuary with its impressive dome, stained glass and marble altar, she felt the enormity of the church and the sadness of the memories of the funerals, especially for her husband. She touched the wedding band on her right hand. It remained a comfort. She watched as one priest in a black robe strode across the front of the sanctuary. He looked towards her, and she hailed him like she was waving at an Uber.

He walked towards her with his shaved head and a smile framed with a horseshoe mustache. She expected an Irish brogue, but was greeted with a distinctive southern drawl.

"Can I help you? I am Father Brian McClung."

"Yes Father. I am Detective Kate Alexander from TPD, and I wanted to ask about your theft from the collection basket."

"I'm sorry that we wasted your time. The report was filed without my approval. If someone is so desperate to steal from the church, I believe we need to have charity in our heart and forgive that person."

"Do you have any idea how much they took?"

"It's impossible to tell. Probably twenty dollars or fewer. The early mass are the diehards, and many of them are enrolled in automatic donations through credit cards. Most of the cash donations are dollar bills."

"Would you be surprised if someone deposited a fifty?"

Father McClung tilted his head slightly. "Occasionally we have a big tipper of a fifty or a hundred. Guilty conscience." He chuckled.

"Well, it was actually a counterfeit bill."

"Really?"

"Did you get a look at the suspect?"

"My eyes are not what they were at your age. He was at the rear of the church, and I was preparing for communion. The volunteer with the basket said he looked homeless and disheveled."

"We arrested an individual named Elmo Price, who said he found the fifty outside in the garden."

"Elmo Price does not the ring steeple bell. I have to say that we will not be pressing charges against the unfortunate soul."

Kate smiled. "I didn't think you would."

"I don't think the boss upstairs would approve. Are you a member here?"

"Me? No. Sadly, I've been to too many funerals here. We have lost five from the department just since I've been here."

"Better to have lived a brief life of meaning and making a difference than a long life of insignificance."

"True. You're not from here, are you?"

"What gave me away?" He winked. "I serve at the pleasure of the church. Eureka Springs, Arkansas, is where I come from. Beautiful northern part of the state, nestled in the Ozark Mountains."

"My partner is from Romance, Arkansas."

"I've heard of it. A small town. A quick kiss on the cheek and you passed it."

Kate chuckled. "Thank you for the time, Father McClung."

"Call me Brian, Kate. I'll say a prayer for your safety. We need crusaders to fight evil."

"Thank you, Brian."

She walked back the short distance to the Blue Monster. Dropping her backpack in the chair of her desk, she turned to Rollins and Felix. "Would you two mind doing me a huge favor? No heavy lifting."

Rollins pulled on his suspenders. "Pick up lunch you bought for everyone?"

"Not hardly."

"Eddy Croissant called me last night."

Felix laughed. "Did he drop F-bombs like raindrops in a thunderstorm?"

Rollins said, "He uses them as nouns, adjectives and verbs."

They all laughed. "Only one time. Maybe because he was talking to a lady?"

Cody jumped in and said, "Whoa. You are a lady? I wish someone had told me."

Kate said, "Big surprise."

Rollins said, "Eddy must be practicing for Lent when he gives up swearing and makes it to the second sentence."

"Cursing aside, he is a helluva cop and always a good laugh. It's in his blood. I would not want him on my trail. So, he pinched a fellow named Elmo Price last night, who tried to pass a counterfeit fifty. Elmo claims he found it in the garden of Sacred Heart. A homeless person did a snatch and run of the collection basket two days ago. This is the first body we have attached to the counterfeit fifties that was being printed by my most recent victim. It's almost certainly a dead end, but I would like to run it out. Could you two do a neighborhood canvass of that block and see if there are any cameras?"

Felix and Rollins nodded in agreement and Rollins said, "For you? No problem."

"Thanks. The best bet is the parking garage next to the church and the parking lot across the street. Not much to choose from."

Rollins and Felix stood and grabbed their jackets as they headed towards the exit.

Chapter Thirty-Five

She returned to her desk, and she and Cody began discussing their strategy. Detective Frank Duffy strode quickly into the office and Kate immediately recognized that not only had he learned to deal with his demons, but his frame had been to the body shop. He looked more fit than she had ever remembered him in the past.

He opened his arms wide and the width of the smile matched the spread of his openness, and they embraced tightly like soldiers returning from combat. In some ways, the weary warriors had, in fact, returned from the toxicity of daily battle. Cody stood there in silence with a smile of admiration.

After they released their grip, Kate turned towards Cody and made the introductions. Cody said, "It's a real honor, sir."

"Knock that shit off. We are all brothers and sisters in blue trying to prevent anarchy in the streets. I've heard good things about you, Cody Danko. So, the honor is mine. I heard you were a camouflage brother of the Wolfhounds in Afghanistan?"

"Yes, sir. 11 Bravo or should I say, 11 bang-bang. Just a bullet chucker and gunslinger. And you?"

"Army potato peeler extraordinaire," Kate and Cody shook their heads in disbelief. "Actually 31 Bravo, MP. Well, now that we've got this reunion celebration over, what do you say we walk over to the Secret Service? It's just a few blocks north of here."

"Sounds like a plan."

The joyous festivities were temporarily halted when The Caveman stuck his shaved head in the door. Kate wondered if this was his feeble attempt at trying to be the alpha dog and lifting his leg on the fire hydrant in an act of defiance to show who was in charge. His face of arrogance quickly changed to contempt when his eyes locked onto Frank.

Frank, noticing the disdain aimed at him, said, "Hiya, Lieutenant. Great day today, isn't it? How are you?"

The Caveman sneered and turned and walked out without uttering a word. Frank shrugged and said, "I was just trying to be friendly."

Kate said, "I don't think it worked. That landed like a stubbed toe. Speaking of which, I can't believe that they pulled Russell Tenpenny to travel to New York. That is like pulling up to the funeral home with the body and being told the mortician is off for the day. But I'm confident that the three of us can figure this out and make a case for us as well as the Secret Service. A win-win for everyone."

Everyone picked up their backpacks and headed for the door. Kate handed a pack of plain M&M's to Frank and said, "A gift for my old friend?"

"A delightful gift. Thank you."

Chapter Thirty-Six

After a five-minute walk, the three detectives badged their way past magnetometers and security guards at the Timberlake Federal Building Annex. Once they arrived at the Secret Service Tampa Field Office, they stood in the reception lobby staring at the service star and portraits of the President and Vice President. Through the bulletproof glass, they could see the administrative staff busy at work.

The middle-aged investigative assistant, Jeff Brasse, pushed open the heavy door and escorted them to the conference room. Brasse had hair that looked like a shoe brush. Flat and course. A guy Kate assumed was one of the two bosses stuck his head in the conference room and said, "Hey, thanks for giving us a helping hand. This was an extraordinarily large gathering in New York and the cupboard is bare here with staff. I'm going to run to the gym for a workout. I'll be back before lunch."

Brasse said, "The ASAIC, Walter Crumbly. He said to give you carte blanche."

Kate said, "That's reassuring." She rolled her eyes. Frank nodded.

Kate thought that a real boss would skip the workout, loosen his tie, and offer to help. Her suspicions were confirmed that too many bosses lacked the leadership skills and were empty suits, like The Caveman. She figured it was probably just as well, as he would probably slow down what she expected would be a fast-moving and rapidly developing investigation.

Brasse went through explaining the process that each fake $50 bill was attached to a government form that merchants or banks filled out. If there were any investigative leads, those would be noted on the form. Such as the identity of the depositor, if known or a description. They quickly realized most forms were filled out in haste and not complete. They pushed those to one pile and then divvied up the other pile with depositor information in three piles for the three detectives. The plan was to call each merchant or depositor to determine if they had more information not included on the form or if video of the transaction was available.

As the three detectives researched each form, they would either call the source or the depositor to determine if there were any leads. What they quickly discovered was because of the high quality of the bills that almost all the bills were not detected until they reached the bank. As each one culled through their pile of forms, they would move the form to the middle of the conference table. Each of their piles were getting smaller, while the pile in the middle of the table was increasing in size. It was a frustrating process, and the disappointment around the table was palpable.

As they exhausted their piles, each one leaned back in their chair and sighed heavily. Kate suggested they organize the piles by merchant. She was hoping to identify one or more merchants that had been scorched in a specific time period. If they could find a victim retailer that fit that profile, perhaps they could view the video for that day to identify any known local criminals or unusual behavior. She acknowledged it was desperation.

Once the piles had been subdivided, they quickly realized that most of the passing activity was occurring at the big box merchant stores. Kate suggested they subdivide the Starmart and Bullseye store piles into individual stores. The Starmart store closest to West Tampa, along with the Bullseye across the street, provided a substantial pile. After going through and sorting those piles by date, she could see a pattern emerging that showed a substantial increase of counterfeit fifties at both stores on the same day.

After grabbing lunch, they would split up. Kate would go to the Starmart, and Cody would go to the Bullseye. Frank would remain at the Secret Service and continue going through forms to see if he could identify any other patterns. Kate knew that typically they could narrow the window and have loss prevention forward the digital recording file, and they could watch it from their phone or desk. That would be impossible in this case and would require in person screening of hours of video.

On their way out, Frank handed the pile to Brasse, who rubbed his bristly hair. Frank updated him on their strategy that he equated to looking in a cornfield for a missing ring. He offered to bring back lunch to Brasse, who declined.

The three walked together to Eddie and Sam's pizza. Long known for having the best pizza downtown, the pizzeria shipped in Poland Springs water from New York as an essential ingredient in their crust.

Cody mostly listened as Frank and Kate walked down memory lane and caught up with each other's lives. As they finished their slices, it was time to burrow like pigs after a truffle. Who would be the winner?

As they walked outside into the September warmth, Frank pulled Kate to the side. "I want to thank you for being a good partner. You saved my life."

"Frank, no need."

"Just listen. I lost the courage to kill myself. I searched the bottom of the bottle for that courage. I wanted to die. You lost your spouse and showed strength and the resilience that I lacked. After Bridget died, I gave up. I would have either drank myself to death or eventually found that courage to end my life. Your intervention that you organized, gave me hope. I miss her terribly. God, I miss her, but I am in a better place of acceptance because of you. It also saved my job. Thank you."

They both mirrored each other with tight lips and eyes welling with emotion. Silent nods of understanding.

Cody interrupted. "Ready to jump in action?"

Kate answered, "Let's go. Let's find some answers."

Chapter Thirty-Seven

After lunch, the three detectives split up to attack their assignments. Kate sat in a hovel that was dark and confining with two other loss prevention officers of the Starmart. Sitting in front of the video screen, she began scrolling through the digital footage from the previous Wednesday starting at noon.

She took a chance that most criminals did not really become very mobile before lunch. Most of their criminal activity was late at night and carrying into the wee hours of the morning. As a result, most slept late. It was best to execute arrest and search warrants as the sun was peeking up over the horizon.

Kate had increased the reviewing speed, hoping that her eyes could remain focused to pick up on anything unusual. Every hour of recording, she would pause, rub her eyes and stand up and stretch. The two loss prevention officers were her constant audience and provided commentary on suspicious activities and observations within the store. Kate was initially distracted by their conversation, but eventually she could block it out.

Her mind had drifted back to her parting conversation with Frank. He had become an out of control speeding train. She watched knowing he was about to jump the tracks and become a full on train wreck. The booze, sloppy in his work, late to work. She covered for her partner as he navigated his grief until she knew it had become too much of a liability. For her and him. The Caveman was head-hunting. Frank was on borrowed time. Kate organized the intervention. There was denials, anger and finally tears. He had been saved.

Her phone rang, and she saw it was Cody. "Yes, sir?"

"I found Johnny Nylon at the register."

"Really?"

"Yep. I almost didn't recognize him without his nylon stocking."

"Good one. Was he passing counterfeit or buying bullets?"

"Better one. I guess if he were still alive, we could ask. This was probably the last photo of him before he landed on the table at the medical examiner's office. I just thought it was a coincidence that he is the one that kind of guided us down this path to begin with."

"Now look at us. The path took us to stiff necks, blinding headaches and red eyeballs."

"True. Keep hunting."

"You too."

After a couple of more hours, Kate leaned in and focused on an individual who was wearing a bright red hoodie in a black ball cap with the brim off to the side. She realized she had seen that same individual approximately thirty minutes earlier in the recording.

She asked the two loss prevention officers if they could pull up the camera view for that individual cash register. Once she did, she could see the individual making a purchase of shaving cream. She watched as the cashier counted out over $40 in change and he walked out. They had an excellent close-up of his image. They then rewound the recording to the previous occurrence. She spotted the same bright red hoodie and off-kilter black hat. Note to self: when committing a crime, don't draw attention to what you are wearing.

This time he had come through a different cashier, but once again made a small purchase of a pack of disposable razors and once again receiving over $40 in change. She also noticed on the close-up that the individual had a beard and was not likely to need shaving essentials.

Calling Frank and Cody, she tied them in on a conference call and told them the promising information. She then shared the image of Mister Red Hoodie to both of them. Neither one recognized the individual. Kate then forwarded the image to the District One police router and asked anyone in District One who might know who the individual was to let her know.

A few minutes later, she received a phone call from Officer Andrea Casale, who had handled the report of finding the Cadillac in the pond. Andrea said, "Without a doubt, that is Roscoe Worthy. He used to run with Johnny Nylon, but I've heard that crew is kind of split up. I've arrested Roscoe twice for misdemeanor shoplifting, some weed, and I know his name came up as a suspect in a burglary. His girlfriend is Maria Lopez and her brother is Jesus Lopez and he runs in a shady crew. He is routinely up to no good. I don't think Jesus has ever been charged with anything. He always seems to skate free."

"Girl, if you were here, I would give you a hug and squeeze you to death. If you could see me right now, I would be like our puppy golden retriever with his tail just wagging away with excitement." Kate thought of Louie wagging his tail when she comes home or in anticipation of a treat.

"Kate, I'm glad I made your day. Leave it to us girls to put our heads together."

"Andrea, we are a dynamic force when we work together."

"Amen."

She backslapped the loss prevention officers and thanked them for their help. In this day and time, they had one of the most dangerous jobs confronting likely thieves. She then emailed the head of the analysts and asked him to find everything on Roscoe Worthy, his girlfriend, Maria and her brother Jesus. She had a viable lead.

Chapter Thirty-Eight

One of the analysts, Ronnie Pulling, forwarded her workup on Roscoe, his girlfriend, and her brother. Ms. Lopez had no prior criminal history and appeared to work at a cellular phone store. Her brother also appeared to be living life without a blemish. Roscoe worked at a convenience store. Kate called Frank and asked him to go through the counterfeit forms and see if the convenience store had been victimized.

A short time later, Frank called her and said that Brasse had checked the database and sure enough, the store had been victimized on at least six occasions. So, either Roscoe was switching out genuine currency for the counterfeit $50's or he was looking the other way allowing a friend to pass what he knew was a counterfeit $50. Perhaps both.

Frank checked into the criminal intelligence bureau database to see what they had on Jesus Lopez. Frank found out that Jesus was also known as J Lo and was associated with several Cuban gangsters. Despite never being arrested, there was plenty of information provided by informants, field interviews, or traffic stops that showed that J Lo was a player. He was obviously smart enough to stay at an arm's reach from the law. This was a new wrinkle, but also explained the concentration of counterfeit activity in the West Tampa area.

Cody and Kate waited for Frank in the parking lot of the Starmart to meet and discuss their next move. After feeling that her eyeballs were going to fall out of her head along with a splitting headache, Kate was feeling re-energized after her hours of watching surveillance video.

She knew, as Tenpenny had told her, that the primary concentration of counterfeit was in West Tampa. They also attributed that truckers might also be involved as they could plot the activity along the interstates in Florida and at truck stops. She knew that most of the dump trucks were operated by those who could trace their heritage back to Cuba. Like many immigrant groups, it was offering a helping and lifting hand to a friend or relative who was looking for a job. Many of the drivers had also moved into larger long-haul trucking, as the need for drivers had increased.

Frank pulled in to the outskirts of the parking lot bordering Dale Mabry Highway and walked up to Cody and Kate and said, "Well, Kick Ass has done it again. She has cracked this case open like a warm chestnut."

"You're killing me. Russell Tenpenny, before he had to leave for the U.N., said the system of passing counterfeit was similar with distributing dope. So Frank, since you are an alumnus of narcotics, how best are we going to tackle this?"

"It's been a while since I was in narcotics."

"Come on Frank. It's like riding a bicycle with training wheels. There is no chance that the hinges are rusty."

"We are kind of like the characters in the Wizard of Oz. You are Dorothy and this certainly is not Kansas anymore. Cody is the lion but does not lack courage. And I am the tin man that needs a little WD-40, so we can all go skipping off arm in arm to find out what's behind the curtain."

Kate clapped her hands in applause and said, "While you are squirting oil into the hinges, let me take a stab at it. We set up at the convenience store and wait until Roscoe leaves and we follow. Just old-fashioned surveillance. Am I getting warm?"

"Warmer than a hot apple pie. Someone can take the eyeball and one will set up to the north and one will take south of the location. When he pulls out, the eyeball will call it out and the rest will fall in line like ducks on a pond. We can do a rolling, rotating surveillance and see where he goes."

"You just needed someone to blow the cobwebs off and start your vintage brain. Something else just occurred to me. A lot of these independently owned convenience stores are owned and operated by people of Middle Eastern descent. In fact, the first time I ever dealt with the Secret Service was when I was in patrol. I helped them serve an arrest warrant and search warrant in one of those stores. FDLE was working a joint case with them and the store had all kinds of fraud where they were processing food stamps or EBT card fraud. I had no idea."

"They do more than protecting the President."

"Apparently. Most of the food product in that store were expired because most of the customers were merely coming in and getting rebates on their food stamps and the store owner was ringing up false sales. So, to think they're running some counterfeit though the store would not surprise me. Especially when you consider our counterfeit printer was also of Middle Eastern descent. I'm thinking the store that I assisted on with the warrants was owned by some Lebanese. I don't want to sound like the town crier that everything is connected to Iran and Lebanon. Frank did you see an abundance of counterfeit at these independent convenience stores?"

"No. Big box merchants, trucks stops and of course the one that Roscoe works at."

"The reality of conducting murder investigations, I don't care where they came from or their religion. Rich, poor, this country or another, I am going to do my best to hunt down the killer. Reza Jaber and his wife Asa deserve justice."

"Well, Mrs. Sherlock Holmes, that is a very enlightening tidbit, and we will have to keep that in mind. No one has ever questioned your tenaciousness. I wouldn't want you hunting me."

"Thank you. We give a voice to the victims and their families. It's all about good versus evil and we have all seen evil up close."

"So true. All right. Let's roll and find out who the wizard is, and who is behind killing your printer."

"Well, let's hope we don't get burned. I remember talking to Greg McGuffin and he told me he was so bad at surveillance and burned so often by the suspect that he needed Solarcaine aloe spray to treat his sunburn. He told me he had been following someone to their house. He watched the suspect go into the house and a few minutes later, someone was tapping on his window. The suspect had gone out the back door and come up behind him and demanded to know who he was and what he was doing. So, McGuffin told him he was a private eye and thought the suspect was canoodling with his client's wife. Needless to say, the surveillance was blown, and he was burned."

"I remember him. Good guy. Sad, his heart gave out like a lot of ex-cops."

Cody said, "Yeah, the accumulation of stress over twenty years takes its toll. Especially on you old dinosaurs. Back in the days when they were still smoking and joking, as well as filling their faces with jelly donuts. Having been in a war zone, even if we make multiple deployments, they are for six months or less. That can be tough. But as cops, we enter perhaps the most toxic workplace possible and there is no reprieve from our deployments. It's every day we strap on our gun and badge and hit the streets."

Frank shook his head and said, "Precisely. I can take the eyeball."

Kate said, "I can set up to the north. Cody, you take south. He lives in that direction. This is going to be fun. Follow the breadcrumbs. By the way, Rollins sent me a message. No joy on cameras looking at the church. It was a longshot. Okay, gentlemen, let's see where this takes us."

Chapter Thirty-Nine

Frank set up across the street in the parking lot of a Cuban sandwich shop. He called the sergeant over the street crimes unit and asked him to send one of his officers into the convenience store to make sure that Roscoe was working. Hopefully, they could find out what time he would get off.

As he waited for the officer to arrive, Frank was excited to be back in the cockpit again. It was a long journey. He felt invigorated to be hunting for bad guys again. Although the demons had been chased from the attic of his brain, he knew they could return at any sign of weakness. He had come to terms with his survivor's guilt and in watching his partner, Rollins, wounded. He missed Bridget terribly and the life they shared. The enormous guilt of not being there all the time with her had exasperated his grief over her loss. Armed with coping skills provided from rehab and the Franciscan Center's Operation Restore PTS program, he felt confident in his positive changes. He is an alcoholic. Sixty-six days dry. A process.

He watched as one of the plainclothes street crimes officers, who he recognized as Jeff Bartlett, walk into the store. He was a legacy cop. His dad had retired and Jeff, like his dad, had a reputation as being a great cop. A few minutes later, Frank's cell phone chirped, and he answered it.

Bartlett said, "Frankie, good to hear you're back in the saddle. Your dude is in there and said he gets relieved at 4 o'clock."

"What's he wearing?"

"A premium lightweight maroon guayabera with detailed satin embroidery and appears to be a cotton and poly blend, although it could be pure cotton."

"Hey smart guy, if I wanted a fashion readout, I would have bought a copy of GQ. You missed your calling. You should have been a judge on Project Runway."

"So, you don't want to know what kind of jeans he is wearing?"

"I should call your dad. You're hopeless."

"Frank, you are welcome and by the way, you owe me for the pack of gum I just bought."

"Jeff, I don't owe you a cent. Put in a requisition with the city. I hope you got a flavor that you like because you're going to be chewing on that for a while."

"Stay safe Frank."

"Thanks, and tell your dad hello."

"You got it."

Looking at his watch, Frank saw it was 3:45 pm and 15 minutes before Roscoe would get off work. He relayed the information to Cody Danko and Kate Alexander. In 20 minutes, Frank watched as Roscoe and his maroon shirt walked out of the store and climbed into a Toyota that looked like it had been retrieved from the junkyard. Frank called the others on the radio and said, "Buckle up, boys and girls, we are off to see the wizard."

They followed Roscoe, south on Armenia Avenue, driving past mostly commercial businesses dotted with fast-food restaurants and doctor's offices. Frank tried to maintain a distance of at least two car lengths and keep one car in between him and the Toyota as camouflage. By this point, Kate, who had set up north of the bodega, had caught up behind Cody.

As they approached a traffic light that had been green for a considerable time, Frank said on the radio, "Stale green ahead. Tighten up so you don't get caught by a red light."

Frank watched as the traffic light turned yellow and Roscoe's car entered the intersection as the traffic light flashed red. Frank pushed the accelerator to add a little extra horsepower to the engine and sped up through the intersection and under the steady red light. He said on the radio, "The light has turned red. I made it through. I take that back. We are done."

Frank looked in his rearview mirror at the overhead flashing lights of a Tampa Police SUV. He knew even if he could contact the officer, the flashing lights may have drawn attention to Frank. He did not want to risk jeopardizing the good lead with Roscoe and shut it down.

Frank slowed down and pulled to the curb, coming to a stop. He rolled down all of his heavily tinted windows and had his badge ready for the arriving officer. In the side-view mirror, he saw the familiar face of Officer Brie Thomas. As she got closer to the driver's window and recognized Frank, a big smile lit up her face. "Frankie, what are you doing running red lights?"

"Brie, under normal circumstances, it would be an absolute delight to see your cheerful and smiling face. Sadly, I was running a surveillance and had no choice but to run the red light. So, we'll just try again tomorrow."

Putting her hands on the windowsill, Brie said, "I am so sorry. I'm not one for writing tickets, but I've got a new sergeant, who is a bit of a ball buster. He asked me to sit on the intersection because they've had complaints from one of the local community groups about red light runners."

"Well, I too am sorry for having you jump out and stop me and thus wasting your time. Now you are empty-handed and no ticket that you could take back to your sergeant. Who is he?"

"Newly promoted. His stripes still have the glossy sheen and he's trying to prove to management that they made the right decision promoting him."

"We all know the type. I would love to stay and visit and catch-up Brie, but I actually have work to do, and I don't want glossy stripes getting mad at you. So, I'm going to scoot and hopefully, it won't be as long before our paths cross again. You're such a joy, Brie."

"Likewise, Frank, stay safe."

Frank passed the bad news to Cody and Kate that their surveillance had come to an abrupt end. Little did he know he was driving through a police dragnet instigated by the concerned citizens of West Tampa and undermining the operation. He directed Cody to drive ahead and drive past Roscoe's house to make sure he had driven straight home. He asked Kate to join him in a parking lot.

Chapter Forty

As Kate pulled up next to Frank, her phone rang, and she looked at the caller ID that identified the incoming call from Detective Ruth Young of the airport police. Kate smiled at the happy memories of her former midnight running buddy and the laughter from the vivacious blonde. "Hi Ruth. Just seeing your name on my caller ID put me in a better frame of mind. Frank Duffy and I were on a surveillance that had just blown up. What's going on?"

"Tell Frank hello."

"I will."

"Well Kate, you know we only share happy memories working alongside each other. Two girls fighting crime and corruption and maintaining our sanity with hilarious antics."

"How could I not laugh with you? We both know how fragile life can be, so let's have some fun on the dance floor while we can."

"You are so right. Regardless if it's a disco ball or an orchestra, my feet are moving." They both laughed. "What I heard was that you're out shaking some counterfeiters related to a homicide?"

"Yep. We sure are."

"So last week, we had five businesses in the airport hit with counterfeit 50s. As you know, there's few places out here at the airport aside from a bathroom stall that you're not under video surveillance. So, I could identify the individual who hit all five businesses and then he jumped on a flight to Miami. His name is Yasmani Guerrero from West Tampa. He couldn't help but spend his pocket full of joy at the airport. He must have wanted to hit the club scene on South Beach."

"I'm on the edge of my seat."

"I distributed an email out through the Tampa Bay Area Intelligence Unit, and I heard from someone you were scouring the earth looking for these desperados."

"Ding, ding, ding."

"Guerrero returned Sunday night. I just sent you an email with all this information, and I just got a warrant for his arrest. I know from previous cases that the U.S. attorney's office isn't interested in small change counterfeit cases. With a combined loss of $250, I knew I could get one from the state attorney's office. If you would like, we can saddle up together like two old gunslingers from the west and go grab Guerrero."

"That sounds like fun. I am dusting off my old six shooter and looking forward to throwing a set of cuffs on Mr. Guerrero with you. Okay, let me look at the email and I'll call you back, so we can coordinate."

Ending the call, Kate opened up her email and started reading the information that Ruth had sent over. She read that Yasmani Guerrero had been arrested several times for mostly minor offenses that landed him in the county jail. He had done a longer stretch in the state penitentiary for a charge of being in possession of stolen credit cards. She also saw he had a commercial driver's license and appeared to be driving for Tito's trucking.

She had seen their trucks on the road, which appeared closely connected to the construction trade. Mostly dump trucks and flatbed transporter trucks for construction equipment. This was perhaps the connection they were looking for. Agent Tenpenny had assumed that some of the counterfeit passing activity was related to truck drivers and truck stops. Could he be deeply involved with the so called "trucker note?"

Briefing Frank about her conversation with Ruth Young, they agreed Kate would join with Ruth and assist with the arrest of Yasmani Guerrero. If the lead did not pan out, they would still have Roscoe that they could resume following the next day. Cody had responded and said that Roscoe's car was parked in front of his house.

She called back to Ruth Young and said that it would be best to make the arrest at Guerrero's house, where he would be more likely to have a stash of counterfeit. This would also not alert the trucking company, who may have been facilitating or acting as a co-conspirator. They agreed to meet at Guerrero's apartment complex.

Chapter Forty-One

Driving past a tire shop, used car lot, and muffler shop, she entered the parking lot of the dingy apartment building that looked like it would not be surprised to see a patrol car from the airport police. Kate immediately recognized the exuberant blonde detective waving in the passenger seat next to the uniformed officer.

After embracing each other, they, along with Officer Stanley Morris and his six-foot four frame, walked towards the apartment building. The aging pink stucco was sun bleached and exhausted looking. The sound of Latin music bellowed from the building, and the rancid odor of marijuana wafted through the air.

Ruth gave a cheerful knock on apartment 107. A man wearing a blue tank top and heavily inked thick arms and a cigarette bouncing off of his lip came to the door.

"What's up, lady cops?" said the man with slicked back black hair.

Ruth said, "Do you mind if we step in?"

Guerrero opened the door as he took a long drag of the cigarette and motioned with his head to come in. "What's going on?"

Ruth said, "Anyone else here?"

"Nope. Just me and the lonely-hearts club."

"Do you mind if we look around just to make sure and for our own safety?"

"Hey lady, unless you have a search warrant, you ain't looking for shit in here. If you're scared, you can step back outside."

"Are you Yasmani Guerrero?"

"Yeah." He sucked so hard on the cigarette it looked like he would swallow it. He then blew the contents of his lungful of smoke towards Ruth.

She smiled. "Okay, tough guy, you can buy your cigarettes at the county jail commissary. You're under arrest for passing counterfeit currency at the airport. You have anything to say?"

"Yeah. Lawyer."

Kate said, "I hope you have a good one. Because it looks like you're taking a bus ride north on I-75 back to the state penitentiary. And I hope this attorney is better than the last one that represented you on your last trip upstate."

Guerrero crushed the cigarette in an ashtray and put his hands behind his back. He knew the drill. Whatever tales or secrets he knew were locked up tighter than a bank vault. Kate's hopes that she would learn something from Guerrero were crushed, like his cigarette. Kate knew there was a strong possibility that he would be back out the same evening on bail. Her concern was that his arrest would tip off the other folks at the trucking company that may have been complicit.

As she watched Guerrero sitting in the backseat of the airport police car driving away, Kate knew that still the most promising lead remaining was Roscoe. They would return to conducting surveillance the next day.

Chapter Forty-Two

Sitting at her desk, Kate analyzed the records of the Tito Trucking. She was frustrated at not being able to get a consent to search at Guerrero's apartment from the night before. He was hardcore and wasn't going to say a word. His lips were sealed to the grave. He would allow his attorney to be his negotiator. So many crooks underestimated the virtue of remaining silent.

There were no associations with Reza Jaber to Tito's Trucking. Perhaps Jaber had printed business cards or flyers for Tito's and that would be the connection. Even if that were true, there would be no proof that Tito was the outsourced distributor of the counterfeit. Perhaps there was a cutout person in between.

Working with the analyst, Ronnie Pulling, she had a link analysis chart of the business operations and all those connected to the business. The chart had a line connecting a person's association with the business or another person connected to the core business. She saw Julio Lopez connected by a single line to Norberto "Tito" Diaz, the owner. The single line had an address connection.

Tito and Julio had jointly owned a house together and now rented the property. Certainly not any sign of a complex criminal enterprise. Tito and Julio had remained free of criminal implications. Kate wondered if perhaps the outside was detergent clean, but grass stains lurked underneath. Julio had been named by others as being associated with criminal enterprises, but was never close enough to be arrested.

All that work and nothing gained. Cody came into the office and told her that Frank and he had sat on Roscoe's car and residence for a couple more hours. Roscoe had settled into his house smoking dope or binging Netflix and no evidence of him leaving.

She told Cody she was going out for a drive and would meet back at Roscoe's work to start surveillance again. As she drove east from downtown on I-4, she cranked up the country music station and sang along like a karaoke singer. She exited on 56th Street and headed north through a heavily commercialized area. The road serpentines outside the city into the county and headed towards the city limits of Temple Terrace.

She drove past Tito's Trucking. A nondescript single level brick building with a fenced-in yard. The enclosure was filled with dump trucks and construction equipment. She could also see the cabs of several eighteen wheelers set up to carry cargo containers from the port. As a homicide detective, she felt it was important to feel the scene. There was just so much you could get from sitting at the desk and Google maps. You had to invigorate the senses. Besides being dusty, the road and area were noisy from the flow of trucks.

Pulling into a nearby truck repair company parking lot, she considered her options. She called a detective with the Temple Terrace Police Department she knew, Al Baca.

"Hi Al, it's Kate Alexander."

"Kate, how are you?"

"Lovely. I was wondering if you folks have seen an increase in counterfeit money?"

"Yep. The sergeant was talking about that yesterday. You know, the typical gas stations, grocery stores being hit. Unless a body is attached, we don't have the time to work with them. So far, no bodies or leads. They never hit the same place twice. We have been sending them to the Secret Service. They are good enough quality that no one notices until it's too late. Speaking of bodies, are you not working dead people anymore?"

"The counterfeit is tied to a cold body."

"Gotcha. If I hear of anything, I'll let you know, and I'll also put out an email to the other detectives. I just remembered that Ruth Young at the airport put out a request for info."

"I was with Ruth last night. We arrested an individual. He wouldn't give anything other than name, rank, serial number and a request for an attorney."

"Smart for him, bad for you guys."

"Indeed, thanks Al."

Ending the call, she put the car in drive. She headed east again on Hillsborough Avenue towards the Seminole Hard Rock Casino. Kate parked outside the massive hotel and casino complex and walked into the Seminole Police office. After identifying herself, Lieutenant Billy Eaglebear, who filled the door frame in his blue uniform, walked out to the reception area.

"Hi L.T., I wanted to know if the casino has been hit with counterfeit lately?"

Eaglebear rubbed his chin and smiled. "Hit? We were crushed Friday night. Our cashiers are well trained, but this stuff was of top quality. I couldn't tell. Multiple restaurants, bars and cashiers were hit. I spoke with Special Agent Tenpenny with the Secret Service. He said that he would stop in after his trip to New York. My analyst, Tracie Robinson, is working through the video to see if there are any commonalities. Do you have any leads?"

"The counterfeit is attributed to a homicide that I'm working on. We know where it was printed in West Tampa. There appears to be a connection to the truckers. The airport police arrested one last night. If Tracie comes up with anything, could you let me know?"

"Absolutely."

"Thank you."

Kate returned to her car. She knew that Tito's Trucking was involved. Perhaps not Tito himself, but knowing that his former roommate's name is associated with Roscoe, who works at a store that received some fake money. Add that a Tito's truck driver was arrested for passing the bogus money at the airport. A lot of the counterfeit money was passed in the trucking company's vicinity. She needed to find the connection.

She called Detective Luis Castillo in the Criminal Intelligence Bureau. He was the resident expert on Cuban organized crime. He told her he was out of the office, but could meet her at La Teresita Café and Bakery on Columbus Drive in West Tampa.

Chapter Forty-Three

Pulling in to the parking lot of the legendary Cuban restaurant, La Teresita Café and Bakery, she drove to the rear parking lot behind the two pink buildings. She looked at the detective in his linen baby blue guayabera, leaning against his car, sipping some Cuban coffee from a small cup. She smiled at the recognition and noticed a few wisps of gray in his bushy beard. As she stepped out of her car, he rubbed his vacant scalp and said, "Kick Ass, so wonderful to see you. How can I be of service to you?"

"I need to pick your brain on Cuban organized crime."

"Since the days of making Cuban sandwiches for lunch at work and rolling cigars at the factories in Ybor, there has always been some criminality within the community. They started the bolita lottery as the major vice and all the ancillary offshoots, such as the betting, bribery, and corruption."

"Okay, fast forward to today."

"Today?" He rubbed the ample beard and said, "Credit cards, gift cards, truck hijacking, auto crash insurance scams, and Medicare fraud."

"Really?"

"Millions. They are experts."

"Millions? How?"

"With the immigration policy specific to Cuba, they basically come and go as they want. They don't need a visa to enter the U.S. and they can stay essentially for two years without harassment. There is no extradition from Cuba. Its a two-hour flight to freedom. They return to Cuba and live like kings while sharing their wealth in the Cuban economy."

"I didn't know."

"We had a big insurance ring last year. We worked it with investigators from Health and Human Services. The fraud ring would smash up cars and file false insurance claims. Go to phony medical clinics and massage therapy. The only thing getting massaged was their pockets. They set up the clinics in someone's name that are at arm's distance from the ringleader. When we went to round them up, they scattered like cockroaches when the lights were turned on. We grabbed some, but quite a few are living the good life ninety miles south of Key West. There was another bunch buying gift cards with stolen credit cards."

"Is Tito's Trucking on your radar?"

"Credit cards, hijacking, and gas smuggling."

"Gas?"

"Yep, the sheriff's office had a huge case using stolen credit card numbers or pulsar devices to bypass the gas pump integrity. They have specially equipped trucks with bladders and fill them with hundreds of gallons of gas. Then they sell at a discounted price to independent truckers trying to make a living. The suspects all had Cuban surnames and made 60K in one night! My family busted their ass coming to this country in the 60's. Floating on a raft for freedom. I hate these guys disparaging our rich heritage. We built Miami and Tampa. Without Cubans, there is no Florida. We are way more than cigars and rum. Our heritage runs deep in this community."

"You are the financial and political machine that drives the state."

"Indeed, my friend."

"Is Tito's dirty?"

"Is it systemic or just some lone actors? Maybe a little of both. The drivers come from Cuba looking for a helping hand. Sometimes that helping hand has conditions. They learn to drive and get their commercial endorsement. The money on side hustles is too big to overlook. The company has legitimate business interests and is a major player in dump trucks and an ever-increasing degree in long haul trucking."

"Do you know Jesus Lopez?"

"J Lo?"

"Yep."

"We can never get him. He has a shitty little abode in West Tampa that he holds court. It's a party house. His actual house is overlooking the Gulf of Mexico in St. Pete. The house is in the name of his dad, who supposedly inherited a king's fortune in Cuba. Can't prove it. That's where he lives with the family. He has soft hands and never gets them dirty, but he is up to his nostrils in fraud. They never tattle on each other because they all have family back in Cuba and know paybacks would be rendered. They do their time or run."

"What about murder?"

"That's your specialty. I think almost anyone is capable as you know. They have some guys that are scarier than Howl-O-Scream at Bush Gardens. Life in Cuba makes you hard. They have lived under some form of oppression for five hundred years. You fight for everything from rice and beans and keeping your '57 Chevy roadworthy, not to mention your honor. We are very prideful people and we don't take kindly to betrayal, especially if it involves family. That extends to your criminal family as well. J-Lo would hire it out. I don't see him doing it himself. He has enough resources at his disposal."

"Like a Russian."

"I suppose. The Cubans and Russians have long running friendship since the Castro days and the Cuban Missile Crisis. There are more than a few Cubans running around with Russian names. So yes, a Russian could be a hired hand. Especially if he wanted it where it wouldn't be tied back to him or his network."

"Any linkage to Iranians?"

He shook his head and took another sip. "No. I've never heard of any."

"The Cubans involved in counterfeit?"

"As in fake money?"

"Yep."

"Why would they? They are making millions in other revenue streams. Who uses cash anymore? I would think it's hard to move." He took a bite of a crispy guava pastry, with flakes crumbling to the ground. "Kate, you need to get you a pastelito from here. Pure heaven."

"Thanks, I'll get some coffee to go."

"Think about it, Kate. It's a lot of work to hustle and move bogus bills. Even at fifty percent take, J Lo could easily make more through one of his scams. Remember, the gas guys make sixty thousand in one night until they got busted."

"We have a lot of linkage back to Tito's Trucking."

Castillo shrugged. "I'm surprised. Maybe the guy that was printing was into something else and he got crossways with them. They killed him and took his shit. The Columbians and Venezuelans have a history of moving drugs and phony bills."

She looked at her fitness watch and realized it was getting time to meet for the surveillance. "Okay. Thanks for the brief on your brothers in crime."

Castillo scoffed. "No brothers of mine. Just like we hate dirty cops that hurt the profession, I hate Cuban criminals."

"I'm going to get some coffee to go. I'll be jacked all night."

"Nothing better than the sweet aroma of Cuban coffee."

"See you later."

She picked up three café con leche coffees and headed toward the meet for the surveillance. As she sipped the frothy and aromatic drink, she pondered what Castillo had told her. Why murder Reza, the printer? Perhaps it had nothing to do with the Cubans and they were merely cleaning out the cupboard filled with counterfeit. The Iranian bullet casing was still a puzzle. Perhaps it was a Russian that pulled the trigger. She was convinced the Tito's was involved as a distributor of counterfeit currency.

Chapter Forty-Four

Feeling like Groundhog Day, the three detectives assembled in the vicinity of the convenience store where Roscoe worked. Frank sat in the same place he had been just twenty-four hours earlier. The only difference was that Frank had switched out with another detective and was now driving a silver Ford Explorer. Kate distributed two coffees to the team and briefed Cody and Frank about the arrest the night before and what she found out about the counterfeit activity near Tito's Trucking.

Kate said, "With what Tenpenny with the Secret Service surmised, they suspected truckers being involved, I am hoping we can catch Roscoe dirty. If not, what other choice do we have? Surveillance on every truck that leaves Tito's or run an undercover or informant inside?"

Frank said, "That will take time and I don't think The Caveman will be patient enough. He will tell you to turf it to the Feds and push this over as an unsolved case unless forensics can come up with something."

"Oh yeah, the valedictorian of the asshole academy. I'm not giving up on this."

"I didn't mean to get you wound up."

"You didn't. I can negotiate cooperation from Guerrero that we arrested last night. I can also do a cell tower dump near the final resting spot of the dead Cadillac, as Benny calls it. We can check for more cameras in the area."

"You're like a pit-bull, you don't give up."

She growled and barked at him. "Nope. I still have Reza Jaber's financials to go through. His cell records didn't show anything interesting. The same for the business phone. He was as a clean as pressure washed deck."

Cody said, "I still think there is an Iranian angle."

"I am keeping my options open, but I would agree with you that the Iranian and counterfeit are interwoven like a patched quilt. We know the Cubans don't fool around. Okay, let's get on our spots and hopefully not lose him again. Frank?"

"Hey, that was not my fault. Brie was doing her job. If you guys had tightened up like I asked, you could have taken over."

"Oh, so now it's our fault. What were we supposed to do? Superglue ourselves to his bumper? Don't answer. Let's go."

Pulling in across the street, Frank could once again see Roscoe's worn-out Toyota was parked on the side of the store. Slipping a piece of gum into his mouth, he took a sip of water. Enjoying his sobriety, he certainly did not enjoy the path he had taken after Bridget's death. He had taken positive steps. Losing weight, he felt more energy and was no longer getting wrapped around the axle over minor issues like The Caveman, who no longer owned real estate in his brain. He had resigned himself to being an alcoholic, one stumble away from losing sobriety.

Roscoe strolled out of the store. With his fade haircut and sipping on an energy drink, the suspect slipped into the Toyota. Frank alerted the others as, once again, Roscoe turned to the left across traffic, heading south. Frank allowed a couple of cars to pass and he slipped out into traffic on Armenia Boulevard.

Once again, they approached a traffic light that had been green, and Frank issued the same warning to Cody and Frank. This caused Frank to fall directly behind the Toyota. He could see in the rearview, the others had also tightened up and had made it through the light.

Frank told the others that he would drop off and allowing Cody to take the eyeball. Frank turned on his right-hand signal and pulled into Fiesta Plaza. In case Roscoe had noticed Frank sitting across the street from the bodega, this would ease any suspicions that he was being followed. As soon as Frank pulled into the parking lot, he immediately circled back around and exited out the parking lot to catch up behind Kate, who had now moved up to the number two position.

Roscoe continued driving southbound with Cody in the eyeball position behind him. Traffic was becoming thicker, as service workers were calling it a day and schools' dismissals had added carpool traffic and buses. Cody watched Roscoe change lanes into the left-hand lane. Cody looked back over his left shoulder to change lanes but was blocked in by a landscaper's truck towing a trailer. A city bus came to a stop at a bus stop and Cody was immediately blocked in by the bus and the landscaping crew passing them.

Kate slipped in behind the landscape truck and passed Cody, only to see Roscoe make a right-hand turn on Braddock Street right in front of the bus. She made the hard right to follow on Braddock Street. The first block they approached was Tampania Avenue. He turned south on Tampania. With Kate providing turn by turn directions, Cody and Frank continued south on Armenia to parallel their movements.

Roscoe Worthy came to almost a complete stop in front of a small block home painted a light lavender. Kate could see that Roscoe was eyeballing the home. She was no longer in a position to stay behind him without looking obvious that he was being followed. She slowly drove around the Toyota and continued south, calling out her movements and that of Roscoe, who was now in her rearview mirror.

The Toyota had once again began moving south but was now behind Kate. Most bad guys would keep their eyes on the side view and rearview mirrors to look at being tailed. Here, he was being tailed from the front, which would remove any suspicion. Sometimes the best plans go awry, but work out for the best. Roscoe turned left on Ivey Street, heading back to Armenia. Kate continued driving down Tampania, as she would now be the trail car in the surveillance parade. As Roscoe approached Armenia, he turned right once again to continue his trek southward. Cody and Frank were once again in position to resume their surveillance positions.

Without warning, Roscoe made a sudden turn into the parking lot of Smooth Spirits Liquor Store. Frank thought perhaps Roscoe was checking to see if anyone was following. He thought of Roscoe's sudden move into the residential neighborhood and then the sudden stop. Now a quick turn into the liquor store. After his time in narcotics, he learned that many times, the person they were following was merely a terrible driver or lost.

Cody continued going south to take up a position further south. Frank pulled in across the street from the liquor store in the parking lot of a body shop filled with dented and abused cars. After a few minutes, Roscoe walked out of the liquor store holding a white plastic bag and climbed back into his Toyota. Frank once again took up the eyeball and asked Kate to go into the liquor store.

Chapter Forty-Five

Entering Smooth Spirits, Kate identified herself to the man behind the counter with a heavy Hispanic accent. He was crowned with a mohawk style haircut with one tattoo on each side of his shaved scalp. On one side was the State of Florida and the other was the Cuban flag. She was concerned that he might be a pal of Roscoe and alert him to the inquiry.

"Could you tell me how the last customer paid?"

"I think that's confidential."

"What's not confidential is when I tell the owner you cost him fifty bucks in counterfeit and you wouldn't cooperate in identifying the suspect."

He stared at her with no emotion. He opened the cash drawer and pulled out a fifty, as Kate had suspected. Knowing the six serial numbers from the counterfeit, she recognized this bill was one of the counterfeit bills manufactured by Reza Jaber. She asked Mr. Tattoo if the video camera was operational. After acknowledging that the cameras worked, she asked to review the recording.

As she watched the video, she saw the person she knew to be Roscoe walk into the store. He picked up a small bottle of Bacardi and paid with cash. Although the video resolution was not sharp enough to see the denomination, the video further implicated and confirmed what they already knew. Roscoe had passed one of the counterfeit $50 bills. She provided that information to Frank and Cody.

Frank closed his distance and was now no longer concerned with being burned. He was what would be referred to as being bumper locked to the suspect vehicle. He called for a marked unit in the vicinity that could catch up and pull Roscoe over.

He updated their moving location as they drove along Cypress Street, heading toward downtown. The road had more pothole patches than acne on a teenager. Never a picturesque drive, it was more of a shortcut paralleling I-275. He recognized the voice on the radio of the approaching patrol car as Doug Elms. Frank looked in the rearview mirror and could see the patrol car screaming up behind him. Frank lowered the driver's window and waved his hand outside, pointing Elms towards the aging Toyota.

Letting off the gas, Frank slowed as they passed the famous Alessi Bakery and allowing Elms to pass him and slip in behind Roscoe. The patrol car's overhead blue lights were activated and Roscoe pulled to the curb. Elms stepped out of his patrol vehicle, checking traffic as cars had to pass on the wrong side of the narrow road.

Officer Elms walked up to the driver's side with his hand on his gun and, standing slightly behind the driver's door, he asked, "Driver's license and registration, please."

"Why did you stop me? I ain't done shit."

Frank, who had been standing on the passenger side of the car, held up one finger to the Doug Elms, pausing the action. Cody had arrived and Frank motioned for him to take his spot while Frank walked around to the driver's side.

Standing next to the Elms, Frank bent down, peering into the window. "Hey pal, why don't you play nice and lose the attitude? Why don't you step out of the car?"

"I ain't got to do shit."

"Roscoe, that was not a request. You can either step out of the car or we are going to drag you through that window. This has to do with Johnny Nylon's death. I'm sure you would love to provide some clarity to why he died."

With that, Roscoe dropped the armor shield and stepped out of the car. They patted him down and found no weapons. In his left front pocket, Frank pulled out a small folding of bills. In Roscoe's right front pocket, he found another fold of money. Frank handed the two wads of money to Cody and asked him to keep those separate.

Frank looked at Roscoe. "So, pal, why do you keep your fifties in one pocket and the other cash in another?"

"I just got them from the bank."

"The bank? Nope. Wrong answer. It's counterfeit. You keep them separate to avoid a mix-up and it also provides proof of knowledge and intent. Officer Elms, if you don't mind, handcuff him and take him to our office."

"Wait! Honest, I got those from my bank."

"Keep in mind, this is federal time you are talking about. No early release. Say goodbye to Maria Lopez. She will not wait around the four years until you get out of the Coleman Federal Correctional Institution."

"Let's talk about this."

"Maria might make the drive for the first weekend or two and then she'll get busy. The next thing you know, Roscoe is history and letters get returned unopened. We can talk soon at the police department."

He advised Roscoe of his rights as Officer Elms placed him in the back seat. Elms called for a tow truck. The two detectives searched through the Toyota and, besides the remnants of a joint in the ashtray, they found nothing suspicious. He removed the bottle of rum and the receipt as further proof that he passed the fifty.

Frank wanted Roscoe to mull over what he had been told. No one wanted to go to jail. The reality of losing his freedom and his girlfriend would cause earthquake like tremors in the ground below his feet. Sitting in the back seat, handcuffed alone, would give him plenty of time to mull over his precarious situation.

The tow truck pulled up in front of Roscoe's car and lifted the front wheels off the pavement to take it to the impound lot. Frank asked Elms to take Roscoe to the Blue Monster, and they would meet him in the interview room outside the homicide squad room.

Chapter Forty-Six

Sitting across from Roscoe were Frank and Kate, who had met them at the police department. Roscoe seemed a little agitated and took on the position of trying to put the cops on the defense.

"What am I being charged with?"

Frank leaned in and said, "Like a game show, you have three doors to choose from. Door number one, I am on a Secret Service task force, and therefore we can charge you federally with counterfeiting U.S. currency."

"You talking some shit, man."

"A wise man would listen to his options sitting in your chair. Door number two, I can charge you on the state level for doing the same thing. Or, door number three, you could name your source and we could tell the state attorney that you were very cooperative and they might not even want to file charges. I can't promise that the state attorney will drop charges, but seeing that the jails in Florida are filling up faster than the maternity ward after Covid, they might be more inclined to go with probation."

Looking incredulous, Roscoe said, "Man, this is messed up. You just playing with me."

"We've got you by the nuts." As Frank looked at Kate. Roscoe sat up in his chair.

With a coy smile, Kate said, "As my esteemed colleague so eloquently said, we have you by the balls. The question is whether you want to cooperate or get a one-way ticket to the Orient Road jail, while we decide to send you by bus to Starke or to Coleman. State or federal. Your choice."

With a dismissive gesture, he said, "You're more messed up than he is."

"Look at this short video." He leaned in as he watched a video on Kate's phone.

"Last time I checked, lady, I blew out the candles on my 21st birthday cake. I merely made a legal purchase of rum, and I was not drinking and driving. I ain't done nothing wrong."

"All true." Kate said. "Let me explain something to you." She looked over at Frank and winked. "You just identified yourself as making this purchase. The store clerk can also confirm that. He also provided the counterfeit $50 bill that you paid for with your liquor purchase."

"Nope. Not me."

"The fake money will have your fingerprints and your DNA on it. Yes, we can get that off of paper. Now the interesting thing is that when my partner here was searching your pockets, he found your money segregated. In your left pocket, which is fake money. In your right pocket was your genuine money. We also know that you've been trading out money at your store. So, all this adds up to knowledge and intent. Not just that you got stuck with a $50 bill and didn't know better, but this shows a scheme to defraud."

The smirk was gone from Roscoe. Kate could see the wheels going round and round as he calculated his choices.

"I don't know nothing. You people must be doing mushrooms."

Frank said, "Well, I guess it's door number one. Four years in the federal penitentiary. One of things about the federal prison system, the Bureau of Prisons, decides where they house you. They could easily incarcerate you at the federal prison in Rochester, Minnesota. You're guaranteed to be in snow up to the ass of an African giraffe. Every time you take a piss, tickle the boys to come out from the shrinkage because of the cold. Temps in the winter are in the single digits. There aren't enough blankets to keep you warm at night."

"This is coercion."

Kate said, "We are merely providing an illustration and imagery of your three choices. Four years' incarceration, or door number three, and you can walk free today."

He sat there once again, going through his options. "Okay, I give up what you want to know?"

"Well, it's not that easy. You wanted to play hardball. So, in order for us to take an eraser to the whiteboard and make this go away, you have to complete three tasks. Since Johnny Nylon is dead, you have no allegiance to him any longer. But you can provide answers to his victims. You're going to give us the details of his knee capping's and his homicide. Like I said, he is dead and we're just trying to clear the slate. Next, you're going to give us the name of your supplier. And third, you're going to introduce an interested buyer to your source."

"So, you want me to narc?"

"You can call it what you want, but it's all about keeping your ass out of a jail cell in an orange onesie jumpsuit. Your choice, freedom, or freeze your balls in a Minnesota jail."

"These are some bad dudes. If they find out that I flipped on them, they will castrate me."

"We will do our best to protect you. You will make an introduction of someone that you did not know was working with the cops."

"Seeing that poor Johnny is dead, I don't suppose he would mind me providing details."

Kate said, "Johnny Nylon is a legend in West Tampa. This will only make him more epic."

"All right. I'll do it."

"Excellent choice."

"Where did you get it from?" Kate asked.

His head dropped like a heavyweight in his hands. In a whisper he said, "J Lo."

"As in Jesus Lopez? The brother of your girlfriend."

He nodded without looking up and after a long pause, he looked up with a panicked face and said, "You can't let Maria know. She can't know that I'm talking to the 5-0 and narcing on her brother."

"He goes by J Lo, like the actress?"

"Yeah, minus the looks, the figure, and the money."

"We can't all be so lucky."

They reassured him they would not be talking to his girlfriend. They merely wanted to make an introduction of an informant to J Lo. They had initially entertained having the introduction made the next day, but decided they did not want Roscoe getting happy feet and going on the run.

He admitted he had a limited knowledge of the counterfeit operation. Roscoe told them that J Lo had offered him the fake money and bought the fake money for fifty percent on the dollar, and that he could only afford to buy $1000 worth. He believed that J Lo was getting the fake money from a couple of dudes from Paraguay through a Russian. He also said that J Lo was moving a lot through his network of credit card skimming thieves and truckers.

Roscoe said, "Unless your guy is Cuban, it won't work."

"What do you meant won't work?"

"It's all networking and if you don't have blood from Cuba, you're out? That's how he stays clean as a white suit."

"You're not Cuban?"

"I'm half. Mi madre is full-blooded. That's my ticket. Besides, we all went to school together, and I'm dating his sister. Exceptions to the rule."

"I think if you sell it, you can make an introduction. He is a businessman and credit cards are king, not cash. If he wants to move it and you provide a buyer who wants a big package, I think he will be like the mouse and the cheese. He doesn't care if it's gouda, cheddar or provolone. Cheese is cheese, and it's food, or in this case, it's profit."

Roscoe shrugged. "Maybe."

While Frank slipped out to arrange for an informant, Cody took his seat in the interview room. Cody interviewed Roscoe about his knowledge of Johnny Nylon's killing and shootings. Roscoe provided information about his knowledge of Johnny Nylon's penchant for knee capping his adversaries. In one instance, his aim was off and he had hit an individual in the femoral artery and the victim, Pookie Williams, had bled out. He said that Johnny Nylon wanted to establish a reputation as being the most feared and crazy man in West Tampa, and to be the most infamous gangster in the neighborhood.

Roscoe told the detectives that Nylon preferred to carry a revolver. Roscoe said that Johnny had heard or watched one of those CSI shows, and he didn't want to leave any bullet casings behind. According to Nylon, each casing could be tied back to the gun used and that they could also get fingerprints and DNA off the casing from whoever loaded the gun. The revolver maintained the casings in the cylinder and then he could dispose of the casing and no evidence would be left at the scene.

Kate's phone buzzed, and she saw it was Travis Longstreet from the Buccaneers. She stepped out into the hallway.

"Hi Travis."

"Hi Kate, I'm sorry that I didn't get back to you sooner. I was waiting for the midnight guard to get back to me. He had some big exam he was preparing for at school and was off for a couple of days."

"I understand."

"The kid said he saw nothing suspicious, but his focus is not on MLK Boulevard. It's on the property and the building. I just wanted to let you know."

"Thank you, Travis."

"Okay. Let me know about getting together for lunch."

"Will do, Travis."

Not a chance. The security guard who had a big exam played into her theory that his nose was probably buried in the books. Unless someone beat on the security booth, he would not have noticed. Probably had his headphones on as well, jamming to tunes. Kate thought about how good police work had unraveled this plot. Officer Doug Pasley had tugged on the nylon fiber of Johnny Nylon, chasing him and his stolen car to the pond. That solved a homicide and three aggravated battery cases. Returning to the pond that claimed Johnny, they discovered the Cadillac with the body of Reza Jaber, which led to the counterfeit operation. Who knew where this was going to lead?

Feeling the buzzing, Kate looked down and read the caller ID said, Ruth Young.

"Hi Ruth. You want to go hunting again?"

"Not unless you have a permit for Havana."

"Why?"

"Yasmani Guerrero has skipped."

"To Cuba?"

"Sure has. He made bail soon after his arrival at jail. Did not stop at go. Went almost straight to the airport and caught a flight to Miami and on to Havana. Adios. We won't see him again."

"I was talking with Luis Castillo and getting quite an education on the Cuban network. He told me these guys scatter like the ashes into the wind after a fire. We have no extradition with Cuba and you are right, we will never see him again. Hopefully, they kicked him out of the clubhouse for being so stupid spending all that counterfeit in one place."

"We can only hope. I just wanted to let you know."

"Thanks. We need to have lunch or dinner when things calm down."

"I'd love too. You have my number."

"You know it. Talk soon."

Chapter Forty-Seven

Years earlier, Frank had worked as a detective in narcotics. Narcotics detectives relied upon developing informants. Most informants were extremely unreliable and mostly filled with drama. They over promised, and under delivered, and were routinely late. Most of them were users or distributors and not much better than the people they were targeting. Their motivations varied from financial incentives to reducing competition, but quite often working off pending charges and arrests.

Chuckles was none of that. He was an eccentric personality who owned a once popular nightclub in Ybor City. The nightclub had his name on the front door, but he had sold out to a group of investors. The club ultimately closed after the magic had worn off with the new investors. But Chuckles laughed all the way to the bank. This allowed him more time to focus on his culinary passions and his relationship with his partner, Jerome.

Frank and Chuckles had developed a special relationship. Frank's own interests in cooking cemented their bond, which morphed into a friendship. Chuckles had initially become an informant with the Drug Enforcement Administration when he was trying to rid the club of a distributor of ecstasy. The introduction was made with Frank and as their working relationship strengthened, Chuckles had less interest in working with the DEA. He was motivated by the excitement.

"Francis, my friend, it's so good to hear from you. How are you?"

"Chuckles, it is good to hear your voice as well. I am well and paroled from the dry-out clinic. I wanted to know if you might be interested in working with me on a case involving fake money?"

"It sounds lovely. We've never done anything with fake money before, but I enjoyed our last caper together with the jewelry and coins. When were you looking at doing this?"

"Tonight?"

"Oh Francis, I love your spontaneity. Let me check with Jerome. We are supposed to go out for dinner. Perhaps I can convince him to get takeout. Is this going to be a long operation?"

"I don't believe so. We will have an introduction into one of the primary distributors, and I'm hoping that they may be close enough that we can shut down the operation."

"It sounds like fun. Francis, I'm excited to see you. Kate has been giving me updates on the new model of Francis Xavier Duffy."

"I'm in a good place. I was a broken man and in a dark place. Thanks to the love and support of my friends, I've made it down the path of redemption. I still have anguish over the death of Bridget, but that's grief I will carry to the grave. I look forward to the day that I see her again, but for now, I have to focus on our two daughters."

"You are too good of a man to have dealt with all of this adversity. We all have only so much time on this earth. Most people will never experience the love and depth of the relationship that you and Bridget shared. You owe it to her to continue to embrace those happy memories and continue laughing."

"Thank you for those kind words, Chuckles."

"I'll text you after I chat with Jerome."

"I'll wait to hear from you."

Frank ended the call. His mind drifted back to his days in narcotics and living a fast life and late nights. It was a crucible that not everyone survived. Bridget provided a safe harbor to come home to and Chuckles was good for levity. He missed his bride terribly, but he smiled at the happy memories. Pastor Rick Malivuk at Operation Restore had recognized the guilt Frank grappled with over all the late nights he missed at home. Malivuk instructed Frank to write his ten happiest memories with Bridget. This helped to reframe his state of mind and focus on the good times. His phone buzzed, and he read the message.

"We have a winner. All sevens on the slot machine. Chuckles is in and on his way."

Kate's phone rang, and she saw it was an 813-area code. "Hello, this is Detective Alexander."

"Hi this is Tracie Robinson from the Seminole Police. Lieutenant Eaglebear said to call you concerning our rash of counterfeit passing."

"Oh yes, he said you were viewing the video and looking for leads."

"It was all different suspects. Nothing really identifiable. One was wearing a black t-shirt with the Tito's Trucking logo across the back. I'll send you the photo collage of the suspects. We have them posted inside the casino in case they return."

"Thank you, Tracie."

This reaffirmed Kate's belief that Tito's Trucking was deeply involved. With the arrest of Yasmani Guerrero, one employee and his sudden flight, and the Jesus Lopez association, she had three direct links to Tito's. She knew the Secret Service referred to the counterfeit as the trucker's note because so much passing activity was along the interstates and truck stops. It would be up to Chuckles to burrow into J Lo and jam him so tight that he would have no choice but to cooperate.

Chapter Forty-Eight

The fit and tanned, diminutive Chuckles showed up at the police department and was escorted upstairs to the homicide office. Chuckles was almost completely engulfed in the larger Frank Duffy's embrace. A friend from his past, Frank, seemed to hug a lost memory.

It wasn't long before, like old friends, they were catching up and discussing recipes and new restaurants on the thriving foodie scene. Frank was right back into his groove with his prized informant.

Chuckles and Roscoe were introduced to each other. Chuckles, after discussing the case with the detectives and Roscoe, sat down with Roscoe to go over their back story together. Any time a major player had an unknown outsider introduced; they would automatically become suspicious. It would be up to Roscoe to ease those concerns. The back story they agreed upon was that Roscoe was a frequent customer of Chuckles nightclub. They had not seen each other since the club closed, but bumped into each other at the Last Drop Liquor Store on Armenia. Roscoe would vouch that Chuckles had been a player and one that was efficient at moving product through the club. It was a plausible story. Figuring that he could get a nice little commission from J Lo for introducing the buyer, it would be a win-win. J Lo could move a large quantity of fake money and Chuckles would make money. Everyone would be as happy as the winners at the roulette table.

Roscoe would be required to assure J Lo that Chuckles had a significant network in the Ybor club scene and money to spend. Any distributor of fake money knew that it was essentially as worthless as the paper it was printed on. So, they were generally salivating over exchanging it for genuine currency. Especially when none of the risk fell back on them, only to the person who is going to be passing the counterfeit.

After going over the story several times, they were confident Roscoe was completely familiar with the story. They asked him to call J Lo on his cell phone and tell him he knew someone that could put a cheerful smile on everyone's face.

Frank had Roscoe practice box breathing to calm himself down. Roscoe made the phone call, which was recorded and monitored by the trio of detectives.

"J Lo, I got a dude that is going to make it rain. You know, before I starting going out with your sister, I was a player on Seventh Ave. My spot was Chuckles."

"Great spot."

"You know it's closed."

"I heard."

"I bumped into Mister Chuckles himself. He moved a lot of product through the club. So, we were discussing how business was in Ybor. He is interested in what we have going on."

"You told him?"

"It's not like that, bro. He was discussing his pill distribution in Ybor and how he was flush with Benjamins from selling his club. I asked him if he might be interested in moving some funny money. He said most of that is shit and not worth the paper it's printed on."

"I'm listening."

"I showed him one of my bills. Man, that dude almost had an orgasm right there in front of me. He wanted to know if I could get more and said that he could move thousands on Seventh Ave."

"Uh, huh."

"Did you hear me? Thousands, like tens of thousands. He is a serious player with deep pockets. He even mentioned possibly north of the border because he is Canadian."

"What's in it for you?"

"I'm just trying to help you out. I wouldn't mind if you kickback a little commission on the deal."

"How much?"

"Whatever your benevolent heart believes that I am entitled to is a just reward."

"Not you. Him? How much does he want?"

"Didn't ask. I thought it best that you two negotiate the terms. I can bring him over now."

"Is he there with you? He isn't listening to you talk, is he?"

"No man. I told him I would get up with you and get the 411 and see if you were agreeable."

"Here is the problem, bro. He is not blood. He is like two thousand miles from having a drop of Cuban ancestry. I like to keep it in la familia."

"Dude, you said that you wanted to get rid of this stock. He is a player with connections."

"You vouch for him?"

"Dude, you know him. The Fucking Chuckles. He is a legend on the Ave. His club was banging man. It was THE spot. He is gold."

"He better be, or I'll kick your ass. I don't play. I don't want no bullshit dick tugging."

"He is money man."

"All right. Bring him over."

"I can smell real money now."

"We'll see."

After silencing the call, everyone nodded in approval. Frank said, "You did good."

The detectives discussed the strategy of setting up for the surveillance. They quizzed Roscoe more on the layout of the house and if he had any weapons. They decided it would look better if Roscoe and Chuckles rode together in Chuckles' Land Rover. It was all about selling the deal, and bling and shiny objects helped to sell the charade.

Chapter Forty-Nine

With the detectives set up in nearby discrete locations, they were close enough to respond while also monitoring electronic recordings of the conversations. They listened as Roscoe introduced Chuckles to J Lo.

Immediately, J Lo said, "Hey, I know Roscoe likes you, but I really don't know you. So, if you don't mind, I'm going to shake you down."

"You know, I find this disrespectful, considering my reputation. I am not armed."

"I don't give a shit about guns. It's a dangerous world out there. No offense, but there is a reason that I've never done time. I'm as careful as driving through a nitro-glycerin factory. I'm sure you can understand my apprehension."

"Are you going to check Roscoe as well?"

The soft bodied and short-haired J Lo finished his pat down of Chuckles. "He is almost blood. We don't discuss business until you follow the rules of my kingdom."

"If you weren't almost blood with Roscoe, I would walk. I appreciate your reluctance since we have not done business before, but I'm a little insulted."

"I'm glad you understand." After the pat down, J Lo held out a black cloth bag and said, "I need you to empty your pockets and cellphone into this bag."

"Is this where you kill me and take my shit? Should I be nervous?"

"Relax, it's a Ferriday bag. In case your phone has been compromised, they won't hear shit. The bag blocks all signals coming and going. It's mutual protection."

"I think this is a little over the top. Worried about the Chinese or Russians?"

"FBI."

"It would have to be the Secret Service for funny money."

"Whoever. I don't take chances."

"Your house, your rules."

"Thank you."

Expecting this possibility, Frank smiled. Crooks were nervous on the first meet with strangers. He knew Roscoe was in his network and less likely to be searched. According to Roscoe, J Lo had never patted him down. They were listening in like it was live TV, with Roscoe being the transmitter and recorder. Frank almost admired how J Lo conducted business. He had never heard of anyone using a Ferriday bag as an added measure of discretion.

With the electronics put away and everyone seated, J Lo began the vetting process. He asked questions about the nightclub, as well as bumping into Roscoe. Chuckles could win an Academy award for the best undercover informant. He could surely walk the red carpet of informants as he had an ability to put everyone at ease and never drew alarm or concerns about his intentions. He talked about everything but the purpose of the meeting to establish rapport. This reflected his days as being an entertainer and facilitator inside the club.

J Lo said, "Hang on a sec."

Walking out the front door, J Lo looked up and down the street. He stood for a moment silently. Looking over the Range Rover, he dropped to the prone position like he was going to do a pushup. Frank could see that he was looking under the rear of the SUV. He stood and turned, walking back into the house.

"I get concerned with new unsolicited business. I wanted to have a look and make sure there were no cops in the area. You never know when the cops slip trackers under your ride. Range Rover is a nice sled."

"You are more nervous than a politician without pockets for donations."

"I'm careful. I'm allergic to jail."

"That makes two of us."

Roscoe said, "Bro. We all appreciate your approach. No one wants to stand behind bars eating shit food off a tray with plastic sporks. I never want to go back and I'm not doing business with someone that I don't trust."

Roscoe was really selling it. It was also setting the stage so that he could plead ignorance when they were all cuffed.

Chuckles nodded and said to J Lo, "So here are my plans. I would like to get a lone sample of your product. First, so I can gauge it's the same quality that Roscoe showed me and second, I'd like to show it to a few of my friends in Ybor. I want to gauge their interest. I am almost 100% positive they will be interested. If I'm going to make a substantial purchase, I need assurances I can move it quickly and efficiently through my network of associates."

"Yeah, I'm usually not down with that. I don't like to let anything walk. But with Roscoe vouching for you, and if the sample is testing the waters for a substantial purchase, I guess I can go along with that. How much are you interested in?"

"It all depends on how much you can move. I could easily move twenty G's or more."

"More?"

"Maybe a hundred."

J Lo looked over at Roscoe, who nodded with an assurance, then looked back to Chuckles. His eyes sized him up, and he finally said, "Okay. Here's a sample."

He pulled one bill out of his pocket and handed it to Chuckles, who put his round framed glasses up on his nose and studied the bill. He held it up to the light overhead and flipped it to its back and studied it like a jeweler looking at a rare gem. His thumbs and fingers massaged the paper.

Then he handed the sample back to J Lo, who asked, "You're not interested?"

"Absolutely. But we need to come to terms with pricing, otherwise it's not worth my time to even leave here with the sample. If I move this package with the quickness and ease that I expect, can I come back for a much larger package?"

"This is like a closeout sale at a store. Once it's gone, it's gone. My supplier does not appear to be interested in a long-term business model. So, I don't know how much more they have left. I would suggest you buy as much as you can and sit on it as an investment package and move it slowly. We want to stay under the radar of the feds."

"That makes sense. How much for 100 G package?"

"For a hundred? I can give it to you for 30 points."

"That's nearly half of what you are selling to Roscoe for pocket change. I expect a substantial discount for volume. I'll give you 12 points."

J Lo scoffed. "27 cents on the dollar. Take it or leave it."

Standing up, Chuckles said, "You can keep your sample, and I understand you are very proud of your product. But unless you are that far away from the printer, you are asking for too high of a price. Especially for a large package. Keep in mind you're selling fake money, and I'm giving you real money. Not all deals go through. Thank you for your time, and maybe we'll bump into each other down in Ybor."

As Chuckles took a step towards the door, J Lo said, "These bills are like museum pieces. You can pass them all day long and unless you're pulling up to the drive-up window at the bank, you're not going to get caught. I am close to the printer. I'm his number one man. So, if you are serious and say that you can move hundred G's, for you, I'll lower the price to 25 points and no lower. The facilitator negotiated a terrible deal with the printer. Any lower than 25 and I may as well donate it to the animal shelter for kennel liners."

Rubbing the back of his neck, Chuckles crinkled his nose. "We have a deal. I'll take the sample. Just out of curiosity, with your Cuban ancestry, I was wondering if these are actually being made in Havana? Very good quality."

"No. The printers are from Paraguay. Local talent."

"Why just a onetime shot?"

"I don't like to ask a lot of questions. The facilitator alluded to the fact that they had limited access to the production material."

Chuckles nodded and extended his hand as they shook on an agreement to the terms. He asked if he could meet at 9 the next morning because he had a business meeting mid-morning. J Lo was amenable to the meeting time. After retrieving his phone and watch from the Ferriday bag, Roscoe and Chuckles walked out of the house and slid into Chuckle's Range Rover. Chuckles circled the block, making sure he wasn't being tailed by any associates of J Lo. He too was careful. Frank also hung back to make sure no one was following.

They all returned to the Blue Monster. The sun had set long ago as they assembled around the conference table in the criminal intelligence bureau. They discussed the developments and everyone seemed pleased at the progress.

Kate turned to Roscoe. "I'm going to release you. You really did well. I will call the state attorney's office and tell them what a great job you did. You are out for tomorrow. If J Lo calls you, tell him your battery died, or you dropped the phone in the toilet and you have to work in the morning."

"I just hope Maria doesn't make the connection."

"You had no choice. It was going to jail, or laying a path to freedom."

Frank said, "By the way, pal. If you tip off J Lo, your head will be placed in the judicial guillotine for compromising the operation."

Kate added, "We will retroactively charge you with each individual count of passing counterfeit money and the possession of the money in your pocket."

"Okay, I'll go over Maria's house and I'll tell her I dropped my phone in the toilet, and I'm going to get another one when I get to the store in the morning. Just in case J Lo asks her."

"Sounds like a plan."

Roscoe left, leaving the three detectives and Chuckles to discuss the continuation and direction of the case. Chuckles assured them he felt comfortable with the operation and that despite J Lo acting like he was on America's Most Wanted, they had developed trust. He would check back the next morning for the finishing touches and ribbon cutting.

Chapter Fifty

Kate began drafting the affidavit for the search warrant that they would need for searching J Lo's home. Kate assumed that she would have enough probable cause to get the warrant. Considering the testimony of Roscoe and Chuckles, along with listening to the conversation, there would be plenty of incriminating evidence. They also bought a sample $50 counterfeit bill, which matched those found at the print shop and being associated with the previous serial numbers provided by the Secret Service for an ongoing counterfeit operation in the Tampa area. She felt confident.

Frank knew that they would have to flash some buy money to J Lo. He discussed with Kate that he would reach out to the Secret Service to see if they had a flash roll of money just long enough to make sure that J Lo indeed had the package. He also said the Chuckles could work his magic and tell him that on such short notice he could only get together enough for a smaller package of twenty-five grand. It happened all the time, customers over promising and under delivering. Chuckles could pause the meeting for another day and he would return with the rest of the money for the full package.

If the Secret Service did not have a flash roll, then he would go to narcotics and see if he could procure a flash roll for the operation. Flash rolls were merely meant to show the bad guys that they had genuine currency ready to exchange. The idea being once Chuckles saw the counterfeit, he would give the buy signal and the arrest team would move in.

Frank, knowing that Russell Tenpenny was still in New York, he decided he would call the Assistant Special Agent in Charge Walter Crumbly and apprise him of the developments in the case.

After listening to the briefing over the telephone, Crumbly said, "Frank, it sounds like you folks have really done a great job on this case, but I'm going to need you to pump the brakes."

"Pump the brakes?"

"Yeah, you're getting a little out in front of your skis on this. Just tell the bad guys that there's been a death in the family and you will be back in a week. This way, our crew will be back in town and can assist."

"A week? How much more will be passed in the meantime? How many more merchants and mom-and-pop stores will be victimized?"

"Frank, I know you're new to this. You understand that these bad guys know that they have a buyer for the full package. They may not want to wait a week, but they're never going to pass up a guaranteed sale. If he says that he has $100,000, he probably has much less than that. It's not like the old days when we took down large operations. Anymore, we rarely have seizures over a few thousand dollars. If he's telling the truth about having a printer here in town, he might have a little more. Remember, the print shop is closed down. The source has been shutoff, so their supply is dwindling. He is probably a little worried about shopping his product around after hearing the printer was killed."

"Well, sir, I may be new to counterfeit, but I worked narcotics for several years. I made some very substantial cases there. I've also been a real cop for a long time. I can tell you that these bad guys know people get cold feet or, just like our informants, they over promise and under deliver. So, if our informant pumps the brakes and tries to pause this for a week, I feel very certain that our bad guy will not feel comfortable being left at the altar. As a result, he will try to move the product by any means necessary."

"I find that unlikely."

"I don't. Keep in mind that this counterfeit has a direct link to a murder. Our bosses will not allow us to slow walk a homicide investigation. We all have to answer to bosses."

"I understand. If your informant is confident and it will help with the murder case, then good luck."

"Talking of the informant, do you have any funds to pay the informant? He is a rock-solid guy."

"We are a little tight. It's right up against the end of the fiscal year. We might come up with a few hundred for expenses for him."

"A few hundred? What about a flash roll?"

"That is another reason to wait until next week. I would have to request one from headquarters."

"I don't think we can slow the arc on this. So, if this deal goes through, we can charge him locally and when your crew returns from New York, they can piggyback off of our arrest and charge him federally. Then our state attorney can drop the charges and allow federal prosecution to continue."

"Well Frank, I would really appreciate if you would slow down."

"I don't believe I'm out over my skis. But I would say the bobsled is out of the gate and hurtling towards the finish line. Our team will be there to greet them. I'll be sure to liaison with Russell Tenpenny when he arrives back home. Thank you for your time." Frank ended the call and turned to Kate and said, "Feds."

Kate nodded and chuckled and said, "And bosses. It doesn't matter what agency. Or even the private sector. Like all bosses go through the same asshole academy. When I worked in banking, I had some good ones and some bad ones. I know Jake said the same thing about the military."

Cody said, "I would agree with that. It was something about getting stripes or bars that made them go through a personality change."

Frank said, "You're right, Cody. Okay, I'll check with narcotics. I'm sure I can get a flash roll to get us over the hurdle. Let's be ready to do this tomorrow morning."

Chapter Fifty-One

The next morning, the three detectives, plus their new sergeant, Benny Thompson and Lester Rollins, were set up in strategic areas nearby the house. Detective Lester Rollins was sitting inside a marked police unit that would provide a show of legitimacy to the raid. Frank, Kate, Cody, and Benny were all sitting snugly in the Toyota Camry.

Benny said, "We should have grabbed my Explorer for a little extra room. Especially when it comes to jumping out."

Frank said, "My legs don't flex like when I was younger. It's a bit tight in the back seat. I might need to go to the day spa for a massage after my legs being contorted like a pretzel."

"You both sound like grumpy old men. Frank, try taking up yoga to stretch your old man ligaments. I like this car. It doesn't scream cop car and besides, it has the new car smell."

Cody said, "Even with the long-legged Kate pushing her seat all the way back, I think this has ample room."

Frank scoffed.

They had already circulated around in the area looking to see if J Lo had posted any lookouts or ambush teams. They weren't as worried, knowing that they were going to his primary business and entertaining residence. If the buy was set up at an off-site by location, they knew there was a chance of a rip-off and something they would have to plan for.

Benny asked, "I hate to be the adult in the room, but what about wifey and little J Lo's?"

Kate answered, "According to Roscoe, this is a crash pad. The family soaks up luxury at his Gulf front retreat. It's like his business HQ."

"Gotcha."

They watched as Chuckle's silver Range Rover pulled up in front of the home. The informant carried a messenger bag that was nearly empty. He knocked on the door and J Lo opened and gave a once over and scanned the surroundings. J Lo broke into a grin that filled his round face and a pumping handshake of his new friend. He virtually pulled him into the house, patted his back. At that point, they had to rely on the electronics to hear the conversation.

Chuckles said, "When this is all done, I'll have to treat you to a nice Cuban meal and we can share a couple of Cuba Libres."

"Talk to me. Show me the money."

"Well, I hate to be that guy. I'm going to have to do this on the installment plan."

"I don't do layaway. What the hell, bro?"

"I was a little overzealous in thinking that I could get the money together so quickly. I brought enough today for one package of twenty-five. But I feel very confident I can come back tomorrow to take the rest of the seventy-five off your hands. Some people that I was looking to invest with were out of town or out of pocket and not available to come up with the money. But for your trouble, I paid you 30 points instead of 25. So here is the $7,500."

They could hear J Lo give a heavy sigh. "I just wish once someone would deliver on their promise. Okay, big man. I'll take your $7,500 and I'll give you 25. When you're ready for the rest, call me. Of course, if someone else walks in that door right now that's ready to take the entire package, I will sell it in a heartbeat. Because this kind of puts a strain on our relationship, if you understand. Cuba Libre aside, I'm not in the drinking mood."

"J Lo, I understand your disappointment, and I apologize for over-promising. I've been pissed when someone does it to me. So, here's the seventy-five."

"Stay right here. I'll get you your twenty-five." The bubbly excitement was replaced with a monotone speech.

The surveillance units moved up closer so that when the buy signal came out, they would be ready.

"Here's your twenty-five."

With that, the surveillance units and patrol car moved up to just on the outskirts of the residence. The four-person crew dismounted from the Camry.

Chuckles said, "I can't tell you how sorry I am. If I got the entire package of a hundred, I was planning to make enough money to go to Acapulco. Now, I'm left to settle for going to Bohica."

"Bohica? Where the hell is that? The Caribbean?"

"It's a state of mind. Bend Over Here It Comes!"

As the door flew open, the patrol officer stepped in with Frank and the rest followed. "Police! Get your hands up! Get down on your knees! Both of you. Jesus Lopez, you're

under arrest." Frank said, "And whoever the hell you are, you're under arrest as well."

His friend pointed to Chuckles, who responded, "I didn't do anything. I was just visiting an old friend. We were going to go out for lunch."

"Save it for court. Cuff him and take him out to the patrol car and keep an eye on him."

They wanted to keep up the illusion to J Lo that he had not been betrayed by Chuckles and Roscoe. They took the handcuffed J Lo and placed him in the chair, and told him they had a search warrant to search his home. It didn't take long to search the small residence. They found the two moving boxes in the closet with what appeared to be a lot more than a hundred thousand dollars in counterfeit money. A second patrol car had arrived to transport J Lo.

Meanwhile, Rollins slid behind the wheel of Chuckle's Range Rover and drove down the street to meet the patrol car. This provided Chuckles with an escape, while Kate looked forward to burrowing into J Lo for answers.

Benny said, "Don't you just love this shit? I got all goose-bumpily joining in this crusade. Thanks for the entertainment."

"Anytime, boss." Said Kate.

Chapter Fifty-Two

In the interview room, J Lo, like so many thugs who'd sat in that same chair, often displayed a look of defiance and would slouch in the chair with an air of indifference to the surroundings. Especially considering the circumstances. But almost without doubt, they would all sit up straight and listen intently as the evidence was laid out in front of them. They had to make calculations of what was in their best interest. Do they stand tall and take the punishment alone? Do they call for an attorney and refuse to cooperate and hope that the poorly paid public defender can negotiate a good plea bargain? Or do they rollover like an eager puppy and start barking names, hoping to save themselves from prison time? This was the time where they would listen intently and start running the arithmetic in their mind like mathematicians. If I cooperate, how soon can I be out? What if I do state time? How quickly will I get paroled for good behavior? If I do federal time, that is a flat sentence.

Well aware of this dynamic, Kate often said homicide detectives were the best salespeople in the world. Anyone could sell a shiny new car or a timeshare to an exotic paradise. In some regard, she was selling a timeshare that provided an all-expense paid vacation lasting years in a 10 x 10 jail cell, with its own stainless-steel toilet and a fashionable bespoke orange onesie. Every cop show on TV told the suspects to remain silent and speak to an attorney. Anyone who had been previously in the system had been schooled by their defense attorneys and the jailhouse lawyers to keep their mouth shut. But it wasn't so easy.

Sliding into their chairs, Kate and Frank looked across at the worried J Lo. She knew he had previously escaped any jail time. He had to know that this was different. He was going to be fitted with a jumpsuit and posed for a mugshot.

Kate said, "I think you are a very smart man. It's obvious that you have a loyal network of business entrepreneurs. Whether it's skimmed credit cards, stolen gas, insurance fraud, or fake money. Being the intelligent business person that you are, you need to show a little more interest in what's going to happen to you over the next few years. It's up to you. If you choose not to cooperate and that is your choice, I will make you a project." She motioned to Frank. "The two of us will make you a project. As careful as you have been, I'm sure there has been some co-mingling of funds between your criminal enterprises and legitimate interests."

He shook his head with defiant confidence.

Kate continued, "We will drill down on every purchase you've made for yourself or your family, including your mother and if we can tie those purchases to ill-gotten gains from your criminal enterprise, we will back the U-Haul into the driveway of your mother's house and your house and seize everything. I'm sure that your mother is very proud of you right now. She won't be when she's humiliated in front of her neighbors, when her car is towed out of the driveway, and she's sitting on milk crates for furniture. The same for your sister. Say goodbye to your gulf front house in St. Pete. Yes, we know about that as well."

Shock exploded across his face. According to the plan, Jesus Lopez set up straight in his chair and leaned forward. "My family had nothing to do with any of this. Leave them out of it."

"The ball is in your court. We are not talking about stealing gas. This is a federal crime of possession of counterfeit federal reserve notes in violation of Title 18 U.S. Code 471. We have had our eyes on you for a while. Since the U.S. Secret Service identified the circulation of your bogus $50 bills. That is a five-year sentence in the federal penitentiary. Maybe you're lucky and you do your time at the Coleman Federal Correctional Institute in Florida."

Leaning forward, Frank interjected. "You see, us Floridians put sweaters on when the temperature drops below 70. There are no guarantees you go to Coleman. You could also land up in Rochester, Minnesota, where it will take the five years of your sentence to get acclimated to the freezing cold and snow. In fact, what is the current temperature in Minnesota right now?" The voice assistant on his phone provided the answer.

"I've been up north before."

Frank said, "Not as a permanent resident."

Kate resumed her line of enlightenment, as she liked to call it. "We know all about Norberto and Tito's Trucking." She let the bluff sink in. In reality, she knew very little.

He tilted his head like a confused animal.

"So, you probably weren't aware that most of these truckers have GPS on them. So, we could identify several of them and determine they were at specific truck stops or hotels when some of these bogus fifties were passed. When they were threatened with being arrested, sometimes being deported and having their trucks seized for carrying counterfeit, we found many of them were very cooperative. We also know several Tito's truck drivers hit the Seminole Casino this past week. Our timing could not have been any better than when we executed the search warrant this morning to find you in the middle of a rather substantial sale. Then, to our amazement, we found a couple hundred thousand dollars in bogus bills in your closet."

"I don't know nothing about those truckers and a friend said he was moving and needed to store a couple of boxes in my bedroom. So, I put them in the closet. I don't even know what's inside them."

Kate recognized this as the last desperate measure of hope. Like someone clinging to a rope hanging on the side of a mountain. "I'm sure you have probably watched at least one or two episodes of CSI. It's typical Hollywood slop, but sometimes they get it right. I want you to think how many times you counted and handled those stacks of fake fifties. Your fingerprints and DNA are going to be all over it. And that was part of your problem as well. You just don't see fifties too often. Genuine or counterfeit fifties are memorable. You should've gone with twenties. No one would've paid a lot of attention. You are like a slice of bread popping up in the toaster. You're done."

"I'm no snitch. I have loyalty." His head raised and his chin jutted out.

"Said every person sitting in your chair. Many were not as smart as you. Let me paint an image for you. You're meeting your sister and mother in the visitor's lounge of the Starke penitentiary. You have your calendar and you're checking down the days until early release because you have been such a good little boy in prison. That is, if your family would have anything to do with you after we have seized most of their assets. The other image is you sitting alone in Rochester, Minnesota, trying to stay warm. Knowing your family can't afford to see you, and you have to flatline your five-year sentence because the Fed's don't give time for being polite. Plus, another three years of parole after. That's a heavy debt. Hey, I'm sure Rochester is a delightful place to live if you are not looking through prison bars. Change of seasons and all that. Think about it. It's your decision now."

Silence fell over the room. The two detectives could almost hear the calculator and J Lo's brain computing his odds. Kate had little inclination to go down the rabbit hole tracking family held assets and tying them to being fruits of a crime or co-mingled assets and seizing their property. She knew the Secret Service may have the additional staffing and resources to do that.

She was also conning about the truckers. She hoped that casting that widespread net about the truckers and the GPS would divert his attention from Roscoe and Chuckles being the primary informants. After all, Guerrero had been arrested two days earlier by the airport police. Since he hadn't cooperated and fled, she would rather point interest in his direction.

J Lo leaned forward and put his hands on the table. Kate knew this was going to be let's make a deal. He was now going to negotiate, but his only leverage would be the identity of his source. "Okay, I know you are only interested in the primary distributor. If I give you that person or persons, you leave my family alone and I walk."

She smiled and nodded. "No one ever wants to do any time. Sadly, that's not the way it works. This is what I will do for you. You tell us everything, and I will charge you only on State charges. We will have the state attorney talk to the government and the U.S. Attorney's office. They won't care as long as you get charged and do time. I will not go after your family. That's not to say that the government doesn't. They like to get assets they can tie to the crime."

"Well, I wasn't the only one."

The last tactic employed for the final cave in was trying to blame everyone else or to share the blame.

"Perhaps that's true. However, as we would say in North Carolina, you are the one in the BBQ sauce. This was your last dance move before we tire of your nonsense, charge you and leave you at the mercy of the court system. To be honest, I don't even need your statement. I was just giving you an opportunity to shave some time off your sentence." This was the closing part of the sale. Like when the salesperson says the price is good for today and this opportunity is only available for a limited time. Call now, our operators are waiting. They scooted back their chairs and stood. She rarely made it as far as the door before the bad guy would ask for a saving hand to pull them off the cliff.

"Okay, okay. I'll tell you what you need to know."

She felt like doing a fist bump and a high five with whoever her interview partner was. Pop the cork on the champagne bottle and shake it all over the room. This is often the time that the floodgates of repentance would open. Sometimes, there was more information than they needed. Then there were other times where they only provided half the truth and accepted responsibility for a limited amount. Like throwing a hamburger to the lion and hoping it would be satisfied. Time would tell how much information he would provide.

"This Russian dude I know made the introduction."

"Russian dude? This is like pulling salt water taffy. I want you to open the door to the vault and tell me everything and don't hold anything back because I probably know a lot more than you think I do. If I catch you lying, this entire deal is off and I'll throw you to the charity of the U.S. Secret Service. And I don't believe they will be as kind as we are."

"Okay, his name is Demetri. Some last name that I can't pronounce. Starts with an M. So, we called him Demetri the Lover, because of the YouTube episode years ago. He was always hitting on the girls and a few times he showed up with some strippers from Russia or the Ukraine. Beautiful girls. Blondes with big tits."

"Spare me the descriptions. I don't need to know that they were wearing bejeweled G-strings. Unless you are telling me they were actually involved, or were they just eye candy in his arms?" She was annoyed at another stall tactic.

"Demetri is from Miami. He and his business partners own some strip clubs in Miami Beach and gift shops in the Keys. I don't know what all they are into, but he comes up here occasionally, and he sells us some numbers."

"Numbers?"

"Yes, card numbers. They steal them from rich out-of-town business executives that are looking to cheat on their suburban housewives. Not the regular clientele. So, a few weeks back, Demetri called and asked if I would be interested in moving some high-quality fake money. He said it was good enough that no one could tell until it reached the bank. So, being the businessman for entrepreneurs, he called me, and I took the meeting. I figured I had nothing to lose, and it was a wonderful party with him."

"Where did you meet him?"

"At a club down on South Howard. We bounced to a few different places. We were having a fun time. Then he showed me a sample of the money. I was impressed. It was as good as anything in my pocket. He paid the bill with the fake money. Bars are good at detecting bogus money, so I thought if he could pass it there, I could move it quicker than love bugs hitting the windshield in Florida. I also knew that credit is king. Not cash. He pleaded with me to move it for him and he would return the favor. Like the cherry on top. He would give a list of credit card numbers gratis to make the deal more palatable."

"What happened next?"

"The next day, he texted me an address. It was in the neighborhood, looked more like a crash pad. In the shadows of the water tower. Air mattresses, beanbags and beach chairs. Place was a dump. Small block home on Pine Street. Linoleum floors. Old inside. But he introduced me to two dudes from Paraguay. One of them was in charge. His name was Alejandro and said to call him Alex. He was the big dog. At least, I think that was his real name. In this business, we're not asking for driver's licenses and passports. Honestly, he could've told me his name was Usama Bin Ladin and I wouldn't have cared. The names are not important, it's what he is promising to deliver. There was another guy named Francisco. He was a little younger and thinner. He didn't talk much."

"What happened after?"

"So, we discussed business. Alex said he was from Paraguay. I told him I had an old girlfriend from Brazil and she lived near Foz and had taken me across the bridge to Paraguay for a shopping trip. He said that he lived near Ciudad del Este. We talked soccer, and we just became comfortable with each other. That's important in business relationships."

"What did they look like?"

"Two dudes. Black hair, olive skin, and fit."

"Fit?"

"Yeah, you know, like they were skipping the rice and beans, empanadas and Cuban pastries. Not skinny. Not muscle heads, just fit. They were, I don't know, maybe 5'9" or so. Alex was in his early thirties and Francisco was mid-twenties."

"Did you see any cars?"

"Yeah, Demetri drives a black Escalade. I saw an older blue Chevy Lumina in the driveway. When we did the pickup, there was a gray transit van."

"Any markings on the van?"

"Not that I saw."

"Was Demetri involved?"

"Not really. He was a facilitator. That's all he does. He facilitates commercial transactions between two like-minded entrepreneurs. Like a lover's matchmaker."

"What does he look like?"

"Spends a lot of time in the gym. Thick chest and his face looks like it was hit with a skillet. Flat, wide face. Bushy black hair. Russian accent."

"Is he from Russia?"

"So, he says. I know he's not from here. I don't know how much Spanish that Demetri knows, but we started the conversation in Spanish. Kind of like the kiss on the first date. No tongue, just a peck on the cheek. Get to know each other. The other dude hardly spoke. He spoke a little about soccer. Then, for the benefit of Demetri, we went back to English. That was it."

"No, that was not it."

"We negotiated the deal. I left and gathered up enough real money to buy a sizable package. I bought half a mill. We made the exchange, and I was on my own. It was now my money to distribute. The two Paraguayans I haven't seen again. I don't know how to get in touch with them. We didn't exactly exchange business cards. Demetri was like a one-way street of communication with them, and he is back down in Miami."

"How do you know he is back in Miami?"

"Instagram. He goes radio silent on social media when he comes up here. He is probably afraid of someone back in mother Russia or up the food chain knowing that he is doing something that perhaps they may not approve of. All I know is that when he is in Miami, he is a posting fool. Always showing off. Big time Russian mobster. I think he is a low wage errand boy that just tries to act big."

"How does Demetri get in touch with you, or how do you get in touch with him?"

"Text message."

"Can you send him a text and tell him you've gone through all of your money and want to know if you can get more?"

"These Russian gangsters are not to be taken lightly. I'm not putting myself or my family at risk. These Ruskies have ways of getting to you, even in prison or going after my family. I don't want to be found in my jail cell with my balls castrated and finger nails ripped out. I think I fulfilled my part."

"Just ask if the Paraguayan's have any more product. Did they say who's printing it?"

"They didn't say. But there was a funky odor like chemicals in the house. I just assumed they were printing at their place. I don't know about calling him."

Kate stared at him with a clear loss of patience.

"Okay, I'll hit up Demetri one time. The rest is on you because I'm not going into that bear's cave, no matter what you threaten me with."

Frank stepped out of the interview room and went through the personal property of J Lo

He retrieved his cell phone and brought it back into the interview room and instructed J Lo to send the text to Demetri. He also told him no codewords and no backdoor shenanigans.

J Lo sent the text to Demetri as instructed by Kate. The two detectives huddled around and saw the bubbling back and knew that he was responding quickly. They hoped that was a good sign. When it came through, they read the message that read, "el heffe, no mas. See you next month." J Lo sent a thumbs up emoji and handed the phone back to Frank.

Kate asked, "He called you the boss."

"Not like his boss. The boss of my crew. That was his nickname for me."

"Okay."

Kate now had the phone number for Demetri. She could track his phone and also search for him on Instagram. She was getting closer.

Chapter Fifty-Three

Picking up his phone, Frank called the Secret Service Field Office and asked the receptionist what agent was available in the office. He was told the Assistant Special Agent in charge, Walter Crumbly, was the only one in the office. Frank's face cringed like it just bit into a lemon.

"Sir, not only did I get out in front of my skis, but I landed and completed the downhill course. We moved on the information that was provided by the informant."

"Wow Frank. Sounds like you hit a home-run. I only wish we could have waited until our people got back from New York."

"I heard you, sir. But unfortunately, this involved more than some worthless paper being counterfeited. If only all victims were large retail merchants that could absorb the losses, but you also had mom and pop stores and everyday citizens. Of course, the detectives assigned to the murder case had to the answer to their supervisors and slow walking a homicide investigation is strictly a no go."

"Okay, I understand. What have you got?" Crumbly asked.

"The informant set up a buy bust. We were able to get a flash role from narcotics. So, to make a long story short, we arrested the individual and seized what appears to be a couple hundred thousand dollars in counterfeit fifties. We have convinced him to roll over and provide the location of his source, who he said is not the printer, Reza Jaber. He said that his source was a Russian mobster tied in with some Paraguayans."

"Okay, you'll have to write a report and give that over to Russell Tenpenny when he arrives back. He is scheduled to arrive back tomorrow. Unless he gets rolled and extended to another assignment in New York or Washington."

"No problem. I don't think we feel comfortable storing a couple hundred thousand dollars in counterfeit money in our evidence vault. I was thinking it would be best if you folks held onto it. After the court case is over, you can dispose of it however, you normally deal with counterfeit no longer in evidence. Did you want to come over here and retrieve it, or would you like me to bring it to you?"

"Yeah, with everyone gone, I'm pretty busy here. Why don't you bring it to us?"

He rolled his eyes and shook his head. "Sure."

"Thank you, Frank. I get a little frustrated with the high tempo of our protection assignments that occasionally strip the office of staffing. Sounds like you guys did a great job. Thank you."

Chapter Fifty-Four

With the phone number obtained from the text messaging with Demetri, Kate prepared a subpoena for the subscriber information and phone records to that number. Once the state attorney had completed the subpoena, Kate sent it off to the telephone company.

She then began preparing the affidavit for the search warrant to search the crash pad on Pine Street. With J Lo unwilling to go back to the Paraguayans or to make an introduction of Chuckles, they had no choice but to kick the door and raid the house.

She knew from the information gleaned from Russell Tenpenny and from Frank that the lower the pricing, the closer to the printer. If J Lo's statement was correct, they were at the doorstep of the primary distributors. If not, probably within two degrees of separation from those closest to the printer. Here, the printer had been murdered. So, it was not an enormous leap to assume that the Paraguayans and the Russian were directly connected to the printer. Thus, they are the primary suspects in his murder.

She wondered why kill the printer? They ended the possibility of continuing a profit stream and diversification of the Russians business that was nearly impossible to detect. Did they get into a payment squabble? The printer could have demanded more money for such high quality. With an Iranian bullet in the back of the head of the printer, perhaps the Paraguayans and Russian had nothing to do with the murder. Kate felt anxious as she contemplated that she might have run down the wrong rabbit hole and wasted a lot of time chasing a red herring.

Completing the probable cause statement for the affidavit of the search warrant, Kate waited for Cody. He was driving past the location of the house where J Lo had picked up the money. She perused the internet and first looked up Paraguay and then the town of Ciudad del Este, that J Lo had described.

In her search, she learned that the area was known as the Tri-Border area and was rife with counterfeit products and corruption. With them counterfeiting U.S. currency, kind of fit with the reputation of the region selling knockoffs of desirable and more expensive products. She also read that there was a heavy influence on an assortment of multinational criminal enterprises and terrorist organizations. It all added up to a conspiracy circling the homicide involving a dead Iranian, a Russian mobster, and two Paraguayans distributing through a network of Cuban truckers. This was like the United Nations of criminals.

When Frank arrived back from the Secret Service, Kate asked him if they were going to give him a trophy or a medal.

Frank responded, "That guy. He tried to appear being too busy but the bottom line was, he was too lazy to walk the six blocks while we are in the middle of a homicide investigation. So, here I am, forcing him to do some work that he would normally delegate. Don't expect me to get an invitation to the office Christmas party this year."

"I guess that is standard operating procedure for that agency. The story I've heard is that they needed to keep a bag packed and ready to drop everything and jump on an airplane. It's another reason I enjoy being a local cop. I know where the pillow is located that I'm parking my head on every night."

"I know they get frustrated, pausing criminal investigations to run out and protect some politician in the name of democracy. They have no control over their lives. Tenpenny told me he has had a career of disappointments. Missed holidays, birthdays, school events and weeks away from home."

"Like being in the military."

"Indeed."

"Hey, I want to show you what I found out." Kate told him what she had found about Paraguay. "Who is our representative on the Joint Terrorism Task Force at the FBI?"

Frank smiled, extended his arms out, and said, "You're looking at him. Yes, I wear many hats in the Criminal Intelligence Bureau. Would you like me to make an inquiry on your behalf about what they might know?"

"Why yes sir, that would be lovely."

Frank put his phone on speaker and called the Supervisory Special Agent over the JTTF, Griffin St. Clair. After Frank made the introduction regarding the background on the case, Kate told St. Clair her suspicions about the connection to the Tri-Border area.

Griffin St. Clair responded, "So, there'd been discussions for decades about the Tri-Border area, also known as the TBA. There has been a strong presence of Hezbollah and an Iranian influence in the region. But over all of that time, they have never shown an interest in coming to the U.S. Back in the nineties, they engaged in some activity and terrorist attacks in the TBA. Of course, with the increase of border crossings at the Southern Border of our country, there's been a fair number of concerns about what nefarious individuals are coming across. There have been several people stopped who were on the watchlist, but none of them were real bad guys. Primarily, the discussion concerning the TBA has always been driven by a bunch of think tanks and foreign policy lobbyists chasing grants and funding. Of course, Pro-Israel groups are typically clanging the alarm that Iran and Hezbollah are staging for an imminent attack. But we've seen no sign or evidence to support any of these theories."

Kate asked, "So, in your estimation, you believe that what we have here is just a straight up criminal enterprise involving counterfeit currency and has nothing to do with terrorism or anything like that?"

"To this point in time, we have seen no sign of that in the homeland or specifically in the Tampa District. After decades of banging the war drums, and no activity to support it, people eventually get tone deaf to the sound of the drum. But if you find that there's more going on, reach out to us or Frank can just loop me back in. Give the Secret Service a call about the counterfeit."

"We have."

"Okay. Thanks for the call."

After ending the call, Frank and Kate discussed the phone call. Kate said, "We have that Iranian bullet casing."

"Yes, but perhaps our Russian or the Paraguayans may have picked up some spare ammo on the black market in Paraguay. Especially considering the price of ammunition these days."

"Who cares where the ammo comes from as long as it goes bang."

"Exactly. But it makes sense what the FBI was saying. Chicken Little screaming, the sky is falling about the TBA, when actually there is nothing to see here. Move along." Frank said.

"Until we see behind the curtain to understand what's going on. My Spidey senses are tingling. We have sadly seen up close the evil that humans can do to each other. Feds have some standoff distance and bad guys are not impressed with the double Windsor knot of the Brooks Brothers tie."

"Not like the old days, when J. Edgar Hoover's name would bring criminals to their knees."

"I agree, but I think sometimes we let our guard down too much as a country. You heard what he was saying with the border crossings. From what I was reading, there have been nearly a million got-aways from the border and we have no idea who these people are. Some that have been caught turned up on the terrorist watchlist."

"True. I just don't think we should sound the fire alarm just yet."

"No, but I am keeping a wide-angle lens open on this. I'm considering all possibilities." She ran her fingers through her hair and sighed.

Chapter Fifty-Five

After presenting and receiving approval from the judge on the affidavit for the search warrant, the three detectives once again met with the uniformed unit close by to the target Pine Street stash house. Cody had previously driven by the home to get a detailed description of the home for the search warrant. Those descriptions were essential in search warrants to get a detailed description so that no mistake would be made. There had been incidents in the history of law enforcement where the police executed a warrant on the wrong home.

Driving past the house one more time, Cody observed no activity and did not see any of the vehicles described by J Lo. The legendary and ornately painted West Tampa water tower was an easy landmark. Towering over the community, the yellow tower had a mural of an old-fashioned cigar band and read, "Bienvenidos a West Tampa." The neighborhood was an eclectic collection of well-maintained homes with prideful yards. The one blemish was the stash house. A pinkish cement block house with ruts for a driveway.

When everyone was in position, Kate gave the go command and they all rolled up in front of the one-story home with a low-pitched roof. The leaner Frank Duffy and uniformed officer Scott Stubenrauch went to the back of the home. Kate and Cody went to the front door along with the second uniformed officer, David Ebinger. Duffy looked at Stubenrauch, who was stroking his mustache. They nodded at each other and Frank texted Kate they were in position.

Kate and Ebinger stood on opposite sides of the door. Cody stood behind Kate. She gave a bill collector's knock on the door and said, "Police with a search warrant! Police with a search warrant! Open the door or we will be forced to knock it down." She gave two more knocking announcements. She couldn't hear any movement inside.

As she listened, she heard protesting wheels of a grocery cart on the asphalt street. A homeless man pushed the cart past the home. He glanced at the officers and continued pushing the entirety of his belongings and a small dog.

Kate thought of the sadness and the simplicity of the man's existence and what his story had been. She also thought about how well behaved the dog was compared to her puppy, who always seemed to be in the zoomie mood. Back to work, she gave one final knock.

"Binger, could you monitor the door?"

"Yep. No problem."

The two detectives walked to the side of the house and looked at the electric meter. There was no consumption of electricity. Kate walked back to her car and extracted a breaching ram.

She handed the ram to Cody. "I'm eager to see your athleticism and knock the door off the hinges."

Ebinger held up a finger to pause the action. He reached up with his left hand and turned the door handle, and it turned. He smiled. "Work smarter, not harder."

Kate nodded as Cody dropped the ram. Ebinger gave a push of the door. Kate yelled, "Police coming inside."

No response. Kate, with her pistol pointing forward, entered the house. Breaching the door while executing a search warrant was the most dangerous time. By this point, the bad guys or girls had plenty of time to be on alert and to arm themselves. She was familiar with one case in Arkansas, where two officers in the same situation were shot. One was killed swinging the ram, as the bullet fired by the suspect entered under his arm. The second officer survived being shot in the head.

Cody followed Kate as they snaked through the house, clearing each room. They radioed to Frank, who was positioned at the back door, that they were clear. Holstering her weapon, Kate opened up the back door and allowed him and Stubenrauch to enter. As described by J Lo, there were two air beds and several beach chairs. They still had price tags attached to the chairs. Kate figured that this was probably another local merchant that was stung by the fake $50.

It was no doubt that the two Paraguayans had abandoned the home. It was steamy and musty inside and Kate adjusted the thermostat to trigger the air conditioning. They found no evidence of counterfeit. It did not take long to search the small barren home.

Hesitating and cringing at the thought of what she would find inside the refrigerator, she pulled the door open. It was empty. She opened the freezer compartment. In it was a partial bag of melting ice. Out of the ordinary was an unplugged standalone ice maker. Most unusual. A standard appliance for a fraternity, but these guys were not hosting parties. The ice tray was empty. Kate and Cody looked at each other and shrugged. They walked outside and found the trash bin and lifted the lid. The pungent odor slapped her in the face, but it was empty.

Stubenrauch said, "Don't get too close. You'll be wearing that scent the rest of the day."

"Eau de Stinko. Not as bad as a ripe body."

"Febreze works wonders."

"Never leave home without it. I always carry it."

She called the owner of the property to meet her at the residence. Approximately thirty minutes later, the owner, George Gentry, arrived. With his hands on his hips, he studied the scene. Kate asked Gentry who his tenants were and how much he knew about them.

Gentry said that they paid cash up front for six months. Including the deposit. He said that they had just moved from Paraguay and had not opened up a local bank account yet. But they showed a driver's license. He told her he had advertised on Craigslist. Kate continued the inquisition and found the landlord wasn't too curious about his renters. Gentry claimed not to have even had a contract or lease with them. She knew with the cash up front he probably would not claim the revenue on his taxes.

She smiled and asked, "Have you deposited the cash in the bank?"

"Yes, I have."

"Was it in fifties?"

"No. Hundreds."

She figured with them running an operation out of this house, they certainly wouldn't want to start off by paying in counterfeit money to the landlord. This could have potentially blown the roof off their operation before they ever got started. He told her they were pretty quiet. In his descriptions one matched that was provided by J Lo. He said that he had seen them driving an older Chevrolet, but he was not sure of what model. She handed him a copy of the search warrant inventory of property seized. Which was blank except for her line through the blank page with her signature.

"What do I do now?"

"I would assume you can list it again after you clean it."

He scoffed as he stood there again with his hands on his hips, shaking his head.

They went door to door canvassing the neighborhood. Knocking on the doors of the mostly well-kept but small homes with manicured yards. The consensus of the neighborhood inquiries, like with previous renters in the home, there was little interaction with the neighbors. They were all relieved that they were quiet and, unlike some previous renters; there was no blaring music or revving of a Harley-Davidson in the front yard. One home next to the stash house had a doorbell camera. They said that they didn't pay to have their footage archived. They did describe that they had seen them driving an older blue Chevy Lumina and a couple of times they had seen a gray van and a black Escalade. Again, this fit with the description provided by J Lo that the Escalade was being driven by Demetri. They had exhausted their leads at the stash house and still were no closer to the identity of the two Paraguayans. Next up was Demetri.

Chapter Fifty-Six

The best lead going forward was to find Demetri, the Lover. Kate laughed at the memory of listening to the audio recording of a person claiming that his name was Demetri and leaving a narcissistic rant about what a great catch he thought he was. He thought it was a girl from a club patron's cell phone number. Instead, it turned out to be a number to a radio station. He eventually became an instructor on how-to pickup girls. When his business came to a failing end, he was subsequently arrested in Canada for the willful promotion of hatred as a misogynist and antisemitic.

They swung by the iconic West Tampa Sandwich Shop. The austere green building, which had been visited by presidents, politicians and served the community for decades, was an institution. The detectives walked inside the busy sandwich shop as the smell of fresh bread comforted the senses. They each grabbed a Cuban sandwich at the counter and returned to the car.

Arriving back at the Blue Monster, Kate dove in on Demetri. With one hand gripping the crispy sandwich, she reviewed the phone records with her other hand. The records came back to a burner phone. The call list was extensive. He spent a good portion of his day either in phone conversations or trading text messages. She knew it would take some time to go through the call history. But there were several 813-area code phone numbers. One was eliminated as it belonged to J Lo. Most of the 813 numbers had appeared repeatedly in his call history over several months. One number appeared for the first time over the previous few weeks. She circled that number as being highly probable that it would belong to his two new Paraguayan friends.

She then went to social media. Just as J Lo had described, Demetri fancied himself as quite the ladies' man and a regular in the Miami Beach party scene. Especially in strip clubs and bottle clubs. His name on social media was Demetri Makarov. Not knowing whether this was another alias, she had the analysts do a dive on his name. Sure enough, he was registered to a black Escalade and lived in a beachfront condo near Miami Beach.

His latest post on Instagram was alarming to Kate. Demetri had posted a picture with an open shirt flashing his well-built chest and defined abs. He was flashing more gold than an Egyptian burial vault. The caption read, "Wishing all my lady friend's warm thoughts. Keep this photo as a reminder of our rocking good times. It's time to fly the coop, but I will return one day."

She was afraid that her best suspect was leaving town. She asked for an emergency location on the phone from the phone company under exigent circumstances to locate the phone for an individual who is a suspect in a homicide. The telephone company responded that Demetri's phone was pinging near the Miami International Airport.

Concerned that he would fly back to Russia and they would lose all hope of finding him, she knew she needed to work fast. She knew that with the hostilities between Russia and Ukraine, there were no direct flights between the U.S. and Russia. She began searching on the internet to see what other likely countries he could fly to from Miami and then catch a flight from that country onto Russia. It didn't take long to see that Turkey was a likely destination. Checking the schedules for flights from Miami to Turkey, she located a Turkish Airlines flight into Istanbul. The flight was scheduled to leave in two hours.

She called the Miami-Dade Police Department station at the airport and asked to speak with the shift supervisor. Lieutenant Oscar Pena was briefed by Kate and advised that he would send some officers to the departure gate of the Turkish Airlines flight.

Pena asked, "Do you have any paper on him?"

"No. I don't have enough yet for a warrant. If you could grab him and ask him some questions would be helpful."

"You know how this works. I'm glad to offer an assist, but if he is not cooperative, there is little that we can do."

"I understand."

She was frustrated that she had no evidence to tie him directly to the murder of Jaber. She only had the testimony of J Lo that he facilitated the introduction of the two Paraguayans. That was a very weak case and under no circumstances did she have enough evidence to do a probable cause arrest.

"That's about all we can do. You understand we can't detain him from the flight."

"Sadly, I do. But once he gets on that plane, I won't even be able to ask questions. So, any help would be appreciated."

"I'll have a couple of uniforms go over there with Detective Jonas. Expect a call from him so that you can provide some background. He will probably tell us to pound sand."

"You are probably right. The Russians are not easily intimidated."

"I agree about the Russians."

She waited for a call back. In the mean time, she prepared a request for records on the one 813-area code number that Demetri had been calling over the last couple of weeks.

Chapter Fifty-Seven

A few minutes later, her phone rang from a 305-area code. "This is Kate Alexander."

"Hi Kate, this is Lenny Jonas. I am a detective with the Miami-Dade Police Department assigned to the airport. My L.T. told me you have some Russian desperado that you need waterboarded."

"I wish. I know there is little that you can do without an arrest warrant."

"We have a couple of uniforms on Segways heading to Concourse E to the Turkish Airlines departure gate. They have his description."

"Segways?"

"The fastest way to move about the airport through the crowds without running. Plus, you have the advantage of looking over the crowd. Like being on a horse."

"We have a couple as well for parades and such."

"I'm going to head over on a golf cart. Not as nimble, but I won't break my neck either. The Segway takes a bit of practice and skill. I fall over tying my shoes. If you could give me the 411, I'll give him a toss and see what we can find out."

Kate filled him in on what she knew about Demetri and his involvement in the case. She would wait for Jonas's call. Kate had the patience of a puppy at feeding time. She began updating the murder book with reports and the chronology. She had fallen behind and this would keep her mind occupied while she waited for the phone to ring.

A few minutes later, Jonas called with an update. "He is not at the departure gate. We confirmed he is on the manifest and flying first class. We are going to check the nearby shops and restroom."

"Thank you. Good luck."

Back to paper work. Kate, like all cops, preferred the action on the street and the hunt and chase. She also enjoyed the satisfaction of completing the paperwork. She took pride in her report writing skills, knowing they would be closely scrutinized by management, the prosecution team, and potentially sliced apart by the defense team. This case file would also be scrutinized by various federal agencies as well.

The phone buzzed again. "Not here in the area. We are heading to the Turkish Airlines Priority Lounge. I'll be over there shortly."

Jonas enjoyed working at the airport. The busiest international cargo airport in the U.S., being the gateway to South America and the Caribbean, and having a thousand flights a day, the airport never rested. He frequently had requests from other agencies to collar a fugitive or to question someone.

Detective Jonas arrived at the departure lounge and met the two brown uniformed officers. They acknowledged they had identified Demetri inside the lounge. Jonas texted Kate that they located Demetri and he would let her know what happened. The three officers nodded to the reception greeter and walked inside the lounge for the premium passengers.

Demetri stood out like the lights on South Beach. In all of his flamboyance, he was holding court with several females. The three brunettes were all laughing. As the detective pointed Demetri out to the two uniformed officers, they made their way through the inquisitive eyes of the waiting passengers. Demetri paused the girl's laughter as he answered a phone call.

As the police presence was made known to Demetri, he told the caller that he had to hangup because the police were there to talk to him. After he ended the call, Detective Jonas asked Demetri to accompany them.

Demetri looked up and down at Jonas, assessing the competition. Jonas, being a veteran detective, held the gaze of his target of interest. "I would like to help the police, but I have a flight."

"This won't take long. There is a room over here for privacy."

After a long pause, "Okay."

Jonas led Demetri to a prayer room that was unoccupied. He asked Demetri to leave his messenger bag with the two officers outside. The room was large enough for only two, and he left the two uniformed officers to stand guard outside. Jonas took the driver's license and passport from the Russian and studied both. "I see you have a condo near Miami Beach in Sunny Isles, also known as Moscow by the Sea."

"If you say so."

"I say so. Lots of Russians live there."

"Sun, beaches and beautiful girls."

"Speaking of the weather, I'm surprised that you are heading back at this time of the year. I hope you packed your winter coat and scarf. With this Ukraine war going on, aren't you afraid of being drafted and sent to the front with a rifle?"

"I have served my time. I have friends in high places, so I'm not concerned. It will be nice to get some quality pirozhki much better than your empanadas."

"Is Sunny Isles like your vacation dacha?"

He shrugged with no answer.

"When do you plan to return?"

"When I get my fill of good vodka. The U.S. has made it most difficult to acquire Russian vodka."

"So, I've heard. Would you mind answering some questions about your recent trip to Tampa?"

"Sure. But first, I must call my attorney. He too lives on how you say, Moscow by the Sea?"

"Sure, be my guest." Jonas knew that this was pulling the plug on the jukebox and their little dance would end.

Demetri spoke for a minute in Russian on the phone. "My attorney wants to know if you have a warrant or am I under arrest?"

"No, to either."

Demetri ended the call and said, "Then, in that case, I have a flight to catch."

"Aren't you curious about my questions concerning Tampa?"

"I am. Send my regards to Tampa. I have no comment." He smiled and said, "Have a nice day."

"Thank you, Mr. Makarov. Have a safe flight and I hope you packed that coat and have a warm greeting when you arrive." Demetri had a puzzled look as Jonas opened the door and allowed the Russian to walk through the two guards to rejoin the smiling brunettes. Jonas hoped to plant an idea that perhaps his reception may not be a greeting of a hero. He wanted that thought to simmer for a few minutes. Jonas walked over to Demetri and said, "Here is my business card. If you change your mind or it's colder than you thought, call me."

Demetri stared at the card, looked at Jonas, and then tore the business card in half. He walked to a trash receptacle and dropped the scraps in the bin and, without a word, returned to the girls.

Jonas knew it was over. He was hoping to plant a few questions that would create a burning desire to find the answers. The Russians had been well schooled. If he had been in the Army or the FSB, Jonas knew he stood a naked man's chance of survival in a Russian winter in obtaining any cooperation. He asked the officer if they had found anything in the bag. They said there was nothing suspicious.

Disappointed in the results, Detective Jonas called Kate and passed the bad news that despite his best efforts, Demetri the Lover would soon be on his way to back to Mother Russia.

"I am sorry, Kate. He lives in a Russian community near Miami Beach. Some are here with good intentions. I question the sources of their money. Most of it is from family, or proceeds from crime or corruption. As many that are wealthy, there are just as many sponsored here that are barely getting by as housekeepers or dancers. The have and the have-nots. I really gave it a good run."

"I'm sure you did, Lenny. Listen, I appreciate your efforts. Thank the lieutenant as well."

"I sure will."

Kate felt frustrated at hearing the news from Detective Jonas. If given another week or even a few more days, she felt confident that she could at least charge Demetri with the conspiracy charge on the counterfeiting. Playing devil's advocate, she knew Demetri would just argue that he had stopped by some friend's house that he had met at a club and did not know what they were into a life of crime. And that he had invited J Lo to swing by and party with them. It would be challenging to contradict that argument.

She had zilch tying him to the homicide of Jaber. She knew Demetri was involved, or why else would he choose now to fly to Turkey and a final destination of Russia? Not when a war was waging between Russia and Ukraine and every able-bodied Russian was being conscripted into the war effort. Unless he had been a Russian intelligence asset and was being summoned home to avoid being implicated in any criminal activity. She would've been willing to negotiate an immunity deal, knowing that he was like an outer planet in the solar system. She contemplated reaching out to the FBI in Moscow, but she knew she would hear nothing but laughter at her request to ask the Russians to interview Demetri. Especially with the ongoing hostilities and tension between the two countries.

Chapter Fifty-Eight

As Kate explained to Cody that Demetri had slipped off the hook and was swimming back across the Atlantic, he held up a finger to pause her conversation. She asked what was going on. He turned up the volume on his portable radio and heard silence. He then picked up his desk phone and dialed communications and asked what was the last call that was dispatched to Bayshore Boulevard. The dispatcher informed him they had received a call for a suspicious vehicle in the parking lot of the Bayshore Bottoms apartment complex facing out towards Bayshore Boulevard. It was occupied by two males. The vehicle was a blue Chevrolet Lumina four-door.

After ascertaining what unit had been dispatched on the call, Cody called the officer responding. He asked them that once they made contact with the vehicle and occupants, to call him. He also requested that they get their identification and to search them as well as the vehicle. Cody also warned them they might be suspects in a homicide and, if true, they would probably be armed with at least one 9 mm pistol. Cody warned the officers to be careful and if they found the vehicle to treat them like a felony car stop. The officer told them they were on the north end of their patrol district and with school traffic it would take a few minutes extra to arrive on scene.

They sat huddled around Cody's desk and discussed getting in their car and starting in that direction. They realized they would be too far away to offer much help unless the officers found the vehicle and occupants. Instead, they sat like nervous family members in the waiting room of the hospital, waiting for word from the surgeon.

After what seemed like an eternity, Cody's phone rang and he answered it. Kate could see the disappointment on Cody's face and didn't need to hear the reason.

Cody said, "They said they drove through the parking lot and the vehicle was gone. They are going to circulate in the area and see if they can find it."

"Do you think it was them?"

"Hard to say. There's not that many of those cars on the road any longer. Maybe it was a coincidence."

"Coincidences rarely occur. It's good police work or in this event a concerned citizen. In Waseca, Wisconsin, a woman was washing dishes and saw a suspicious juvenile entering a storage facility. She called the police. It turned out the kid was using the place as a bomb factory and planned to attack his school."

"Do you want to find the complainant on the call and see if it could be them, or am I just shooting off rounds into the darkness?"

"Nope, just good detective work. I'm just shocked that you heard that on the radio. I tune out everything aside from hearing my unit number. Everything else becomes almost white noise. I could probably use the police radio as background white noise to help me sleep better. Until you hear the excited voice of someone needing help. And then, the adrenaline instantly kicks in."

"I guess my alert level and situational awareness were heightened when I was in Afghanistan. So, my brain rarely shuts off. I can't explain why I picked up on that. Perhaps it was when they mentioned Lumina that my ears perked up like a German Shepherd on alert."

"With your brain staying engaged, do you have trouble sleeping?"

"Sometimes. But I try to get in a good workout in the gym, have a nice early meal with my mom, and get some gaming in. Then I spend a little while with my mother conversing or reading, which allows my brain to quiet my body. By then I am hoping my brain is fatigued enough to submit to the call of slumber."

Cody picked up his portable radio once again and listened. This time he heard the patrol unit checking out with a vehicle in Ballast Point Park, not too far from the apartments where the original suspicious vehicle call had originated. The patrol unit was asking for an additional unit as backup. That was all the two detectives needed to hear. They jumped up and headed towards the parking garage and started in that direction.

Cody keyed up his microphone on his portable radio and told dispatch that the vehicle was possibly occupied by two-armed homicide suspects. He knew that would send the calvary to the officers, who were now busy dealing with their tactical approach protocols.

As they ran towards their car, they could hear the cacophony of nearby patrol units sensing the danger and notifying communications, that they, too, were on their way.

Cody and Kate made their way across the bridge from downtown Tampa and turned south on Bayshore Boulevard. With lights and siren engaged, they zigzagged through the heavier than normal afternoon traffic. Not being in a marked unit, they had to be careful in traffic. A zoned-out driver not paying attention could change lanes and hit them or, worse, slam on the brakes, resulting in evasive action.

Kate and Cody arrived at the entrance to Ballast Point Park, which was now congested with onlookers and other police cars. As they made their way up to the primary unit, the officer asked, "Is this your guy?"

Cody and Kate looked at a Hispanic male on his knees with his fingers interlocked behind his head. The lone male occupant was wearing white painter's pants which were speckled with an array of paint colors. His rounded belly looked like it had been fed a steady diet of starchy food and beer.

Next to the suspect were the remnants of an ice cream cone and its contents melting into the pavement. His physical description certainly did not match with the physically fit Paraguayans. The man spoke very little English, and what he could speak was heavily accented.

The officer began questioning the individual and found that his name was Pablo Garcia. His driver's license confirmed that, along with the registration on his Chevy Lumina. Pablo told the officer that he had been painting a nearby house and had stopped to get an ice cream cone at the park refreshment stand. He denied having been parked at the apartment complex and told them after leaving the painting job, he had come directly to the park. He enjoyed eating the ice cream while watching the horses at the stables across the street, which reminded him of when he worked on a ranch in Mexico. The officer dialed the owner of the paint company and verified Pablo's story. Kate peered into the car and saw that, in fact, the backseat contained painting equipment and drop cloths.

Kate took the keys from the ignition and opened the trunk. As she lifted the lid, she saw more painting supplies. She looked at the calm water of Tampa Bay behind them and thought there was no calmness in the park. She looked at Cody and they both shook their heads.

Cody bent down and asked if his favorite flavor was vanilla. Pablo nodded in agreement. After asking Pablo to sit back and lean up against the car, he walked over towards the refreshment stand. A couple of minutes later, Cody walked back holding a large vanilla ice cream cone and handed it to Pablo, who said, "Gracias."

Cody asked an officer, named Diaz to explain to Pablo why he had been stopped and to apologize for being accosted. Pablo, who was already licking his cone, smiled and stood up. He thanked everyone and resumed his position in his car, eating his vanilla cone that had been so rudely interrupted.

The two detectives thanked the officers for their help and told them they could return to service. As the police cars retreated from the park, so to did the onlookers that appeared disappointed at the lack of excitement and tucked their cell phone cameras away. Cody called communications to find out the address and phone number of the complainant on the suspicious vehicle call.

Chapter Fifty-Nine

Cody steered out of the picturesque park past a group of palm trees that stirred with a gentle breeze off the bay and pointed at the horse stables across the street. "You ever ride there?"

"Perennial Farms?"

"Yep."

"No. It's part of the Yacht Club, but open to the public. My horses are in Brandon at Over the Moon Stables. Closer to the house."

"Why horses?"

"Jake and I loved being outdoors. Smell the fresh air and feel the strength of the horse under you and the wind blowing through my hair. It's the freedom. I can go slow and enjoy the scenery or gallop and feel the power. It is exhilarating. I have no worries in the saddle. It's an escape and Duke, my equine friend, never asks for much. Just a little hay and an occasional sliced apple."

"Sounds good."

"Besides, Brittney and I get to spend awesome mother daughter time together."

"Now you have the puppy."

"Yes, animals are magnificent. They only ask for a little love and have tremendous loyalty. Speaking of love, that was very nice of you to buy a new ice cream cone for Pablo."

"Poor guy. Just minding his own business. Busting his ass working all day painting, and wanted a little treat. Next thing he knows, he is being jacked up for nothing."

"You're a good man."

He smiled and continued driving the short distance to the apartment complex and parked the Camry. They walked up to the apartment of the individual who had called to report the suspicious vehicle. Cody gave an official knock. A man of average proportions with a tight haircut introduced himself as Hector Marino. He told the detectives that he had just arrived home and noticed the car. He said he had never seen the car there before and it just looked out of place. This drew his attention to the car and the two occupants. From his apartment, he continued to periodically looked out of the parking lot and just thought that it was odd. So, following the advice to see something, say something, he called the police. He told them shortly after making the call that he looked out again and the car had left. He did not see what direction they went.

Cody asked, "Aside from sitting in the car, were they doing anything out of the ordinary?"

"No, they were just watching traffic. They weren't doing anything inside the car that I could see. Not like they were eating lunch."

"How could you tell they were just watching traffic?"

"They were like watching the volleying of a tennis match. They would look towards the right down Bayshore and follow cars, passing their location. Then their heads would shift back to the right until the next car came along and then they would fall for that. They were only watching what was coming north on Bayshore."

"This is the first time you've seen them? Did you get a look at them?"

"They looked like Middle Eastern males."

"Are you sure about them being Middle Eastern and not Hispanic?"

He shrugged and said, "I am in the Air Force, and I have spent a lot of time in the Middle East. With my surname, I tend to recognize Latinos. I couldn't be hundred percent sure, but I would lean towards them being Middle Eastern."

"You didn't see anything distinctive on the car like bumper stickers, body damage or the license plate?"

Marino smiled and said, "Nothing distinguishing, but here's the license plate number I copied down."

Cody and Kate thanked him for being so attentive and for calling the police. They walked outside and Cody called communications to run the license plate number. It was registered to the stash house on Pine Street to Alejandro Duarte. J Lo had mentioned that the primary Paraguayan was named Alex. They now had the registered owner, who sounded more Hispanic than Middle Eastern. This was a huge break.

Cody said, "I have an idea."

"I'm all ears."

Chapter Sixty

Cody said, "I have a hunch. None of this has been adding up. So along those lines, let's take a drive south on Bayshore towards the base. And let's see what could they be watching."

As they drove south, they passed residential neighborhoods, expensive condo complexes and glimpses of Tampa Bay to the left. They had seen nothing that would raise their suspicion. Bayshore Boulevard ended at one of several security checkpoint gates leading to the MacDill Air Force Base. The military base was home to the U.S. Central Command (CENTCOM) headquarters, which directed all military actions in the Middle East theater. In addition, they also housed the headquarters of the Special Operations Command (SOCOM) which oversaw all actions by special operators worldwide. A lot of activity is under one roof. The tip of the spear, as they would say. The airbase also housed a military refueling wing that would conduct midair refueling of U.S. military aircraft.

Cody said, "With these dudes conducting surveillance on Bayshore, we might want to let OSI know, so they are aware."

"That's a great idea. I like the way you have your thinking cap on. Who knows, they could already be working something on base and we wouldn't know."

"Yep."

They pulled up to the security booth. They were greeted by a young female Air Force security officer with her blond hair tied in a bun under her navy-blue beret. After inspecting their identifications, she provided directions to the building of the Air Force Office of Special Investigations. While the security forces at the gate would act like the patrol officers for the base, Air Force OSI was the investigators or detectives of any crimes occurring on base involving military personnel. They were also involved with counterintelligence.

Cody weaved through the base and asked Kate if she had ever been on the base. She replied, "Yes. When Jake was alive and assigned to SOCOM, we spent a lot of time out here. An occasional round of golf, renting a boat, eating at the club, and shopping at the PX. I still come out here shopping. I replaced the sad memories with happy memories. That took a long time."

Parking in a lot for a nondescript brick building, the two crime fighters saw the building resembled most of the other architecture on the base. There was nothing exciting. Once inside the glass doors, they asked the individual sitting behind the desk if they could speak with the commander. A few minutes later, a petite Asian female appeared at the door and introduced herself as Lucy Ming. She escorted them back to her office, which was decorated with various certificates and awards, along with a substantial case displaying her collection of military challenge coins.

Cody and Kate apprised her of the circumstances of why they had come to her. The Russian, the Paraguayans, who might be Middle Eastern and from the Tri-border area.

After hearing what they had to say, Lucy said, "Wow, that's a lot of drama. Sunken car, murder, counterfeit, alligators, tigers oh my."

They all chuckled.

"As the commander out here, if one of my special agents brought this case to me, I think I would put in my papers to retire. I have a migraine just thinking about this case."

Kate said, "I'm living it and it feels like I have a marching band parading through my head right now." They all laughed. "Have you had any reports of anyone conducting surveillance on the base or personnel assigned here?"

"When there's a significant event anywhere in the world, we usually have a spike in reporting activity. People get paranoid as they start to see terrorists behind every bush, but that's not a bad thing. I am not aware of anything recently reported that would raise my concern. With CENTCOM and SOCOM based here, we are a target rich environment for bad actors. After 9/11, the threat level was extremely high and continued on that scale after the bin Laden raid. After the withdrawal from Afghanistan, we have not been on the radar as much. The current landscape, of course, is focused on Russia, Ukraine and European Command."

"Where is that command located?"

"Stuttgart, Germany and thankfully a long way from here."

"Are there any personnel who might be a target?"

"Who isn't a target? A jealous ex-spouse. A jealous current spouse. Or look at anyone who has a security clearance on base, or any of our partner countries that are participants, in particular the Israelis. We have a Ukrainian liaison to CENTCOM."

"Ukraine?"

"Just a temporary posting. There were some concerns about Russia recruiting assets from Syria to fight in Ukraine. So far, that has not materialized. I'll reach out to them and advise them to know that there was a Russian in the neighborhood and to exercise situational awareness."

"Well, Commander, thank you for your time. We will let you know if we develop anything else that is focused on the base."

"Please, call me Lucy, and yes likewise, I'll push out a notification of possible targeting of the base to the security forces. If we get any intel back, I'll be sure to give your ring."

"Thank you very much."

Cody and Kate walked out to the car. Squinting into the sun, Kate thought of someone that might help reveal more about Alejandro Duarte.

Chapter Sixty-One

Kate called a friend that she had in one of the local DMV offices. She'd cultivated the friendship after responding to a burglary at her house. Kate had tracked down the offender and recover the property that was taken from her, including a vintage ring from her grandmother. Although Florida's sunshine policy exposed most public records. Periodically, Kate would need to do some additional research, and she could rely upon Tabatha to help speed up the process.

Calling Tabatha, Kate asked her to research the transaction involved in the registration of the Lumina. Tabatha said the Lumina was purchased at an auto auction by Paradise469 LLC and transferred to Alejandro Duarte. She could determine that Duarte had recently got his Florida driver's license after surrendering a Texas driver's license, which had an address in San Antonio.

Kate asked, "Was the Texas driver's license genuine?"

Tabatha said, "It appears to be a genuine driver's license. Duarte got his driver's license the same day that the vehicle was bought by Paradise469 LLC from the auction."

"Tabitha, thank you so much."

"Anything for you, hon. That was easy."

The timeframe coincided with the approximate time of when the counterfeit appeared in the city. The previous Texas driver's license for Duarte listed an address in San Antonio.

After speaking with Tabatha, Kate called one of analysts, Ronnie Pulling, and asked if she could do an inquiry on Duarte and the address in San Antonio. The analyst determined that a person with the same name and date of birth was killed in an automobile accident in San Antonio. He had died three days before Duarte got a new driver's license after claiming he lost his. The address that he provided came back to a homeless rescue mission. A transient facility where no one paid much attention to people coming and going. Unless they were causing problems.

Kate deducted that someone had either got a legitimate birth certificate or counterfeited a birth certificate along with additional identifying documents, knowing that the real Alejandro Duarte was dead. The real Duarte name would not have shown up in the death registry quick enough to prevent this imposter from stealing the identity of man sadly laying in a grave. The new Alejandro Duarte would then show up in Florida, purchasing a relic from the auto auction.

Massaging her temples to ease some of the stress, Kate felt the pounding of a headache. She was at a loss, not knowing who the fake Duarte really was, since the real Duarte was now six feet under the sod. How was this guy connected to Demetri, who had fled the country? She leaned back in the car seat and sighed heavily.

Cody asked, "You look like you could use a drink or some ibuprofen."

"Do I look that bad?"

"Worse."

"Just what a girl wants to hear." He reached into his backpack and she heard the pill bottles rattle. "What do you have in there?"

"I am a rolling pharmacy."

"Good to know. Let's head back to the apartment complex and work north."

Chapter Sixty-Two

Heading north from the apartment, they were trying to find any cameras that captured the Lumina. They were hoping to see if they could determine if the car was actually following someone. The skilled investigators both realized that this was going to be a long shot.

Pulling into a row of merchants, they canvassed each one. None of them had coverage of Bayshore Boulevard. They found an eatery, Chubby's Super Subs & Pizza, which had a camera looking over the shoulder of the cashier towards the front door. The iconic South Tampa eatery had just announced that after four decades, they were hanging up their aprons and closing. The manager was kind enough to allow them to review the footage.

They rewound the recording to the time the call was made to report the suspicious vehicle. It didn't take long to spot the Lumina, but the obstruction of the glass and the distance would not allow them to see the occupants. It appeared the traffic was pretty heavy, and they were following behind a van that they could make out that said Bob's Plumbing.

Opening her phone, Kate did some research and found the website for Bob's plumbing. The motto was "We keep your pipes clean." Kate called the number from the website and a female answered, "Howdy, Bob's Plumbing. This is Bonnie. How may I help you?" Kate could hear a dog barking in the background of the phone call. She asked Bonnie if she could get in touch with Bob and have him call Kate on her phone.

A short time later, Kate's phone rang. Bob returned her call. He told her he had been on a plumbing job off of Bayshore, and was heading north. She asked him if he had seen anything suspicious, or noticed that a Chevrolet Lumina following behind him. He advised he had neither seen anything suspicious nor had he noticed the Lumina trailing behind him. He said that he continued north on Bayshore Boulevard from the retail center Kate described and made a left on Gandy Boulevard. Bob did not notice anyone following him. He said that the focus of his service calls was all over South Tampa. He had just left the installation of an outdoor pool shower at a residence off of lower Bayshore.

The thought crossed her mind that perhaps Bob's plumbing truck could be used as a ruse to provide cover to conduct an attack or break into a house. No one would think twice about seeing a plumbing truck parked outside a home.

She provided a warning, "Bob, if you don't mind, keep an eye out for an older blue Chevy Lumina. Two guys are driving it. Do you know what a Lumina looks like?"

"Sure do. They haven't made them in twenty years. Not many left on the road."

"You are right. I just don't know if they were following you or someone else, so if you see one, please call me at this number."

"I sure will."

Kate was silent for a moment as she considered her conversation with Bob. These people, whether it be Demetri, J Lo or the two Paraguayans, they had been careful. Was the murder of Reza Jaber disposing of a loose end or more? Regardless, why risk hijacking a plumbing truck and the driver and potentially expose the entire operation? Too high of a risk for a group that had been running for weeks without getting compromised.

Realizing that Bob may not have been the focus of Duarte and the Lumina. Just like they had conducted surveillance on Roscoe, most people conducting surveillance would try to stay back behind the vehicles and possibly looked at Bob's plumbing truck as being the perfect screen between the Lumina and whoever their target was. The target could easily have been two or three cars ahead. Or they weren't following anyone. Perhaps they were there to merely make a counterfeit money exchange.

Kate sighed heavily with frustration. "You ever have one of the Chubby's steak bombs?"

"Sure. Guaranteed to want a nap after. Another institution fading into the past."

"Let's head back to the office."

Chapter Sixty-Three

Cody received a phone call from communications. The dispatcher told him she was aware of the homicide and counterfeiting operation. She said that a patrol unit had just been dispatched to a camping store for a possible passing of a counterfeit $50 bill. The dispatcher provided the location and the responding officer's name and phone number. Cody told her how grateful he was and told Kate.

They both wondered what they were purchasing at the camping store, and who was making the purchase. Could it be Duarte and his pal buying the air mattresses and beach chairs? Or was it one of J Lo's associates?

The camping store was close to the West Tampa neighborhood, where most of the activity was occurring. Cody called the responding officer and asked him when they arrived if he could provide an update. The officer said he was approximately five minutes away from being at the scene.

Cody and Kate pulled into the parking lot of the camping store. The patrol SUV was already parked in a spot close to the front door. There were several small RVs in the parking lot, along with several other cars. They walked in and met with the uniformed officer, Mike Victor. The bit of hair left on his scalp was cut short and gray, and he had a big smile on his face.

"Mikey V!" Cody said.

"Smiling Mighty Mike!" Kate said.

They all fist bumped at the smiling Corporal.

Cody said, "You get tired of being the mayor's shadow?"

"Change is good, sometimes. More regular hours back in uniform. Let me introduce you sleuths to the manager. I'll take the fifty and place it in evidence."

Thomas Small greeted the trio. His heavy cologne reached the group before he shook hands. His bright white smile contrasted with his black hair and well-trimmed beard. He told them an alert had been sent out by the bank that there had been an uptick in counterfeit $50 bills being passed in the Tampa area. As he was preparing the deposit, he inspected the lone $50 bill. He told them they received almost no cash and almost all purchases were made via credit card.

Cody asked, "Mr. Small, do you know who handled the sales transaction, and do you have any video?"

Mr. Small answered, "That won't be a problem. But you will have to get a subpoena."

Kate leaned in closer and said softly, "I understand you have bosses to report to, and I also understand you do not want to get into any trouble. Obviously, you have a very established client base and you're not looking to get anyone in trouble. This investigation is linked directly to a homicide investigation. If you would rather, we can have all of your employees, including yourself, subpoenaed to appear in front of the grand jury. You may not be aware, but the Florida's grand jury normally only hear evidence in murder cases. Because this is involving counterfeit currency, one of our associates can do the same with the federal grand jury. Now I realize this would be a major inconvenience to your business and to your customers. I am sure you would like to avoid that hindrance to your business continuity. You and your business are victims of a fraud by whoever used this counterfeit $50 bill. I would also think your client base would not appreciate that you stood in the way of a cooperative request concerning a murder investigation."

Small looked like a school child being called to the front of the class and disciplined by the teacher. He massaged his beard. The smile was gone. "Well, since you put it that way, I didn't realize the magnitude and I appreciate you providing me with insight. By all means, let me get that information for you and just to show you I'm not a bad guy, let me give you one of our VIP swag bags we give to our loyal customers."

Kate peeked into the bag like a Halloween trick or treater and saw some logo pens, memo pad, lint cloth and hand sanitizer. She said, "Mr. Small, we really appreciate the offer, but a gift is unnecessary. We don't want anyone getting the wrong idea."

"Oh my, I didn't even think of that. I am so sorry. Let me go find the records that you are requesting." His cologne lingered like a fog.

As he shuffled off into the office, the three police officers looked at each other and simultaneously rolled their eyes. They had all faced similar circumstances and knew that Mr. Small was coming down on the side of caution. Everyone these days was afraid of being sued. A little common sense injected into the argument typically cleared up the reluctance and miscommunication.

A few moments later, Mr. Small returned and said, "It came out of the cash drawer for Freddie Suarez." He pointed to a man with graying hair in his late fifties stocking the shelves with cans of emergency tire inflator's.

"Thank you, Mr. Small. We appreciate your help." Said Kate.

After making the initial introductions and asking Suarez if he remembered the cash transaction, he said, "Oh, sure. It was two customers that bought some hexamine tablets."

Kate asked, "Hexamine?"

"Yes, it's used in camping stoves for fuel."

"And you're sure that's what they bought?"

"Yes. I used to be in the car business. So, you get to read people. They just didn't seem like the outdoorsy camper types. I asked them where they were going, and they said they were going to meet up with some friends in Georgia. They said that they were asked to pick up some fuel tablets for the friends. Maybe they were or maybe they weren't."

Kate asked, "How do you mean they didn't seem outdoors people?"

"They were not interested in any other camping or hiking supplies. I asked them where they were going in Georgia and they said they were going to Tacoma. I asked if they meant Toccoa, Georgia and if they were going to climb the mountain? They had that lost look and said yes."

Cody said, "Currahee Mountain?"

Kate chimed in and said, "Hi ho silver. Three miles up and three miles down."

They all nodded at the reference from the Band of Brothers training camp. Suarez said, "When I asked them about Currahee, they nodded and said yes. But it was like being at a party and someone talks about a new movie that you haven't seen, but you kind of nod and B.S. your way through. That's what these guys did. You could tell they didn't want to chat, so I took them to the register."

Kate asked, "You don't think they were going to Georgia?"

"Nope."

"Can you describe them?"

"The one who did most of the talking was older, fit, thirties maybe. The other one was leaner and in his twenties. They both had an accent. They said they were from Paraguay. I asked how long had they been here, but I could tell they weren't wanting to talk."

Cody asked, "Could they have been Middle Eastern?"

"I never gave it any thought. To be honest, they both seemed a little dodgy. Certainly, with the fake bill, proves my suspicion. Nothing you could tell me about them would seem surprising."

"Mr. Suarez, thank you for your time."

They exited the store and said goodbye to Corporal Victor. Cody had a revelation to share with Kate.

Chapter Sixty-Four

Once Kate and Cody returned to their car in the camping store parking lot, Cody turned towards Kate in front of the Camry and said, "I hope I'm wrong, but I've got a bad feeling about this."

"What are you talking about?"

"Things are starting to not add up to a good outcome. Hexamine, which is found in those camping stove fuel tablets, is a precursor to RDX."

"RDX as in the explosive RDX?"

"Yes. Although in Afghanistan we didn't see it nearly as much as what they saw in Iraq, but convoys were being seriously targeted by IED's. They became much more deadly when used as explosively formed penetrator's known as EFP's. They were built by Iranian knowledge and imported by demolition trainers loaned out by the IRGC."

"So, how does the EFP differ from the typical roadside bomb?"

"EFP's are a more focused detonation. Kind of like a bullet coming out of the barrel of a gun. Except this time, it's about the size of the mortar tube firing as a shaped charge made of copper, which forms into a projectile. It will slice through just about anything, like a hot knife through a frozen popsicle."

"So how does RDX fit into this and how do they make RDX from the hexamine?"

"The RDX would be the explosive charge behind a copperplate like the gunpowder behind the bullet in the shell casing. Hexamine gets mixed with the nitric acid. It's challenging to make, but remember at the stash house they left behind an icemaker? That's necessary for temperature control during the mixing of the chemicals."

"Remember, J Lo said, he smelled chemicals and thought it was ink. Perhaps they were mixing chemicals, because we know they printed the money at Mr. Inky."

Kate combed her fingers through her hair and sighed heavily. "So, we have an Iranian national who was counterfeiting U.S. currency that is murdered. We know that probably the two Paraguayans are involved not only in the counterfeiting but probably in the Iranian's murder. We also know that Paraguay falls in the Tri-Border area of South America where there are a lot of Iranian and Hezbollah influence. Now we know one purchase made by the Paraguayans was used to purchase a potential precursor to RDX. We also know that the Paraguayans were conducting what we believe could be preoperational surveillance near the MacDill Air Force Base, home to Central Command and Special Operations Command. Perhaps we have Demetri the Russian operating as a puppet master, making introductions for these Paraguayans. Then the Russian suddenly jumped on a flight and headed back to mother Russia. None of this adds up to a simple homicide investigation. I've have said that the motive for murder almost always tracks back to love, money or revenge. I'm not sure this time. This is about as bad as you can imagine."

Cody looked down as he kicked a pebble with his foot and, shaking his head, he looked back up at Kate's eyes and said, "I don't like to be an alarmist, but this is scary."

"Okay, before we ring the bell of hysteria, let's get a K-9 to go through the stash house and see if he picks up any scent. We can also start checking on suppliers of nitric acid. If I'm not mistaken, I think they use the acid in the jewelry business."

"How would you know that?"

"An old boyfriend from college. We also knew each other in high school, but his family was in the business. I was around their business operations frequently enough to know they used nitric acid to extract gold from metals."

"Was this like a high school sweetheart turning into a college sweetheart?"

"I'm not going there. The city is on the precipice of being blown to bits and you want to rip the curtain open to my previous love life?"

Cody grinned and put his hands up in a surrendering gesture and said, "You are the boss."

Chapter Sixty-Five

Returning to the stash house, Kate and Cody parked at the curb. Kate had once again called the owner, George Gentry, and asked him to meet them at the stash house. She also called for crime scene to meet them there and then asked dispatch to put her in contact with a patrol sergeant for that area.

When Sergeant Paul Smalley called, Kate answered, "Hi Sarge, I'm out here with Cody Danko on a stash house on Pine Street. We suspect that there may be some residual residue from explosives. Do you have any bomb dogs available? It's a small house and won't take but ten to fifteen minutes, tops."

"Good God. Sure. I can send you K-9 14, Troy Neal. He is just finishing up checking a school for a bomb threat. He has to be at a function to search for an event with the Governor later today. Will that work, Kate?"

"Yes. Thank you, Paul."

Within thirty minutes, all the parties were assembled once again in front of the stash house. Kate explained to Mr. Gentry that they had evidence that the renters of the property may have been involved with mixing dangerous chemicals.

He said, "Dangerous chemicals? Like meth or something?"

"Probably not. More like nitrates."

"English please."

"Explosives residue."

"Like for a bomb?"

"We don't know. They may have only had some chemicals. Like fireworks."

"Oh great! It's bad enough that I rented to a couple of lowlife criminals. Now you're telling me they may be terrorists as well? This day has gone straight down the shitter."

"We don't know. Since we left after the execution of the search warrant, we would need your permission to enter."

"Fine. I have a migraine now. Here are the keys. Please don't destroy the house."

"You'll not even know that we were here."

Kate turned to Dee Hanna of the crime scene unit that, despite processing the scene earlier, she now wanted them to take swabs in the kitchen for possible explosive residue and forward them to the FDLE laboratory.

Dee said, "Small kitchen, small job. I'll check the counters and faucet handles. Anywhere else?"

"That should do it. Maybe the door handle as well."

"Easy. They should have the results pretty quick."

"Thank you. If you don't mind, K-9 is on the way. Let them get a clean vapor scent."

"No problem. I'll check my social media feed while we wait."

They turned towards the barking excitement of bomb sniffing K-9 partner Repo. The smiling Troy Neal stepped out of the SUV, leaving Repo behind. Dressed in his black tactical BDU's and ball cap, he held out his arms and said, "Paul Smalley told me something about a bomb factory. Should I put my fingers in my ears and you call me after it blows?"

"I applaud your humor. You and Repo have an audience with the Governor today? I thought you and Repo would have matching tuxedos?"

"I'm in black and this is as formal as I get. We like to leave before the politicians arrive. Helping FDLE on a sweep of an event space this afternoon before he arrives."

"I like to stay clear of politicians as well."

"Has the house been sealed?"

"It was, but we did a search on it. It's been sealed since. Problem?"

"No. The longer it's sealed, the better the containment of vapors for Repo. Like a spaghetti dinner when you walk in to a closed house as opposed to a house with doors and windows open."

"So, Repo is going to sniff for a spaghetti dinner? I hope he doesn't get sauce on his nose."

"Ha! He will smell the tomato, basil, garlic, olive oil, wine and each ingredient. His nose has an encyclopedia of odors."

Neal told them that since time had elapsed once again with the house sealed that whatever vapors present would once again be easily recognized by the dog, who'd been specifically trained to pick up the scent of explosives. Even if those explosives were no longer present.

"Okay, let me get him." Troy walked back to the SUV and put the leash on his partner. The dark colored Belgian Malinois bounded with the enthusiasm of a teenager on their birthday. Troy led Repo to the front door, whose tail was wagging with joy. Troy reached up with his free hand and turned the doorknob while holding the leash with his other hand. He pulled the door open and commanded Repo to go to work. The K-9 took a step inside the door and sat.

Neal turned to Kate and Cody. "Winner, winner, chicken dinner. There is definitely explosives residue inside. I can't tell you what type. I can only tell that one odor that he has been trained on hit his alert signal." Neal reached down and began praising his partner and gave him his reward toy.

Neal said, "You can count this as a positive response for a K-9 trained in explosives detection for your report and that he has picked up the scent of explosive residue in and around this residence. Strong enough that he actually alerted before we ever entered the front door. There is no doubt in my mind that sometime recently, there were, in fact, explosives inside this residence."

Kate said, "Well, that may not be good news, but it confirms our very strong suspicions. Thanks for coming out, Troy. I just bought a puppy. Could I hire you as a trainer?"

Troy Neal laughed and said, "I think I'm past the puppy stage. Good luck with that Kate."

"You're a lot of help. Stay safe and say hello to the Governor."

Troy Neal waved a goodbye, and he nudged Repo back to the Explorer. Kate extended her hand to Dee Hanna, showed she was free to enter the house and swab for the residue. Kate was confident about Repo's nose, but continuing forward, she would need scientific corroboration for the court.

Walking over to George Gentry, the owner, she handed back the keys. He asked, "What's the verdict?"

"We collected samples and will send them off to the lab."

"What about the dog? He hit on something?"

"The lab will prove conclusively."

"Sweet mother of God."

"I ask you to please keep this to ourselves. We don't want your former tenants going into hiding, or worse."

"Worse?"

"Calm down. I don't want to speculate. We really need your cooperation. Some agencies like the IRS could land up following the money trail of these two guys. If they follow the cash rent payment to you, I can vouch for your cooperation if you understand what I am saying?"

"The IRS? Good grief! All I did was rent a vacant home."

"I'm just saying if the IRS gets to tracking the scent, they could land up nosing around your accounts. Everyone gets a panic attack with the IRS, myself included, so I could let them know the trail ends here because you were cooperative and kept quiet about the investigation."

"My lips are sealed like Velcro."

"Thank you, Mr. George."

Cody arched his eyebrows, looked at Kate, and asked, "What is the game plan now?"

"Well, this just became very sticky. We went to the FBI, and they told us there's nothing here. Move along. We spoke to OSI at the base and they said they were not aware of any threats or potential targeting. The Secret Service was short staffed guarding kings and queens in New York. But I would say that you and I had just stepped into a huge steaming pile of horse manure with flies buzzing all around. I think probably the best course of action is to call Benny and ask him to have a joint meeting with all the players that could have an interest. I would say that were probably looking at all the alphabet agencies. FBI, OSI, USSS, ATF, HSI. The problem I foresee is they will try to wrestle this case away from us in the interest of national security. Once we lay it all out in front of them, it will be like throwing out a bowl of dog food amongst the litter of puppies. They will all be pushing and shoving and jockeying for position. In some ways, if it wasn't for the seriousness of the investigation, it would actually be entertaining to sit in the cheap seats, passing the popcorn and Junior Mints as we wait for the dust to settle and see who the victor is."

"You know that once we make the grand reveal, they will go nuclear."

"Most definitely. They only have themselves to blame. We tried to share the information with them. I will say, OSI was interested and willing to take some preemptive measures by notifying some folks to be more vigilant."

"What about The Caveman?"

"He will have to attend. And he will lose his shit. He won't say anything until after the meeting to present a united front, but watch him during the meeting. He will look like he just ruptured a hemorrhoid."

Frank parked at the curb and with a little spring in his step, walked towards the two detectives. "I heard the radio call for K-9 14 to this address. I knew you two were up to something. A colossal shit storm?"

"Yes."

Kate was distracted by a familiar sight down the street as she looked past her fellow detectives. "You both stay here. I'll be back in a minute."

Cody and Frank both turned to see what caught Kate's attention.

Chapter Sixty-Six

Walking briskly down the street, Kate was almost at a slight jog to catch up with the focus of her attention. She caught up and slowed to a walk as she approached the same homeless man, she had seen earlier pushing a shopping cart with the small dog. He was still wearing the same black frayed and faded hoodie, camo shorts, and a knit hat. The disheveled man's hat barely contained his mop of hair and a furry beard lined his face.

"Excuse me, sir?"

He stopped the cart filled with blankets, tarps, and a sleeping bag. Perched in the child seat was a terrier like white dog sitting like the king of the castle. The man and the dog simultaneously looked at Kate. The pungent smell of body odor slapped her nose.

"What is the name of your dog?"

"Sarge."

"Well. Hello Sarge, my name is Kate." She held out her hand for the dog to sniff. Sarge's tongue licked her hand. "He must smell my dog."

"Sarge likes you."

"He is a cutie. How old?"

"I don't know. I adopted him and he adopted me."

"Sarge? Are you a veteran?"

"Yes."

"My husband was in the Army. What branch were you in?"

"I was Army. 10th Mountain, 1st Battalion, 87th Infantry Regiment."

"The 10th? Ft. Drum, New York?"

"Yep. You a cop?"

"Why do you say that?" As she stroked Sarge on his head.

"I can tell. Besides, I saw you at that house kicking the door."

"Guilty. You travel this area much?"

"Yep. The streets are my home. Until I can get General Motors interested in my water combustion engine. The car is powered by electricity after the conversion of water into a gaseous mixture of hydrogen and oxygen. No more gas. All green. Big petroleum is fighting me and the Chinese. My idea hurts the Chinese in providing batteries for EV's. The green lobby is against me too because of all the subsidies they receive. Seventy percent of the earth's surface is water. You could fill the gas tank at the kitchen sink for free. The industrial complex won't allow it."

As he stroked his beard, she could see the spark in his eye and the enthusiasm in his voice.

She said, "That has to be frustrating. Have you taken your idea to the VA? Perhaps they can help you?"

"Oh sure. The VA only wants to throw a net over me and put me inside, along with a bucketful of pills. Too many rules. Worse than when I was in the Army. They won't allow Sarge. We need each other."

"Man's best friend. You support each other. I wanted to ask…"

"Pete. Peter Comiskey, sergeant." He saluted Kate.

"Yes, Pete. Did you ever see any activity at that house that we were at?"

"You mean with the two Arabs and the Russian?"

"Yes. Why do you say, Arabs?"

"I heard them speaking to each other. It wasn't Dari or Pashto. Maybe Farsi, but I wouldn't swear to it."

She was stunned. "How could you tell?"

"I picked up enough while I was in that hellhole. Before they kicked me out of the Army and into a straightjacket."

"Could they have been Hispanic? From Paraguay?"

He shrugged. "Don't know. I made them for Arabs."

"What about the Russian?"

"I only heard his accent. He looked Russian. Could have been from any of those countries. Ukraine, or any of the former satellites."

"Any other visitors?"

"Cubans. Locals."

"Did you see anything suspicious?"

"Nope. Just coming and going. I mind my own business and they left me alone."

"Pete, thank you for your help. Thank you for your service as well." She handed a twenty to Pete. "Treat yourself and Sarge to an enjoyable meal."

"Thank you."

She watched Pete and Sarge move down the road. She thought about how fit and virile Pete must have been as a young soldier in Afghanistan. Fighting the Taliban for harboring terrorists and a noble warrior. Somewhere, his brain unraveled. Was it the result of combat or, like many in that age range, mental illness began to manifest. Now he slept under the same stars he looked up at from the mountains of Afghanistan. He now felt abandoned by the system, like so many other veterans that are merely a shell of the person they once were. Sad.

She walked back toward her partners, both veterans, to provide a sizable nugget of information.

Chapter Sixty-Seven

The three detectives huddled together to discuss the strategy going forward and what the next step would be. Kate shared the information that Sergeant Pete shared. This was now the second reporting of the two counterfeit salespeople as being Middle Eastern. The Air Force member that reported them in the car, whose first impression was they were Middle Eastern and now Pete heard them speaking a Middle eastern dialect. Despite being homeless and suffering from a mental illness, she believed his observations. This again was now providing further evidence of perhaps Iranian involvement from the Tri-Border region.

Cody said to Kate and Frank, "I have a hunch."

Kate said, "Like a hunger pain hunch?"

"Ah no. I am going to forward a list of pipe companies in the Tampa area. I'm looking to see if anyone purchased any steel piping within the last week. Preferably, the steel piping we are searching for is type 40 piping. If we don't get any joy from the pipe company's then maybe we can try with the junkyards that might have some scrap piping that they could sell. But most junkyards are selling old appliances and junk cars."

Frank said, "Where are you going with this Boy Scout?"

"If my hunch is correct, this whole Iranian connection has me thinking that they might construct an EFP."

"An EFP?"

"Yeah, so I was explaining to Kate earlier, an EFP or explosively formed penetrator is constructed like a mortar shell. In the back of the pipe, the explosives, in this case, would be RDX placed in the pipe's base, and then they put a copperplate inside the mortar shell at the front opening. When the explosives detonate, the copper plate comes out at an extremely high velocity and can even penetrate armored vehicles like we saw with Humvees in Afghanistan and Iraq. The Taliban was using them after being schooled in the manufacturing by Iranian Quds Force."

Frank said, "Okey-dokey, let's get back to the office and start the telethon."

Kate entered Benny's office and plopped in the seat across from his desk. Benny leaned forward and looked over the folders piled on his desk, and adjusted his glasses.

"Just so you know, you look haggard. Or am I not allowed to say stuff like that anymore?"

"Thanks for the compliment. I could say the same."

"I just wanted to coast across the finish line into retirement. Now, I need to look over all these files to see what you cops are up to. The lieutenant is nipping at my ankle like a neurotic dog, and then your case is a full-on train derailment."

"The train derailment is going to be worse."

"Like clusterfuck worse?"

"Worse."

"Let me hand you my gun and just shoot me. Son of a bitch. Okay, bring it on."

"You might want to start off with a clean page on your notepad."

After providing the up-to-date details of the case, she watched the grimace on Benny's face and shaking his head. She knew he was considering how best to package this and present it to The Caveman.

He said, "Before I go to the corner office with this, I have to know if the rumors are true?"

"Rumors?"

"About you and Cody manscaping The Caveman?"

With a sly smile. "I don't know what you are talking about."

"That just made my day. Like an umbrella on a rainy day."

Back at their desks in the homicide office, Cody and Frank began phoning through the list of pipe companies. Kate began researching the sources of nitric acid.

They found quickly that most of the pipe company's either were not open to the public or sold only to established construction companies. Eventually, Cody hit pay dirt with the Ybor Metals and Pipe Company.

He turned to the others and said, "Sadly, we have a winner. The pipe company on the outskirts of Ybor City said that they are open to the public and made a sale to two Hispanic males. Both of them match the description from the camping store and from J Lo. The company said they sold the 12" x 24" steel pipe with a capped base. They also bought a sheet of copper. According to the salesperson, they said they were buying it for an interior decorator who was working on a rehab of an industrial loft site conversion into residential units. They did not know what the purpose of the purchase was for, but they were provided a shopping list by the interior decorator. The salesperson said the sale was unusual but became stranger when they were notified by the bank that their deposit contained counterfeit $50 bills."

Kate said, "So essentially they would make what would be commonly used for shooting fireworks into the sky, but instead of having fireworks, they're going to shoot this copperplate out."

"Exactly." Cody answered.

"I remember Jake attended a school on international terrorism at the base. He was telling me some stories, and I remember one case was an assassination of a German finance or banking guy who was assassinated by the Red Army Faction. They detonated a shaped charge into his armored Mercedes and killed him."

"An EFP works like a shaped charge, except it's much more lethal."

"This is Friday the 13th, scary bad news."

"Yes, one part of me is thrilled to make the connections, but mostly I am terrified at what this means."

Frank said, "Wait until the cop world gets a hold of this. They will all be all participants at thirty-five thousand feet and in a sheer panic."

Kate said, "Nitric acid is too commonly found. Jewelry supplies, fertilizer, etching electronics and chemical companies. So, that's a dead end."

Chapter Sixty-Eight

Kate walked up to the whiteboard and erased some earlier scribblings. She placed the eraser back in the tray and picked up the black marker and wrote across the top EFP. She turned to Duffy and Cody and said, "Let's do some brainstorming. Who would they be targeting in Tampa?"

Duffy said, "It could be any politician, but we know not one of high importance is coming to the area since the Secret Service is all still in New York. My money would be on someone at MacDill."

"I know we never like to make assumptions, but with what we know, let's just assume that perhaps it is focused on MacDill. Who then would be the target? Considering that these Paraguayans are from the so-called Tri-Border area, which is a hotbed for Lebanese and Hezbollah and with a gumbo mixture throwing in a Russian and an Iranian, who do we come up with as the likely target?"

The three detectives all looked at each other and said simultaneously, "Israel."

Kate said, "The Iranians have openly called for the extermination of Israel, as have their main terrorist outreach through Hezbollah, which is based in Lebanon. We know the Tri-Border area has a sizeable population of Lebanese. Recent news reporting suggests that the Russians are working with the Iranians on drone technology against Ukraine. So, it's not a stretch to say that the Russians are providing some introductory handshakes and logistics support in a community that the Iranians did not have a previous presence."

Cody said, "All this because of Johnny Nylon and the Cadillac."

Frank said, "I'll track down someone over at Customs and Border Protection to see if they have anything in the sights of their binoculars.

Kate walked into Benny's office. She came to realize that the just-moved-in-look and disarray was probably going to be a permanent motif. Benny was leaning back in his chair and feet on a free spot of his desk. She noticed the sole of one loafer had a worn spot. He adjusted his glasses as he lowered a report he was reading and motioned for her to come in. He sat up and put the report down on his desk of papers.

"More?"

"Yes. We identified a company in Ybor that sold them a cast-iron pipe to be used for an..."

"EFP? Yes, I was listening."

"Exactly, and our money is on targeting the Israelis."

"Well, that's no great reveal. They hate each other. Keep it up Carmen Sandiego."

"Count on it."

Chapter Sixty-Nine

Frank thumbed through his contacts looking for a local contact with CBP. He found Randy Sutton's name that he had met at various networking events.

"Randy, it's a good day to be in Tampa as opposed to being at the border."

"Any day not at the border is a good day and it's not as hot as my last posting in Vegas. So, how can I help you?"

"We are picking up some bad juju locally about some characters that came out of the Tri-Border area of South America. Are you picking up anything here in Tampa?"

"Nothing locally. We have a vibrant Lebanese community around the University and up in Temple Terrace. They keep a low profile since the two professors were arrested on terrorism charges in 2003. The professors were eventually acquitted and deported. Another of the group had fled earlier and became the head of the Palestinian Islamic Jihad. The community has been law-abiding since and has raised no concerns. Hell, that was twenty years ago."

"Before my time. But otherwise, all quiet on the Gulf Front?"

"Yep. Since you mentioned the Tri-Border, there was an intel bulletin that came a while ago that they fished someone out of the Rio Grande that had a waterproof backpack. Inside the backpack were U. S. currency printing plates and a Zoaf PC-9 pistol."

"A Zoaf?"

"Yeah, apparently, that is an Iranian rip-off of the Sig Sauer 226 model. His passport was from Paraguay in the name of Moises Benitez."

"Well, stick by your phone. I think the JTTF will sound the bugle to assemble the troops."

"I can hardly wait."

Kate's phone rang, and the number was from the FDLE.

"Hi Kate, it's Christina Bentham from the crime lab."

"My savior on identifying the soil samples from a homicide scene to a pair of shoes. That was the clincher in helping me with arresting suspect in murder of the family. Are you calling with good news?"

"Probably not. Dee Hanna said these swabs from a house on Pine Street were a rush."

"Yep."

"I won't bore you with all the tests involving chromatography or spectrometry. That will be in the report. All you need to know is the swabs had positive traces for RDX."

"So, I have a positive result for a boom?"

"Don't get too close."

"Holy smokes. Thank again, Christina."

Kate turned to Cody and gave him the news from the crime lab. Frank shared his discerning news from CBP concerning the Iranian pistol recovered from the drowned border crosser, who also had counterfeit printing plates. This confirmed the Iranian involvement along with the bullet casing.

Frank said he would send out an email through the router for the Regional Domestic Security Task Force along with speaking with the RDSTF boss at FDLE, Jim Born. Frank wanted to make sure that all the agencies were aware of suspects. He feared an officer who pulled over the Lumina for a traffic violation and was not aware they were dealing with explosives and armed suspects, would end badly. He also told Born that there would be a meeting the next morning and it would be an all-hands-on deck. Born said he would notify the director of the Tampa regional office.

Cody advised he would call one of his former trooper buddies that now worked at the Bureau of Alcohol, Tobacco and Firearms. He and Gray LeMaster had both attended trooper school together. LeMaster jumped from nailing speeders to catching arsonists with ATF.

"Hi Gray, hear any booms lately?"

"I like to stay left of boom. I'm more focused on burning for bucks. Never an end to the supply of arson cases. Especially with failing business from the pandemic. Insurance helps save an owner whose business is on life support. What's going on? I haven't heard from you since our class reunion."

"I wish it were an invitation, but I have some scary news."

Cody provided the details to LeMaster and told him there would be a meeting the next morning at Tampa P.D. for all the bosses to get on the same sheet of music. All the major players in the law enforcement community had been notified. The detectives knew it would be a restless night and a full court press the next day as the bugle was sounded for the charge of the calvary.

Chapter Seventy

The next morning, sitting around the large wood conference table, Kate was disappointed in her selection of seats with her back against the windows overlooking the Tampa skyline. She had first intended to occupy the seat directly across the table, but Benny Thompson tugged on her arm and gave her the head bob to sit next to him. Cody had the much better view and The Caveman and his baldhead set at the head of the table.

Although the conference table was left over from the previous building's occupant, it was enormous enough that it easily accommodated twenty-five people. All the movers and shakers from the local alphabet law enforcement community were present. Kate surveyed the audience. Some familiar faces. Most displaying curiosity. Except for one. Griffin St. Clair from the FBI. His face looked clenched and tight as molded plastic. He was not happy.

The Caveman stood and sounded like a politician at a campaign stop. "Good morning. For those that don't know me, I am Lieutenant Jack Willard of Major Crimes. I want to welcome all of you here today. The presence of all of you at this table is a clear indication of the synchrony of our law enforcement partners within the Tampa Bay community. We have asked you to assemble here today in the spirit of cooperation as our homicide squad shares with you some quick developing incidents surrounding a case that started as a homicide investigation. However, we now believe that this deserves the attention of all of you, our partner agencies. Without further ado, I'd like to turn it over to Sergeant Benny Thompson of the homicide squad."

He sat down and Kate noticed a flash of contempt from The Caveman directed towards Benny. She admired the oratory skills of the lieutenant, his one redeeming quality.

Benny stood up and adjusted his glasses as he looked down the length of the table. Kate was surprised that Benny had not even taken the time to tighten his tie up around his neck. He looked around, put his fingers on the table and said, "I don't want to be a speed bump in this presentation because I would rather that you hear it directly from the detectives that have been working this case. They have uncovered this unsettling information."

He nodded at Kate. It was her queue. Despite having a runner's pulse rate, she could feel her heart beating like a kettledrum in the orchestra. Her throat tightened and her mouth became instantly dry. She thought quickly about trying to do some tactical breathing, but knew there was no time. Taking a deep breath, she held it for just a moment and exhaled, calming her public speaking nerves.

She started off by telling everyone that she would run through the case and to hold all questions until she had completed the narrative. As she went through the various aspects of the case, she watched various participants become agitated and saw flashes of annoyance. Kate knew each one would have to address their superiors why they were not included and did not know about this information earlier. When she concluded her narrative, she asked for questions.

The first question came from the FBI supervisor, Griffin St. Clair. He asked, "As Jack Willard so clearly laid out during his introduction, the law enforcement community in Tampa enjoys a very close working relationship with each other. We have invested a great deal of time and energy in fostering that relationship. Frankly, I am stunned that we are just now hearing about this case and we are already in the eighth inning of this ballgame."

Kate cleared her throat and started to respond when, to her relief, Benny bolted to his feet and leaned on the table, looking at the FBI supervisor.

"I believe at the very early stages of this investigation, the detectives reached out to you with concerns about possible Tri-Border activity, and you immediately discounted it as a bunch of political hogwash, and said there was no substance to that reporting. Something along the lines of 'saber rattling for decades and nothing but a paper tiger for grant writers and lobbyists.' So, let's not come in here and try to erase the whiteboard with the facts that are already up there. You had no interest in this case until, as you said, it is now in the eighth inning and now you're worrying about what your supervisors and the folks in the Hoover building are going to say. So, we have that notification documented. The Secret Service was also notified very early in this investigation, but they were short staffed, so we took the ball and ran with it. But thankfully, my detectives pushed the gas pedal to the floor and now uncovered this potential terrorist attack. The Air Force showed interest and pushed out information to the base to be aware. So, you can save your indignation for the folks in Washington, but that won't wash here. I think everyone needs to swallow some nice pills and let's put our running shoes on to work together for the common good to stop this game before it hits the ninth-inning."

The FBI supervisor's jaw clenched, and he too took a deep breath before he responded. "Sergeant, you're right that our focus right now is to bring this case to a rapid conclusion. We can address all the oversights after the case is resolved. I will assemble all the members of the Joint Terrorism Task Force at our office and we can have a full briefing over there and discuss our strategy from now on." He closed his clipboard, stood up and adjusted his tie, which needed no change, and said, "Expect a phone call shortly concerning what time to be at our office."

Kate understood the pin had been pulled on the hand grenade and many people would catch fragments when it exploded. She knew from experience that most times the upper echelon of all agencies will throw the foot soldiers under the tracks of the tanks, and they would fall prey to becoming roadkill. In a very public setting, she witnessed her new sergeant, not only standing up and supporting her but also standing out in front of the tank like a single protester. It was quite apparent he had little regard for his career advancement.

As the meeting broke up, Benny leaned over towards Kate and whispered to her, "I want the date and time that you notified ass wipe because I've seen people of his ilk before. He is squirming as if his tighty-whities are crushing his balls because he knows what's coming down the pike, and he wants to throw shade on us. That guy has never been in a street fight with me. He won't know what hit him. Get that information and meet me in my office."

She nodded with a smile as she watched Benny lumber off and The Caveman approach her.

"Kate, could I have a moment, please?"

"Yes, sir."

"I'm afraid this case has created a circus environment and, unfortunately, our federal partners are deeply offended. I told Benny to give this case to the Feds and let them get to the bottom of it and figure this Rubik's Cube out."

"Sir."

He interrupted her. "We don't know how much longer Benny will be assigned to us. He is eligible for retirement, so he could go, especially if he has an attractive offer or he just tires of draping a tie around his neck. You know, for someone as bright and articulate as you are, I watched with great admiration at your delivery. It's quite clear that you're going places. There is no glass ceiling for talented people like you."

"Thank you, sir."

"I would be very careful which racehorse you want to align yourself with. Some of us are going to be here all the way to the finish line. I would appreciate if you would keep me in the loop on what's going on and try to remove your sergeant as a filter. Because, as you've seen, people can get very upset when pertinent facts are filtered out or water down. If there is any fallout from this case, I can provide cover for you, whereas I don't believe Benny has the bandwidth or the connections to look out for you."

"Jack, you don't mind me calling you Jack, do you?"

"No, Kate."

"Well Jack, I don't know whether you're aware of it or not, but I am an animal lover. I have a couple of horses and an exuberant puppy. You know what I love about these animals?"

"No."

"Their loyalty to me. They show me unconditional love, and they don't love me one day and not the next. They love me every waking minute of the day. And if we're being candid, you have never been one to cover for anyone but your own ass. So, thank you kindly for the offer. Even if Benny is perhaps an old nag and won't get me to the finish line, the least that he did today was show me unconditional love and support and he had my back. Nice chatting with you, Jack."

"Be careful Detective."

"Lieutenant. I love my job. I love my family more and I know what's more important in life. When I reach retirement, someone will take my place. I will be a distant memory to this department. But my family will be there to greet me at that finish line. And that's the horse I know will complete the race. Have a nice evening, Lieutenant."

Cody was waiting at the elevator landing and asked, "I saw your RBF on full display."

"My Resting Bitch Face? Did I roll my eyes as well?"

"Maybe a little."

"I would be a terrible poker player. My face lights up like a big screen TV."

"Yes. It does. What was that about?"

"He wanted me to become his snitch and bitch."

"Really?"

"He can go fuck himself. Excuse my language."

"So much for de-escalation. Good for you."

"I was walking a tightrope with him. Between my friendship with Duffy and our manscaping fragging of him."

"That was my doing."

"Yes, but I was a willing co-conspirator. Now I have really pissed him off. I am in his forever doghouse. Perhaps actually buried under it. When Benny cashes in his chips, I may as well move my tent, because life will become miserable for me."

"You get results. He respects that because it makes him look good."

"Not in this case. I just told him the emperor is not wearing clothes."
"You'll look good wearing the blue polyester uniform again."
"Thanks and no more call outs and phone calls disturbing family time."

They returned to the homicide office and entered the sergeant's office. Benny already had an email typed up addressed to Griffin St. Clair and the Special Agent in Charge of the FBI. It read, *"As per our conversation this date pertaining to the briefing conducted at the Tampa Police Department, I wanted to remind you of your conversation via telephone with Detectives Duffy and Alexander in which Detective Alexander advised you of her concerns and suspicions about the connection to the Tri-Border area and this homicide case.*

According to her report of that conversation, you responded that for decades, the Tri-border area has a strong presence of Hezbollah influence in the region. But over all of that time, they have NEVER shown an interest in targeting the U.S. You expressed concerns about the increase of Southern border crossings. You diminished concerns about the TBA as being driven by a bunch of think tanks and foreign policy lobbyists chasing grants and funding, as well as Pro-Israel groups that are always "clanging the alarm" that Iran and Hezbollah are staging for an imminent attack. According to you, the FBI has seen no indication or evidence to support any of these theories.

Detective Alexander specifically confirmed with you that "in your estimation, you believe that what we have here is just a straight up criminal enterprise involving counterfeit currency and has nothing to do with terrorism or anything like that?" You responded that to this point in time, the FBI has seen no indication of terrorism in the homeland or specifically in the Tampa District. After decades of banging the war drums, and no activity to support it, people eventually get tone deaf to the sound of the drum. But if you find that there's more going on, feel free to reach out to us and Frank can just loop me back in. Thanks for the call.

As the trajectory rapidly developed in this case, and once our detectives knew the homicide of an Iranian was connected to a counterfeiting ring that connected to individuals from the TBA and possibly acquiring pre-cursers to an explosive device, we immediately contacted your office. We look forward to bringing this case to a successful conclusion with your help and cooperation."

Benny said, "I know how these folk's work. The knives will come out. If the case ends well, the spotlight is all on them. They have a huge PR machine in DC. If their nuts are in a squeeze, you can guarantee they will launch a full-on assault against us. Now, this might affect you if you ever plan to apply for a job at the FBI."

"Nope. That train left the station a long time ago. Thank you for standing up for us."

He waved dismissively in the air and said, "That was more fun than watching a mongoose attack a King Cobra. Oh, I saw The Caveman bending your ear. Probably playing nice with you to prepare to throw me in a pre-dug grave."

"Sort of, yes."

"Well, that tombstone has not been inscribed yet. He better be careful or he may be pushed into that hole. You two get out there and nail these sons of a bitches. If this goes sideways, we are all going to the morgue for former investigators. The microscope will be shoved so far up our ass, we will all be choking on our own vomit. Get the hell out of here and find them!"

Frank called Kate from the FBI office and told her he had just heard that the JTTF had received an alert from the CIA. The alert was for general information and no specific threat reporting. They'd picked up a conversation from Lebanon in which they had received information that a bad guy said to put a lid on all operations for the next week. What that meant was that the hierarchy within the terrorist community did not want to jeopardize or compromise a major operation that was planned. Kind of similar to when cops had surveillance or a buy bust set up and told patrol to stay out of the area so that the bad guys did not get hinked up.

Kate knew this was another piece of a disturbing puzzle that showed an attack was imminent.

Chapter Seventy-One

Discussing their next steps, Cody and Kate were both in full agreement that probably the Paraguayan's were perhaps Iranian assassins and were originally part of a three-man team that had crossed the southern border from Mexico into the U.S. weeks earlier. According to what Frank heard from CBP, probably one suspect drowned carrying an Iranian manufactured pistol and plates for counterfeit currency. With the current state of the border, it was very easy to cross undetected and to evade capture. The two Paraguayans then met up with the Iranian counterfeiter, who was extorted to work with them to provide the release of his son from an Iranian prison. The counterfeiting would fund their operation under the radar of the various U.S. financial watchdogs. For whatever reason, the Iranian printer was murdered, and he and his Cadillac were dumped into the pond. If not looking for the missing gun from Johnny Nylon, they may have never known about the operation.

A bullet casing from Iranian manufactured ammunition also provided the context that the printer had been targeted by someone within the Iranian community. After uncovering and backtracking on the counterfeit money operation, they could identify the Russian, who made the introductions into the Cuban trucking syndicate and the purchases to the precursors of an Iranian inspired explosive formed penetrating device. They knew that since the Iranian revolution of 1979, Iran's vehement enemy was Israel, and their leaders had commonly vowed for the annihilation of the State of Israel.

Kate called Lucy Ming at the Air Force OSI. She told Lucy, "I know you had planned to put out an alert to the security forces and warn the Israel representative for added vigilance. If that individual lives off base, we can provide added patrol to that area. We might get the street crimes unit to set up surveillance to provide over-watch."

"Yes, that would be helpful. His name is Commander Moshe Cohen, and he is the son of the former Mossad Director. It makes sense that if you can't get to the father in Israel, why not go after his son and send a message? This attack would shock Israel. Meanwhile, in Iran, they would celebrate after the successful assassination of the son of the former director of the Mossad. The same man who is responsible for killing so many brothers of the revolution. It would also embarrass the U.S. despite not attacking a U.S. person."

"That cruise ship left port when they killed Reza Jaber, the printer, who was a U.S. citizen."

"You are right. I have already sent a couple of agents to the Israeli's home. He lives in a condo complex at Interbay and Bayshore. I spoke with Griffin St. Clair and he will send some additional folks from the JTTF, once they have their briefing."

"That is good to know."

"You know he is livid."

"Yes. As you heard at the briefing this morning, we reached out to him, just like we did with you. He has selective memory."

"I know. You gave an excellent brief this morning, especially knowing that St. Clair would like to have you in front of a firing squad. This information you have developed makes it a scary situation, and I'm going to feed this up the chain."

"Cody and I will swing out there now to look and coordinate additional security for Moshe Cohen. We'll see you at the FBI meeting."

"Thank you, Kate. Despite the insolence of Griffin, we are grateful that you ran this case to ground and uncovered this plot."

"Thanks, we will be in touch."

Chapter Seventy-Two

The FBI office building was locally referred to as the Taj Mahal. It was in a beautiful standalone building on prime real estate overlooking Tampa Bay and under the flight path of the Tampa airport. As Kate and Cody made their way to the conference room at the FBI, Kate ran into her onetime nemesis and now friend, Special Agent Roxanne Snelling.

Roxanne asked, "Are you on the way to the war room?"

"I guess you could say that. I don't think St. Clair is in my fan club."

"He has buried a few bodies along the way. The Bureau has tremendous resources and us street agents love to work and put bad guys away. He is not an agent. He is a politician."

"Take his gun away and give him a bumper sticker and campaign button."

"Exactly. Now and then, we get a boss like St. Clair, who only has one agenda."

"Himself?"

"Yep. He is looking for a quick promotion here. I heard he has one foot in the bear trap over this case, which means he could still be dangerous. Keep your distance."

"Just like a toxic relationship or a gunfight. Distance is your friend."

"Sage advice. Kate, are you not going to introduce me to your bodyguard?"

"I am so sorry. Yes, Roxanne, this is Cody, my police partner, and Cody, this is FBI Very Special Agent, Roxanne Snelling. Even her badge says she is special."

After the smiles, nods and handshakes, Roxanne said, "It's all my pleasure."

"Likewise." They held each other's gaze.

Kate said, "I'm sorry that I didn't call you first, Roxanne. Frank made the call to St. Clair. You and I speak cop and could have teamed up again."

"Girl, I'm telling you. It's best to start in the trenches with the street agents. Live and learn, right?"

"Copy that. Shall we go in?"

It was standing room only in the conference room of the Joint Terrorism Task Force, at the FBI field office. Some in suits and khakis and most of the local cops in jeans or shorts.

Kate, Cody, and Frank stood with their backs against the wall. Every seat was occupied with a few folks standing at the far end of the table. The chair at the head of the table was vacant while everyone waited for the JTTF supervisor. The crowd was becoming restless as the meeting was supposed to start at the top of the hour. Now 10 minutes past, and Frank Duffy was looking at his watch and sighing heavily as he looked over at Cody, who nodded and rolled his eyes.

Cody had little tolerance for the lack of respect coming from superiors. When he was in the Army, he was often inconvenienced by a particular supervisor, who was never on time for briefings. Hurry up and wait.

The FBI supervisor, Griffin St. Clair, with his slicked back dark hair, finally walked in and closed the door behind him. He provided an insincere apology for being late, stating that he had to brief the top floor. Cody assumed he meant the bosses in the penthouse suite were probably now in full panic mode as they had made calls to the Hoover building in Washington.

St. Clair sat down and flipped open his notebook. His mouth twisted with the annoyance of someone who had just bit into a sour apple. He took a deep breath and said, "Well folks, I'm sorry for the late notice and lack of planning, but this was like watching an accident occur in front of you on I-275. One of those in which all you can do is watch as you witness the car crash unfolding in front of you. We were just advised by the Tampa Police Department that they had stumbled onto a possible terrorism case that appears to be targeting the Tampa area. I'm going to turn it over to Detective Kate Alexander, who will provide the briefing on the case."

Thinking to himself, Cody thought St. Clair didn't even have the decency to honk the horn before he threw the Tampa Police under the bus. Cody could only imagine what Griffin had told the penthouse, knowing that St. Clair was doing everything in his ability to cover his own ass.

Listening to Kate go through the summary of the case, Cody inside was laughing harder than the audience at a comedy show when Kate said, "Similar to 9/11 when the government was focused on domestic threats, they were lulled into complacency on the threat from international actors." Pause for effect. "Specifically, in this case, the Tri-Border area, which until today was discounted by some in this building as merely being the beating of drums by grant seekers, politicians, and the Israelis. We now know that is not true and that these individuals coming out of the Tri-Border area are an imminent threat to the Tampa Bay area."

St. Clair squirmed in his chair. Cody smiled like a child on the playground who was just told by a chum that the girl across the way liked him. He admired Kate as a colleague and especially her tactical maneuvering through the political morass that encompassed most bureaucracies. He thoroughly enjoyed how she had sliced Griffin's nuts with no one else understanding the meaning behind her statement, other than the intended target of her dagger.

Cody also knew that St. Clair's career was listing to the starboard side after getting hit by Benny's torpedo to the front office. St. Clair was one of those types that he knew would never be content with a picturesque corner office overlooking Tampa Bay. He had plans to return to the Hoover Building for another promotion. This albatross of a case may as well have been custom fitted cement shoes fitted to him and tossed off the Skyway Bridge. This was a potential career ender for him and he might move out of the corner office, but it wouldn't be on a relocation to the Hoover Building. Probably the moving van would be headed up I-75 to a much less desirable and certainly less tropical location.

Cody thought about the three amigos holding up the wall and thought that he stood in good company, sandwiched between Kate and Duffy. They, like him, had no aspirations to move upward and, therefore, focused on being good cops. Like most of the cops and FBI agents in the room. St. Clair and The Caveman were cut from the same cloth. Spineless politicians only looking out for themselves. Cody looked around at everyone in the conference room and assessed that they too were mostly soldiers in the trenches fighting to keep the community safe. The bosses from this morning's briefing at the Blue Monster had all returned to their posh offices and delegated the hard work of chasing leads and conducting surveillance through the darkness of night.

He looked over at Roxanne and they traded smirks, and he winked. He approved of her air of confidence. Attractive, she had the IBM executive look going. He preferred not to fish off the company dock, having been burned by his ex-wife, but Roxanne was with a different agency. Perhaps she would be agreeable to exchange phone numbers for a Buddy Brew Coffee date.

St. Clair had regained his composure and now sounded like a general, barking orders to his army. He divided the conference room up into small groups with specific assignments to conduct surveillance on potential targets.

Cody said to Roxanne, "Hey it was so nice to meet you. Here is my card. Perhaps we can share a cup of coffee at Buddy Brew."

"Or something stronger at the The Pearl in the Channel District?"

"I like the way you think."

She handed her business card to him and said, "Call me."

Cody winked and smiled.

St. Clair told Kate, "Thanks for the briefing. We've got it from here. You don't have a security clearance."

"Clearance? Who do you think developed this case and brought it to your attention? If there was any information pertaining to classification, it has already been exposed to me."

St. Clair put up his hands in a calming gesture and said, "I understand. You have done excellent work on this case. However, because of the nature of this case, especially involving possible Iranian involvement and perhaps even Russians, we have no choice to include only personnel who have received a security clearance. We will keep the police department wired in through the inclusion of Frank Duffy, who has received a clearance and is assigned to the JTTF."

Kate pointed her finger at Griffin and said, "That's bullshit. You are just pissed because you were embarrassed. Your ass is redder than sunbathing at a nudist beach."

St. Clair said nothing, but flashed a slight smirk.

Cody said, "I had a clearance in the Army. Would that allow me to have access?"

"No. A clearance is only good for five years after the certification. Unless you are still in the reserves, you obviously have been separated from the military for over five years and the time counts from when the initial certification was completed."

Grabbing Cody's arm, Kate said, "Let's go, Cody. Since we don't know the secret handshake, let's give them their privacy in their cone of silence, and they can turn off their blinking light that shows the unwashed has vacated the premises."

Cody felt the sense of rejection that he was not worthy of acceptance and had been unceremoniously shown the door. Kate was absolutely correct that this conspiracy would've never had seen the light of day had it not been through their tenacious investigation. No one would've been the wiser until the boom happened. Now, after bringing it to the light of day, they were no longer worthy of participating in bringing the closure of the case. There was solace in knowing that Frank Duffy was on the inside and could look out for their vested interests.

He followed Kate from the building toward the visitors' parking lot. He knew she was part furious and part dejected from being excluded. This wasn't just a slap in the face, but a hard uppercut with a fist to the jaw.

Cody knew that there would be a time lag for the JTTF to assess surveillance points for each location, make the assignments, and deploy the resources to the field. This would give the two detectives a small head start. St. Clair said nothing about standing down from the investigation. He only said they could not take part in the FBI investigation. As a plane roared overhead, Cody picked up his pace and caught up with his partner. He put a consoling arm on her shoulder and leaned down towards her ear and said, "I have an idea."

Chapter Seventy-Three

Sliding her visitors pass under the bulletproof glass separating the receptionist from the visitors, Kate retrieved her driver's license from the receptionist with a polite smile. Kate did not return the smile, nor did she wait on her partner as she pushed open the exit doors and headed towards the visitor's parking lot.

Kate was seething. The case began in a happenstance manner. While searching for the murder weapon used by Johnny Nylon, they discovered the dead Cadillac submerged with the body. It was because of her investigation that she not only uncovered a counterfeit operation, but a murder by Iranian assassins. That connected to a Russian and a Cuban criminal enterprise that funded the Iranians' procurement of explosives.

Having been completely transparent and willing to share the information, she was dismayed with her federal partners. She felt she was now the target by bureaucracy at the expense of the investigation. The FBI was initially dismissive. The Secret Service was too busy and at least the Air Force, who wasn't aware of any threats, at least was putting out a warning to stay vigilant. Now she was getting the stiff arm from her own investigation.

It was still her investigation, and it was up to her to speak for Reza Jaber, who'd come to this country in pursuit of freedom and the American dream. It appeared he had been extorted to enter a criminal counterfeiting operation to win the freedom of his son, who had become a political prisoner in Iran. Or was his son specifically targeted to gain the cooperation of his father?

Kate thought about her own daughter, Brittney. If she had been arrested in a foreign country, Kate would've stopped at nothing to win her daughter's freedom. She would be relentless as a hornet in the side of the U.S. government. Would she pay a ransom or engage in criminal activity to buy that freedom? Perhaps if she knew, it would win her daughter's release. She could not stand in judgment of Jaber. Despite engaging in criminal activity, he did not deserve to die.

There was a murder to solve and two prime suspects to arrest. If that investigation collided with the JTTF investigation, then both cases would be strengthened by each other's findings.

The Caveman would probably be in the fetal position in his office, afraid to answer the phone from upper management, waging complaints against what he perceived as insubordinate detectives. Kate knew she had the full backing of Benny Thompson and was convinced she could bring this across the finish line before the feds.

As the plane roared overhead, she thought to herself that once they arrived in the privacy of their city car, she and Cody could brainstorm on how to advance this case. She was comforted with the fact that Frank would have her back and keep her updated on the progress of the federal investigation.

Deciding her next move would be to go to the address of where the Israeli military liaison was living and to meet with him. She felt it was imperative that she follow through with the duty to warn and notify him personally of the likely dangers.

Cody's shadow came up alongside of her, and she felt the comforting hand on her shoulder as he whispered into her ear, "I have an idea."

Looking over at Cody, she held up one finger, motioning to hold on, and pointed towards the visitor's parking lot. Cody acknowledged the gesture by nodding his head. An airplane roared overhead.

Chapter Seventy-Four

Once comfortably sitting in the quiet confines of their city car, Kate's paranoia of being overheard had been eliminated. She turned to Cody and said to her apprentice, "What say you?"

"I think we should return to MacDill and speak to the Israeli and then swing by his residence and get an assessment of where he lives."

She smiled and nodded and said, "I hate to say the old cliché, but great minds think alike. Because of your rapid ascent to quickly winning the Sherlock Holmes award, I'll even let you select the music."

His face exploded with excitement as his finger reached up to change the radio from Kate's country music selection to a heavy metal station. Cody looked over at Kate's cringing face as he began air drumming to the beat. With his head bobbing to the beat, he put his car in drive and put the FBI building in the rearview mirror.

Shouting over the music, she asked, "Isn't this song a little old for you?"

"Nah. Great jam song. Classics never get old. *Run Through the Jungle* by Creedence Clearwater Revival. It's so appropriate today."

"I suppose you are right." Kate answered. "By the way, what was that swiping right on Roxanne?"

"We were merely exchanging business cards."

"She was picking wedding gowns."

"What are talking about?"

"She caught those blonde locks and broad shoulders. Then you flashed your pearly whites at her. Her knees almost buckled."

"Stop."

"Uh, huh."

"What is she like?"

"When she was new, she was so tight, she squeaked when she walked. She was sipping the J. Edgar juice and a power junkie. It took a bit, but Frank and I loosened her up. Like most FBI street agents, she has moxie. I like her, and

I would call her a friend. She gave me a warning about St. Clair. That tells you how she is now."

"That's an endorsement."

"The Pearl?"

"Oh you heard. You ever been?"

"No. Trent wants to go."

"Great spot. Awesome vibe, drinks and food. The Chanel District has got it going on."

After making it through the security guard gate, Cody drove the meandering route to the simple building housing the Air Force Office of Special Investigations. After being escorted to Commander Ming's office, they waited for her return. Kate and Cody were like two kids at a museum looking at the collection of photos and awards and memorabilia adorning the office walls. Kate knew her nickname was Kick Ass, but as she admired the career achievements of Lucy Ming, she thought she was a badass. Some of the action photos were definitely taken in war zones and various foreign postings.

Lucy Ming walked back in and Kate said, "You have an impressive record of achievements." As she pointed towards the walls.

"The wall of fame or the wall of shame. We collect these items over our career and to spare yourself of blank walls, you hang some mementos to remind you of the journey. This is my last stop. After this, they all get put into a box and moved up to the attic."

"Your career at the end in retirement may be reduced to a few moving boxes, but you know and your colleagues know you are a contributor to a life well lived and making a difference."

"As you can see, I've made some stops in places where there were no t-shirt shops or postcards. Many, that I have no desire to return to, but there are places where I would've never have traveled to if not for this job. Throughout the Middle East, Iraq, Afghanistan. Wherever there is an Air Force Base, we have a presence." She looked at Cody and said, "You were in the Army, right?"

"Yes, ma'am, the 27th Infantry Regiment. Also known as the Wolfhounds."

"Kunar province?" Cody nodded as the Lucy continued, "It was a pretty hot zone. Speaking of hot zones, it appears we have one here in Tampa. You folks have done a great job on unearthing this plot. Their biggest mistake was killing Jaber. That was the thread that you two tugged that unraveled the entire scheme. We still don't know with clarity the intended targets, whether it's the base, the Israelis, or an Iranian ex-pat that has nothing to do with us."

"Definitively, no we don't know the exact target."

"Regardless, I have elevated the security posture at the base. Last evening, I assigned a team to Moshe Cohen's apartment complex up on Bayshore. It's pretty secure from the street, it has some vulnerabilities from a water born assault. But we have assets in place to take care of that as well. We provided an escort for him to the base this morning. He is currently in a meeting at CENTCOM, which they expect to break up in the next hour. He has already been advised of the potential threat and the added layer of securities at his apartment complex."

Kate said, "We can drive up to his apartment complex just so we can be familiar with the layout, but we won't compromise your security plan. Then we can meet Cohen out in front of CENTCOM."

Lucy Ming said, "Sounds like a plan. By the way, if it's any consolation, Griffin St. Clair isn't high on my Christmas card list either. He's one of those headquarters parasites who comes out to the field and sucks the lifeblood out of the troops and returns for a promotion. I have seen the same in the military as well. I'm sure it's the same thing at the police department. St. Clair made a mistake of displaying his indigency to your sergeant, who quickly pulled his pants to his ankles, exposing him. Just be wary if the opportunity presents itself, he will steamroll right over the top of you and smash you like a bug on the asphalt."

As they stood, Kate nodded and said, "Thanks for the warning. I'll have my driver and his heavy metal music take me on a brief tour."

"I'll call you when Cohen is out of his meeting, and I can meet you there to make the introductions with Cohen."

"Great, thanks."

Chapter Seventy-Five

As they cleared the guard gate to the entrance of the base on Bayshore Blvd., Kate was on the phone updating Benny Thompson on the developments. Cody's mind drifted to how many times he entered and exited similar military bases over the years. The entrance to his forward operating base in Afghanistan was much more modest and greeted with a machine gun post.

As they drove away from the base, Cody recognized the disparity of the accommodations living on base as opposed to those off-base. He looked to the right at scraggly oak trees and palmetto palms overlooking Tampa Bay. The water was as calm and flat as a pressed shirt. There were a few vacant boat piers. To the left were mostly modern mansions that had replaced simpler homes. The further north, as the land to the bay-side increased, the green grass was taken up by expensive homes with a grand water view.

They approached the Bayshore Bottoms apartment complex on the left. The location where they had received the complaint of the suspects possibly conducting surveillance from the parking lot. Cody's mind drifted considering what exactly the suspects were up to sitting in the complex. Was it indeed watching traffic or possibly waiting on a resident.

Across the street from the apartment complex on the right side was a yet to be developed vacant lot. Cody looked at a dark gray transit van parked in the grass parallel to Bayshore Boulevard. The description matched what was previously told to them by J Lo in the counterfeiting operation. He noticed the discoloration on the side of the van. A section appeared to be a darker shade of gray.

As Kate continued talking on the phone, Cody's eyes scanned back to the left towards the apartment complex. He noticed a bicycle that had been chained to a street sign. It was then that he made the connection.

He yelled to Kate, "Hang on!"

Seeing a clearing in the oncoming traffic, Cody mashed on the gas pedal of the car and turned the wheel towards to the left. The Toyota Camry blasted across the oncoming lane of traffic, hitting the bicycle and the traffic sign.

He ran over the obstacles like they were on mountain terrain. The exploding airbags slapped their faces like boxing gloves and then quickly deflated.

He steered the car through the grass and along the sidewalk, paralleling the street they had just been traveling. As horns honked, he ripped the steering wheel to the right, crossing the two-lane road. He slammed on the brake and came to a sudden stop, blocking all lanes of traffic.

"What the hell are you doing?" Kate said.

"Jump out on your side, stop the traffic and have them turn around and go back in the other direction. I'll stop the traffic up here and reroute them back going towards the city. Stay away from the van. It has a bomb inside."

Cody watched helplessly as a Chevy Lumina, like the one described, pulled out of the driveway a half a block away and escaped on Bayshore Boulevard away from the scene. He looked back at the mangled bicycle.

Depressing his microphone on his police radio, he provided his call sign and put out an officer needs help call as well as requesting a K-9 and the bomb squad to their location. He knew that call would rally all the troops and have them headed in their direction. He also put out the description of the fleeing Lumina.

When the first two units arrived, Cody instructed one to go north and block traffic towards the city at Tyson Avenue, and the second unit he told to go south and block traffic at Interbay Boulevard.

As they cleared out the cars and cut off traffic, Kate asked, "Are you going to tell me what the hell is going on?"

"The eye of Allah."

"The eye of Allah?" Kate asked with her hands on her hips.

"Yes." He pointed across the street to the gray van. "I believe that is the transit van that they talked about. If you'll notice the discoloration of paint on the side. It appears there is a square hole that has been covered up with some pretty bad bodywork. I didn't initially notice it, but there is a small hole in that repair job. This bicycle has an infrared sensor mounted on the frame between the handlebars and the seat. Although we didn't deal with it in Afghanistan, in Iraq, the Iranian made EFP's using infrared sensors that they could turn on remotely. The bomb would be triggered by a passing car, breaking the beam and triggering the detonation device. Similar to the beam with an automatic garage door opener."

"So, you're saying that we are probably staring at a bomb in that transit van?"

"Yes. Keep in mind an EFP is almost as precise as a gunshot. Albeit a hypersonic shot coming at a speed equivalent to Mach 6, which is over four thousand miles per hour. That copper cone will come out shaped more like a tadpole traveling at 2,000 meters per second. In comparison, a 50-caliber bullet being fired from a rifle travels at 900 meters per second."

"Unbelievable."

"I definitely saw a Lumina driving north."

"Do you think it was them?"

"Yep. Because of the traffic on Bayshore, they could not just turn it on and leave. Because any car passing would trigger the device. They had to manually turn on the infrared beam as they observed their target approaching. They're targeting someone, probably the Israeli military attaché. There's a good chance he's driving in an armored vehicle, which would not stand a chance against an EFP. So, they had to be close enough to turn it on remotely while seeing him approach the van. It would've been lethal."

"Okay, so the next patrol unit that arrives, we need to have them go across to the apartment complex talk to the manager. Ask if they have some way to communicate with all the residents and start knocking on doors to evacuate. Benny is on his way to the scene, and I'll also call OSI and let them know what just happened, so they can harden up around the Israelis apartment complex. At least they can keep him on base where he will be safe."

Chapter Seventy-Six

K-9 14 parked the Explorer on the mostly vacant Bayshore Boulevard, aside from the various police vehicles. Officer Troy Neal, who had searched the stash house with his furry partner, Repo, walked towards the two detectives.

"Twice in two days. Cody, we are seeing you more often than your Tinder dates. And Kate, it's always a pleasure to see you."

Kate said, "Thanks Troy. I think we have a live one here. The scent that Repo picked up on Pine Street leads to here. Let the blonde Boy Wonder explain."

Cody said, "We think the bomb they were working on may be inside that van. I spotted a bike with an infrared sensor aimed at the van, which has a hole in the side panel. You might not let your partner jump against the van or it could go boom."

"I guess this explains your wild-ass driving?"

"Saving the world."

"Sure, Boy Wonder. Okay, I'll get my partner."

Cody could hear Repo barking with excitement as Neal returned to the Explorer. He opened up the back door and clipped a leash on his collar. The Belgian Malinois enthusiastically bolted from the confines of the SUV.

Kate said, "Are you sure he is not a German Shepard?"

"Repo is deeply offended. Just because he is a dark shade, there is no mistake that he is a highly skilled Malinois. Right Repo?"

Repo gave an authoritative bark.

Kate said, "I apologize puppy. I wanted to get a rise out of your human partner."

"Okay, Repo, let's go to work."

Neal gave the K-9 his commands to search. As soon as Repo reached the rear bumper of the transit van and sniffed, the dog sat proudly. The officer looked at Cody and Kate and nodded. He reached down and vigorously rubbed the dog's chest while praising him and giving him a treat. He immediately tugged on the leash and escorted his partner to return to the safety of the backseat of the Ford Explorer.

Looking at each other with synchronized looks of yikes, they both understood the gravity of the situation. This was for real. Kate considered the fact that Cody had just interrupted the triggering sequence for a bomb. Being on the passenger side of the car, she was within feet of the bomb. She took a deep breath, knowing this was too close of a shave, and she would like to avoid facing danger this close in the future. She also considered, had Cody not put all that together, what would have happened?

Kate called Frank Duffy and apprised him of the unexpected developments. She asked him to inform St. Clair of what happened and where the active scene was located. She understood that St. Clair would explode through the rooftop and will probably need a parachute for a safe landing. This was indeed a big deal. She knew that once Benny told The Caveman, he would scamper up to the 10th floor hoping to beat the patrol supervisors, who had just been notified of the officer needs assistance call and the bomb squad call out.

Chapter Seventy-Seven

The box truck of the bomb squad rolled up and parked on the now vacant Bayshore Boulevard. Towed behind the truck was the total containment vessel, which would secure any explosive device. Lieutenant Shawn Morman, along with two of his fourteen officers, arrived on the scene. He stepped out of the passenger side of the truck and rubbed his bald scalp. Morman began scanning the surrounding area to ensure that there weren't more secondary explosive devices that might be planted in the area.

He was aware that terrorists had in the past, plant a secondary explosive device. This would target first responders arriving at the scene of the first explosion to intentionally kill the public safety practitioners. There was nothing but an empty, undeveloped lot that the van sat on. The apartment complex, with all the cars in the parking lot, gave Morman concern.

He walked over to Troy Neal, who cracked his window and spoke through the small opening. "Shawn, it sure is hot out there. I am trying to keep the cool inside my unit. You know it's all about Repo."

Shawn shook his head. "Nice one. Maybe I'll pull you through that crack of the window."

"Don't you have a bomb or something to play with?"

"Yes, and I hate to disturb your furry partner, but I need you two to run a search of the parking lot."

Troy looked back at Repo, who was sitting up in the backseat. "You hear that Repo? He wants us to go to work. What do you think?"

Repo barked once.

"There is your answer, Shawn. Just for you, he said he will give up the comfort of the air conditioner and look for another bomb."

"You two are the best."

Neal guided Repo on a search of the cars in the parking lot. They moved from car to car, clearing each one. When the search was complete, Neal gave a thumbs up to the Lieutenant and he and Repo returned to the air-conditioned comfort of the SUV. Despite the K-9 search of the apartment complex not detecting any additional explosives, they continued with their plans to evacuate the neighboring area.

In the meantime, the bomb squad pulled the robot out of the bomb squad truck. Shawn Morman agreed with Cody's assessment on the EFP. Especially, after assessing the carcass of the bicycle and its infrared beam. Using binoculars, he could see the hole in the van's side about the size of the water bottle. He could also see the opposing Eye of Allah that would trigger the high velocity explosive device when the beam from the bicycle was broken. He knew the lethality of such an attack targeting.

The robot would open up the rear doors of the transit van. They hoped the Iranians had not booby-trapped the doors. Robots had virtually eliminated the need for the technician with the bomb suit to be placed in such precarious and potentially deadly positions.

Rolling up to the driver's window, the robot with its camera began peering into the inside. A curtain had been pulled across the divide to the cargo section. The robot's camera did not see any tripwires or anything else suspicious in the passenger seating area. The robot was then dispatched to the rear of the van. With its mechanical arm, the robot slowly opened one of the rear doors. Once it was cracked open, the camera lens scanned the opening. No trip wires were seen.

The robot carefully opened the door the rest of the way. Huddled around the camera's monitor, the bomb squad members, Kate and Cody, viewed the images. The image was that of the cast-iron pipe sitting in a wood cradle with one end facing towards the fake panel on the side of the van. Confident that they located an EFP, the bomb technicians recalled the robot so they could go over the game plan of how best to render safe the explosive device.

Chapter Seventy-Eight

Rick McMahan, an athletic looking special agent with the OSI, arrived on scene and received the briefing as to what had occurred. He told Kate the commander was keeping Lieutenant Colonel Cohen isolated at the base. He also said that the JTTF was on the way.

Kate got Cody and McMahan together and asked, "Do you know who else besides Israelis that the Iranians hate?"

Simultaneously, they both answered, "The U.S."

"Yes, but I've been reading up on Iran. The MEK. Mojahedin-e-Khalq. The Peoples Mojahedin of Iran. It started as a bunch of middle-class college kids looking to overthrow the Shah in 1979, but lost out in a power struggle during the revolution."

McMahan said, "The U.S. Embassy debacle and takeover."

"Exactly. So, the MEK was run out of town and landed in Iraq where they could launch attacks against Iranian leadership. Since the fall of Iraq, the MEK has moved to Albania. Financially backed by Saudi Arabia, the MEK backs internal protests and opposition. Iran hates the MEK. Iran blamed the MEK working in concert with the Israeli Mossad with the assassination of a senior official in the Iranian nuclear program. The U.S. gave the United Nations funding to resettle the MEK to Albania from Iraq. Now based in Albania, the MEK continues to look at overthrowing the Iranian government."

Cody asked, "You think Albania could be on the hit list?"

"Last year, the Iranians allegedly launched a cyber-attack on Albania, and as a result Albania cut diplomatic ties to Iran expelling Iranian diplomats. Albania is U.S. and NATO supported and with ongoing hostilities over the nuclear negotiations, you could see Albania being targeted."

Cody said, "Remember what Duffy found out from Customs and Border Protection? They recovered the drowned body with the Paraguayan passport but also carrying an Iranian manufactured gun? It was going to be three assassins. So, you wonder if they were content with one target or multiple targets?"

Kate pointed to the unmarked SUV being driven by Benny Thompson arriving at the scene. She could see The Caveman was with him. "Oh great, The Caveman is on scene." She turned to McMahan and asked, "Do you have an Albanian representative at CENTCOM?"

McMahan said, "Even though Albania falls outside the area of responsibility for CENTCOM, they are part of the coalition nations. Let me call back to the office and get some details about who that liaison is and where they live."

Kate turned to Cody and lowered her voice, "Once we brief up Benny and The Caveman, we will get Benny to loan us his car and we can go to the Albanians home. Hopefully, there's not a second EFP set up for him."

Cody nodded and said, "The Albanians are probably not in an armored car unlike the Israelis, who live with a target on their back worldwide. You know the Albanian thinks he won the lottery being assigned to MacDill in beautiful Tampa, and probably feels he is out of harm's way."

"Well, let's find out. This bomb scene and continuing circus is going to last for a while. Wait till The Caveman sees your new car. He'll have you on an electric bike from now on."

"You're probably right."

Kate briefed both Benny and The Caveman, whose mouth was doing more twisting than a washing machine on the spin cycle. His eyes looked at the van, back to the twisted bike, Cody's car, and finally to Kate. He was furious. They both listened to the description of how Cody, with his prior Army experience, could recognize the Eye of Allah focused on the suspected EFP in the transit van.

The Caveman said, "We will all have a discussion about this case after this scene has been resolved."

Benny said, "I believe the locating and apprehension of the assassins is more important than giving attaboys to Cody and Kate for a job well done. I think your accolades, which are greatly appreciated, can wait until the community is safe." He winked at Kate and gave no ability for The Caveman to respond. "You guys single handedly found the bomb and kept it from exploding. Hell, they'll have you on one of the Gasparilla Floats tossing beads, and the mayor will give you the key to the city. I know the chief is having a fan fest with the mayor over this."

Glaring, he said, "That's not what I'm talking about." He looked over and saw the two majors over District 1 and Criminal Investigations. The Caveman walked towards the bosses for face time.

Kate gave a gentle tug on Benny's arm and whispered into his ear regarding her plan to drive over to the Albanian attaché's residence. Benny nodded and said, "Good call and good luck. I'll keep The Caveman busy after he is finished ass kissing."

"Point him towards the cameras when they show up."

Benny handed his car keys to her and winked. "Don't let Cody drive and destroy my chariot."

She smiled and nodded.

Chapter Seventy-Nine

Kate walked over and rejoined her partner and Special Agent Rick McMahan, who had found out the physical address to where the Albanian Army officer lived. He was also made aware that, like the Israeli, the Albanian would also be kept on the base in a secluded, safe location. They agreed to take separate cars.

Kate and Cody piled into Benny's SUV and called McMahan, who was driving his blue Chevy Tahoe. Cody put McMahan on speaker as Kate followed the Tahoe. They drove north for a short period until they intersected with Interbay Road. Making a hard right turn on Interbay, which more or less paralleled with Bayshore Boulevard, the trio now drove back south.

McMahan told them that the mid-rise white condominium to the left was where the Albanian lived. The Smugglers Cove Condominiums surrounded by a white privacy wall, the complex enjoyed a view of the bay. As they passed the entrance, parked inside the gates, was the Chevy Lumina.

Cody pointing through the windshield said, "That's it. That's the suspect's car." Cody looked over at Kate as they drove past. "How do you want to handle this?"

"Just like a car stop. We will stop from behind. Cody, you go up the right side towards the passenger side. Rick, you pull in the front to block him from driving forward. I will go up the driver's side. Watch our crossfire."

They turned around at Crescent Drive and returned to the Smugglers Cove. McMahan leading the way, entered through the walled opening. He steered the Tahoe around the parking lot and pulled in the front. "I only see the driver. He is alone."

"Keep an eye out for the second. We don't want him ambushing us."

Kate pulled in behind the suspect's car to block him from backing up.

Kate said, "Go!"

All three quickly exited their cars with weapons drawn moved quickly onto the suspect vehicle. Kate took up the lead and using the trunk as a barricade on the vehicle parked next to the Lumina. Cody took up a position, mirroring

Kate viewing the passenger side. McMahan aimed his SR-16 rifle across his hood directly at the driver.

The second suspect might be within an earshot or view of the takedown. He could flee the area. She was really concerned that he would circle up behind them and shoot Cody and herself. Or had he gone to another location?

The thought crossed her mind that the driver, being an Iranian assassin, would come out shooting or worse, detonate a bomb inside the car, taking all three with him.

Pointing the barrel of her gun directly at the driver's head, and yelled, "Police! Open the door." Her heart felt like a sledgehammer beating against an iron plate. She took a deep breath through her nose and exhaled slowly. The door slowly opened, and the suspect had his hands in a surrender position facing her.

She yelled, "Sal del coche. Manos arriba. Date la Vuelta y camina hacia atras hacia mi voz." (*Get out of the car. Hands up. Turn around and walk back towards my voice.*)

He followed her directions and raised his hands, turned facing forward and walked backwards towards her voice. Once he got to the rear of the car, she asked him to get on his knees and lay flat towards the front of the car. He understood Spanish and English commands.

She paused and looked around. No sign of number two.

With McMahan and Cody covering her, she holstered her gun and pulled out her handcuffs from the small of her back. Kate grabbed his hand and thumb twisted behind his back. With her knee in his back, she pulled the free arm to connect with his left arm and she snapped the cuffs on his wrist.

She began searching his body and found a semi-automatic handgun in a holster attached to his waistband, which she handed off to Cody. Cody and McMahan continued scanning the area.

Cody, examining the pistol, said, "Zoaf."

"The Iranian gun. Perhaps the murder weapon."

Feeling confident that the suspect had no more weapons, she rolled him up to a sitting position. She asked him, "Where is your friend?"

"Asylum? Asylum!" and with a wisp of an accent, said, "No English."

Kate said, "You followed Spanish and English commands perfectly."

He shrugged and cocked his head like he didn't understand.

McMahan spoke with a Middle Eastern dialect and conversed with the suspect briefly. He turned to Kate and said, "In the sandbox, I became a student of Arabic. I explained to him I didn't believe he could not speak English and that to be considered for asylum, he would have to cooperate fully and speak in English or we could interview him in Spanish."

Kate said, "I'm impressed."

"Don't be. I speak enough to order hummus at a restaurant and conduct a simple interview. Fortunately, he speaks English. So, you're free to ask away."

"Good, because I exhausted my Spanish vocabulary."

The suspect was now sitting on his bottom with his hands cuffed behind him. He looked up at Kate. She crouched down to look at him at eye level and asked, "Are there more bombs?"

He looked at her with defiance. She nodded and smiled. "I'm only going to say this once. You can either answer each of my questions truthfully or I will send you on a slow boat to Israel." The defiance dropped quickly as his eyes became larger. "You cannot do that. You cannot send me to Israel. I am in custody in the U.S."

"I don't have time to play your silly ass stalling games. Your mission has failed. One of your associates drowned in the Rio Grande River. Your bomb has been discovered and is being defused and dismantled. Your counterfeit operation is over. Wherever you face trial and imprisonment would be up to the Israelis and the U.S. government to decide. For any cooperation to sway the U.S., you better start talking right now. Are there more bombs?"

"No, just the one on Bayshore." In perfect English.

"What is your name?"

"Firouz Noor."

"Who and where is your Iranian Quds associate?"

They could see that Firouz's mind was racing like a high-speed computer as he processed the reality of the situation. "His name is Ali Azar, and he is at the Saudi attaché's home."

Kate looked at Cody and McMahan with a questionable expression. McMahan nodded. "Make's sense. I've been to that house, so I know exactly where it is."

Kate asked Firouz, "Is he going there to kill the Saudi Attaché?"

"Yes."

"Okay, I will go with Rick. Cody, would you stay here with Firouz until you can get a patrol unit for transport?"

"Will do. I'll also keep my Glock close by in case he is lying and Ali is hiding nearby."

"Be careful."

"Likewise."

Chapter Eighty

They passed the Israeli complex at the Bay Boulevard condominiums. The contemporary complex featured white and turquoise accents. The modern looking complex, which looked very secure to begin with, was now an armed encampment with federal agents and long guns posted as additional security. She could see police markings from several agencies, including the FBI.

As McMahan drove the Tahoe past the Israeli complex, the view opened up to the right, exposing a panoramic view of Tampa Bay and the city skyline in the distance. Just as soon as Kate saw the wide berth of the bay, they made a quick left turn on Hawthorne Road.

Driving down the narrow road under the canopy of oak trees with dangling Spanish moss, they were surrounded by an eclectic group of multi-million-dollar homes. All with lush green landscaping.

McMahan slowed the car and pulled up against the curb on the left-hand side. He pointed a few houses up on the left and said, "That's the Saudi's attaché. I accompanied the Sec-Def to a party there once."

"You know anything about him?"

"Like all of them, he is connected to the Royal Family. A pilot. He flew bombing missions into Yemen against the Houthi rebels, backed by guess who?"

"Iran?"

"Yep. I know Iran and Saudi are trying to kiss and makeup, but Iran may have a little angst against a pilot that killed a bunch of Houthi soldiers. Let's be honest, Iran only cares about themselves and has repeatedly violated conditions of human rights against protestors, nuclear arms, and seizures of tankers in the Gulf of Oman."

"Scary that they have come here to wreak havoc."

Looking at the 2-story contemporary home with straight line architecture, a lot of glass, steel railings and cream stucco, Kate figured the home was north of a few million. She figured the price tag for most of the homes on the street exceeded $2 million. She shook her head and said, "Not too shabby."

"The Kingdom and its oil and money."

"I don't see anything but let's call for some additional backup. I'm just going to take a stroll past the house and see if I see anything. Keep my portable radio safe. I want to blend not stick out."

"Copy that. The task force has more bodies running around here than moonshiners in Kentucky. It won't take them long to shake a few bodies loose."

After McMahan placed the call for backup, Kate slipped out of the passenger side of the Tahoe and began an easy gait towards the attaché's home. If she had been in her car, she would've had her ballistic vest on and an oversized jacket to cover it. She texted Benny and Cody the address she and McMahan were watching and that they were waiting for backup from the JTTF. She then called communications to notify them of her location as well.

Her mind wandered as she contemplated what the owners of these homes did for a living. Were these inheritances from generational wealth, hard-working entrepreneurs, or lucky Powerball winners? As she walked along, she admired the stately oak trees whose trunks were pushing against the disheveled curbs of the street. One oak tree had a toddler's swing suspended from the tree. She smiled at the thought of when she and Jake had suspended a similar swing for Brittney and the joy that it brought to their child and her parents. They eventually replaced it with a hammock swing.

Chapter Eighty-One

Kate pulled her shirt over the top of her holster and badge, hoping that no one would pay attention to the lone female walking alone. As she walked past the Saudi's home, she thought of the wealth that it took to build such a home. The modern square architecture was not to her liking. As she approached the driveway, she heard the crackling of leaves within a swath of landscaping with various short palms and plants.

She assumed it was a squirrel or lizards. It was then she saw the head of a man. This tropical garden directly across from the garage was a perfect assassin's nest. A clear line of sight for an ambush as the attaché arrived home and pulled into the garage. He would never survive. She planned to continue walking past the house and then called McMahan on the phone. Kate figured she would take up a position next door where she could monitor the front of the house. There was another stirring in the garden and she looked over and made eye contact with whom she suspected was Ali Azar. His gaze narrowed at Kate as he stood fully, exposing his concealment. They froze, staring at each other like two dueling gunslingers.

Ali turned and hurried away from Kate towards the gate of the privacy fence to the side of the home. Fearing that he had determined that she was a cop, she knew she might not have another chance to capture him. The thought of the trained Iranian assassin on the loose in Tampa was unacceptable. He was there to kill.

She turned towards Ali and, taking cover behind one of the large oak trees, she withdrew her Glock pistol from her holster. She raised the weapon and aligned her sights with her finger just outside the trigger guard. Aiming at the center mass of Ali, she yelled, "Police! Stop or I'll shoot."

Ali gave a quick look over his right shoulder and broke into a run as he reached the gate and extended his hand towards the handle.

Kate once again yelled, "Police, stop!"

Signaling to McMahan, who was parked in his Tahoe two houses away. Kate motioned for him to come in her direction. Kate sprinted the length of the short driveway past the tropical jungle and towards the slamming gate. She took a quick peek over the top of the gate, hoping he was not sighted in on the gate. One shot would've ended her life. She pushed the gate open and lowered herself into a combat position, peering through the opening.

The pathway down the side of the house was the width of a bowling alley. Kate knew that if the assassin was waiting at the corner, she was most definitely entering the fatal funnel. With her gun in the ready position, she hurried towards the end of the house. She tried to close the distance as quickly as possible to get herself out of the immediate kill zone.

She reached the corner of the house and pressed her back against the warm, stubbly stucco. Her left hand felt the rough surface. She took a deep breath and blew out slowly. With her gun tucked into her midsection, she took a quick peek around the corner.

As she pulled her head back in, two shots rang out, striking the corner where her head had just been, spraying her with shards of stucco and dust. From her quick peek, she knew the shots were coming from a pool cabana in the backyard and perhaps he was using a lounge chair for concealment.

She instantly lowered herself to her right knee and took up a firing position. Following a sight picture through her gunsight, she quickly peeked around the corner. Knowing she had a fraction of a second, she pulled the trigger three times, aiming the rounds into the cabana. She felt the recoil of her pistol. Kate watched the chair cushion rip apart with the impact of her rounds and could see his head move behind the chair. She altered her shooting position, knowing he would target her position.

Standing like a group of spectators at a hockey game, all the police personnel watched with intrigue as the bomb squad robot motored towards the gray transit van. They were close enough to see the robot, but far enough to maintain their safety. They crowded around the video screen, which was displaying the view of the robot, which continued its assessment of the explosive device and the van's undercarriage.

Everyone's attention was distracted by the sound of gunfire in the distance. They all traded glances and looked back towards the north and listened in the distance. Benny recognized immediately this wasn't just some random gunshots, but a sustained gun-battle. He knew from the updates that Cody had one in handcuffs and sitting in the backseat of Benny's car. Knowing that Kate and the agent from the Air Force were a few blocks away from the bomb site, Benny jumped into action.

Grabbing one of the uniformed officers and he said, "Come on, let's roll to Hawthorne Road. An officer needs help."

The Caveman interrupted, but Benny told him, "Stay here. I'll keep you updated."

As he jumped into the patrol SUV, Benny barked into the radio, "Officer needs assistance. Shots fired. On Hawthorne Road off Bayshore. Plain-clothes officer is female. Suspect is unknown male."

Chapter Eighty-Two

Watching Ali sprint the short distance to the right from the cabana to the far corner of the backyard, Kate took aim from a kneeling position. Ali began firing wildly in her direction, meant to keep her in place. She heard the rounds striking the fence. She felt the spray of plastic splinters exploding behind her and showering her back. She was still trapped in the alley with limited movement. Since he was running towards her right, she was hoping his aim was not accurate. She dropped into a prone position. Trying to lead the fleeing suspect, she fired twice more into the corner of the backyard. She watched as he bounded over the six-foot white PVC fence.

Using her athleticism, Kate stood and quickly covered the distance. Clutching her Glock, she half scaled and half vaulted over the fence. She dropped off the top of the fence. Immediately, she assumed a crouched position and ready to fire. Watching her suspect sprinting away across a vacant lot towards the busy Gandy Boulevard, he was in a full gallop with a slight hop. Perhaps he was injured.

Kate, with her gun in her right hand, took off in full stride and closed the distance on Ali. She once again yelled at him, "Stop, police!"

He looked over his right shoulder and saw that the hunter was gaining on her prey. Suddenly, he stopped to steady his platform. He turned and fired four times at the closing Kate. Watching him stop and turn, she recognized the threat and dove towards the ground.

Cringing, she waited for the impact of the bullets. She knew she had to counter or risk being a stationary target for the approaching assassin. Lifting her head through the tall grass, she raised her gun.

Aiming at the killer, she placed her forefinger on the trigger and tightened the grip. She pulled the finger against the trigger and squeezed off three rounds. She watched as her rounds impacted the chest of her target.

Ali's face revealed what his body had not yet told his brain. He was defeated. His mission was over. His left hand reached for his chest. The Zoaf 9mm pistol dangled in his right hand as his knees slowly buckled, and his body collapsed to the ground.

Slowly, Kate stood up with her Glock and focused on the target. Kate moved cautiously towards Ali. She kept her sights aimed at the fallen man. Both hands steadied the pistol. She moved her left foot and brought the right foot up, maintaining her balance and shooting platform. Never crossing her feet.

She saw no motion as she approached the body of the assassin. She was prepared if he was playing possum. Keep your guard up. Be prepared for a counter-assault.

She now stood directly over the killer. Flat on his back, his white linen shirt looked like red paintballs had hit him. The blood soaked into the cloth. She looked at the stubble on his face. Not even a grimace. She stared for a moment. His life had vacated his body.

Reaching down, she felt for a pulse. She knew the answer. Nothing. His heart was no longer pumping. Kate slid her weapon back into the holster. She snapped a photo on her phone to document his final pose. A second closeup of his hand and gun. Kate reached down and picked up his Iranian made pistol and moved it away.

She looked back and saw McMahan running across the field after dropping off the top of the fence. His rifle slung over his back.

Using her cell phone, she called communications, advising them she had been involved in a shooting and the suspect was down. She was okay, but needed an ambulance to arrive at the open lot on Gandy.

She called Benny and advised him of the situation and where she was located. He told her he was moments away.

McMahan, winded from the long run and climb over the fence, asked, "Are you okay, Kate?"

"Yes. I think so." She hadn't even thought that she might have been hit. She looked over at herself as best she could. McMahan looked over as well.

"Looks like you're good. No blood. What the hell happened?"

"I'm not so sure myself. He was hiding in the bushes. He saw me and ran. I couldn't let him get away. He shot at me, and I returned fire."

"You did what you had to do. I'm sorry I wasn't closer."

"Then it would have been both of us shooting."

She knew that this would be the first of many accountings of this story that she would have to provide to internal affairs, the state attorney's office, the FBI, and who knows how many others.

Chapter Eighty-Three

Blue lights flashed on the patrol SUV as it parked on Gandy, blocking a lane of traffic. She could hear other sirens approaching and watched as her sergeant lumbered through the thick grass. Benny walked up to her and gave her a gentle nod, and then hugged her.

He whispered into her ear. "Breathe. Just breathe."

She took a deep breath through her nose and held it for a few counts and slowly breathe through her pursed lips. She repeated this process four times, knowing that she could slow down her heart, which felt like a jackhammer on asphalt.

Benny released his grip and rested his hands on her shoulders and said, "He gave you no choice. You survived and get to go home today. That's all that matters. Before they erect the circus tents here and the entire zoo shows up, I want you to walk over there and call your family and let them know that you're okay. This whole thing will be big news and everyone in your family will be terrified, so it's best to hear it directly from you that you are okay."

She nodded. "Thank you."

Following the sage advice of her supervisor, she walked away to give herself some privacy and called Trent. After one ring, he answered. "Are you okay? I've been watching the news updates about the suspected bomb on Bayshore."

Hearing his voice broke through her stoic veneers. Kate wanted him to hug her, hold her tight and for her to just collapse into his arms and sob with emotion. She did not have the liberty of losing it at a crime scene surrounded by her fellow cops, who would stand in judgment. Taking a deep breath, she gave a staggered exhale through her pursed lips.

Trent asked, "Kate? Are you all right?"

"Yes." She paused for another deep breath and said, "Thank you for answering the phone. I'm okay. I don't have time to go into everything right now, but I wanted to call to let you know I am okay. If you don't mind going over to the house and letting mom know that I'm okay. Stay with them, keeping them company. I'm sure this is going to get a lot of news coverage, but I've been involved in a shooting, and I killed a man today."

"Oh, my gosh! I'm just glad you are okay. You are not hurt in any way?"

"No, I am physically good. I just have to process the emotions, and I'm hoping that you, Professor, will be there waiting for me when I get home, whatever time tonight."

"Guaranteed. I'm here for you. I love you and I'm leaving right now for your house."

"I love you too, Trent. I've got to run now, but I'll see you tonight."

Ending the call, and she looked over and could see the ambulance crew running across the lot carrying their trauma bag. She figured they would not have to open the kit once they assessed him for vital signs. She also saw several others wearing FBI markings making their way across the lot as well. Recognizing one as Griffin St. Clair, she walked back over to stand next to Benny as if he would be her protector.

As St. Clair arrived and looked over at the bullet riddled body, he shook his head and looked with disgust at Kate.

Before he could say anything, Benny said, "Did you bring your spokesperson with you? You can thank us, and specifically Kate, for bringing this to a successful closure. No bombs went off. No one was killed except for the bad guy here."

He pointed to the ground as the EMTs shook their head establishing Ali had not survived his mortal wounds.

Raising his arms and illustrating an arc above, Benny continued. "I can see the news headlines now. The FBI and other local partners dismantled a terrorist operation targeting foreign military members. So, I'd say you came out smelling better than that fake air freshener they spray inside the car at the car wash. Yup, you'll be on your way to the Hoover Building in no time now. Hell, they'll probably pin a fucking medal on your hairy chest."

St. Clair moved his hand to make sure his hair was in place. He stared at Benny and then glared at Kate before looking at the dead Iranian. His lips tightened as he looked back and nodded at Benny and said, "You're right. We disrupted this plot. Thanks for your help."

Kate had just witnessed a game of chicken. Two sets of headlights converging. Benny had already displayed that he was unlikely to swerve. Then Benny did a remarkable thing. He tossed an opportunity for St. Clair to save face and preserve his ego. Just like a politician, Griffin St. Clair jumped at the story-spin that would save his career. He was on his way back to headquarters, a hero. He would steal the credit and dole out a few crumbs to the locals. The sergeant's narrative spin would save the squad from the buzz-saw of politicians and allow Kate to stay in the obscurity of the shadows.

Chapter Eighty-Four

Frank Duffy arrived at the scene and immediately ran up to Kate, who was sitting in the passenger side of a patrol car. Officer Marco Conelli was keeping her company. He was talking fast with his New York accent about his budding musical career and cooking interests. Her sullen face lifted at the sight of her old partner.

She stepped out, and they embraced. Frank said, "I'm here for you, Kick Ass. I know what you're going through. I am the peer support person assigned to you. So, whatever you need regardless of the time, you call me. If you can't sleep tonight because you're too wired, call me any time."

"Thank you, Frank. You are dear friend."

He waved at Marco, "Thanks buddy."

"Anytime, Frank. Stay strong Kate."

"Thanks, Marco."

Frank said, "Just to give you some updates that I received on the way over here. You apparently hit him at the pool cabana in his left arm. You hit him again in his ass as he was going over the fence. Obviously, you hit him in the field three times."

"I'm glad to hear that all the time on the range and all those drills that Brett Bartlett and Julie Dickey put me through saved my life today. I remember getting annoyed at the repetition of the drills. Julie and Brett yelling to do it again. Those firearms drills saved my life. Well, they were right."

"Eagle eye Brett and Julie were the best combat firearms instructors we had."

"I agree 100%. Julie was a pioneer and an inspiration to the rest of us females."

"She was the original bad ass."

"Absolutely. Hey, have you heard any updates from Cody?"

"Yes. The FBI took custody of your guy, Firouz. They let Cody sit outside the interview room. Between what he gleamed from the last man standing and what the Bureau has got, I guess Firouz was a little worried. He faced going back to the Republic of Iran with total mission failure and humiliation. I'm sure being turned over to the Israelis or Saudi's, were not good options. His best alternative was going to a maximum-security prison in the U.S. He was not as hardened as his two co-conspirators. Apparently, he was brought onto the team because of his language proficiencies in Spanish and English."

"I guess Ali, here was the triggerman."

"Not anymore, thanks to you. While we are on the topic, be aware that many will exalt you as a hero and how you took this guy out. It's not lost on me the weight of taking a human life. Good guy or bad, your actions will weigh heavily upon you. Many of these knuckleheads will high five you. Make sure you follow through with a therapist."

"Thank you."

"Back to Cody. He reaffirmed everything that the two of you had uncovered about these guys coming from Iran to Paraguay and landing in Mexico to cross the river. One operator drowned in the river crossing. Apparently, the one that drowned was the boss and wouldn't listen to Ali and Firouz about the river current. Sounds like a boss. Right?"

"Yep."

"Firouz said the counterfeiting was to fund their operation and to stay under the view of law enforcement. The Russian was merely here to make introductions for him into the Cuban community for the distribution."

"Why did they kill the printer?"

"He said that was Ali's decision, and he didn't agree, but Ali was afraid Reza would compromise and disclose the operation. He accused the printer of stealing and spending some of the counterfeit money. Firouz was concerned he might be eliminated at the end as well. He said they had left a stash of some counterfeit and genuine money left over from the operation, and he thought about taking the money and making a run for it. Seemingly, he no longer looked at the U.S. as being a land of infidels but instead a land of prosperity."

"Why Tampa?"

"The Israeli attaché was the number one priority. For Cohen's father's attacks on Hezbollah and the Iranians. It's more challenging to target the father with the enhanced security in Israel, but his favorite son would be a much easier target in Tampa. They knew he was in an armored vehicle, so they needed to use an EFP to take him out. They set up in a rented garage near Ybor, where they kept the SUV that they drove from Texas. Also in the garage, they kept the Lumina and the van. It's where they assembled the bomb."

"They improvised and expanded their target list?"

"The hat-trick of the three goals would've been to take out the Albanian and Saudi Arabian, who were not on the Ramadan card list for Iran. Along with the Israeli, it was always the three targets. It would've garnered huge media attention worldwide. Imagine staging the attack outside the base that houses

Central Command operations against the Middle East and the embarrassment that it would bring to the United States."

"Well, it would've been a huge operation if they had pulled it off."

"But you stopped them. The bomb was removed from the van and placed it into a containment vessel. Lieutenant Morman felt, after a diagnostic assessment, that he was comfortable removing the device and blowing it elsewhere. Who knows how many people that could have potentially killed? Keep that in mind when you question what you could've done differently. Your actions speak for themselves. The bad guy chose his actions and forced you to react. You saved countless lives."

"I could sure use a glass of rum with Trent this evening, but I am afraid one glass could turn into four or five. I think I will substitute a big bowl of mint chocolate chip ice cream."

"Having found refuge once before in the bottom of the Jamison's bottle, I would strongly embrace the ice cream method. You're going to be okay."

"I know."

"Have you checked your fitness watch to see what your pulse was during this?"

"Let's see... 132."

"Well, within the optimal range, before you lose your shit in the 150s. You kept it together."

"Goes back to my training and my fitness. I wasn't terrified until after. My knees went to jello."

"All normal. You stopped evil today. Dave D'Agresta once said that using deadly force is the ultimate in de-escalation. A lot of truth to that statement. Let me tell Benny that I am going to take you back to the Blue Monster."

Chapter Eighty-Five

Like a slow-motion replay during a football game, Kate's mind replayed the shooting like it was a repeating Instagram reel. Unlike a football game with her winners and losers, Kate felt like they were only losers. A man had failed in his mission and was now laying dead in a field with bullets from her gun. She had hoped that despite the many times she pointed the barrel of a gun towards danger, she would never have to feel her finger pull the trigger, or feeling the recoil, while watching the impact of the bullets striking the assailant.

Like being in a car wreck, the mind plays the what if game? What if she left later that morning? What if she had taken a different route? What if she weren't so eager to speed up from the traffic light?

Kate's mind mulled over the what if decisions? If only she had disconnected from the case after briefing the FBI. If only she and Cody had stayed at the bomb scene and not gone to the Albanians residence. If only she had stayed in the car with McMahan and waited on backup. If only she had waited for McMahan to catch up before she approached the backyard.

The slow-motion reel began replaying once again. The knot grabbed her midsection as she also considered the possible legal ramifications. She knew the likelihood of being sued by the victim's family was virtually nonexistent. Kate understood the Monday morning quarterbacks would review every decision she made like a jeweler through a magnifying glass. Internal affairs would review whether she complied with the department's rules and regulations. The state attorney's office would investigate for consideration of any criminal charges. Last, the news media would spin their own narrative. Was she a trigger-happy gunslinger or a hero stopping a terrorist? That story had yet to be printed.

Frank touched her on the shoulder and said, "I know exactly what's going through your mind right now. It will take time for that slow-motion replay to stop. I know you are also thinking of how you could've avoided the encounter."

Her brown eyes met the eyes of her wise mentor. He knew. Frank had lived it himself. He had walked in her shoes. They had been partners in homicide and now they were partners in a club that no cop wanted to join. She thought for a moment and hoped that her actions this day had not caused Duffy to revisit his own demons and begin a downward spiral again.

"Frank, you are spot on."

"Sadly, I've been there. Twice." He paused and smiled at her. "You're probably terrified that you will land up like me and becoming a drunk that had to go through rehab."

"No, not really."

"My finding refuge in the bottle had more to do with a caretaker's daily struggles for my dying wife and Bridget's ultimate death. I processed both of my shootings fairly well with my decisions to pull the trigger. There was some survivor's guilt over Rollins being shot."

"I figured."

"They call us the thin blue line for a reason. We are the sheepdogs that protect society from evil and anarchy. That asshole terrorist planned to inflict carnage in our community and you stopped him. You know, if he got away, there is no telling how many more people would've been killed."

"I know."

"You gave him an opportunity to surrender, and he chose not to give up and forced you to stop him. That's what you were trying to do was stop him. The fact that you wounded him and he continued is evidence that the only way to stop him was to take him out. At the end of the day, you survived and you get to go home to Brittney, your mom, and the Professor. Don't forget that Louie's puppy's tail is going to be wagging for you when you walk through the door."

She turned and embraced Frank. She marveled at his therapeutic insight. "Thank you."

She took out her phone and thumbed through her contacts. She pushed the button and heard the voice from her past. "Hi Kate, to what do I owe the pleasure?"

"Melvin, I've been involved in a shooting and need legal representation."

"Kate, don't say anything to anyone until we have time to meet. I'll meet you at the police department."

"Thank you, Melvin."

"They are not your friends! Remember that. Don't say a thing. Not a word. Seal the lips."

She rolled her eyes. "Got it. I promise."

Frank said, "Good decision. Melvin Storms is the best defense attorney in town. Better to go with a shotgun than a flyswatter. The PBA would provide a freebie, but you can't beat having Melvin Storms at your side. Our attorney will be a specialist on use of force. You will have your own legal dream team."

"Hopefully, Melvin will give me a discount. Let's roll."

Chapter Eighty-Six

As Duffy drove Kate towards Bayshore Blvd., Kate pulled out her phone again and began scrolling through text messages and voicemails. Messages had already accumulated from concerned well-wishers within the law enforcement community. She knew everyone met well, but she couldn't deal with the influx and certainly did not feel like sharing her story with anyone. A person was dead because of her.

There was one voicemail that was an outlier and she read the partial transcription. She then played the voicemail and listened to an insurance investigator. "Hello Detective Alexander? This is Lucas White from One-Shot Insurance Company. We had received a death claim for Reza Jaber. Apparently, the victim of homicide. We want to establish if the claimant could be considered a suspect before we process payment. If you could call me back, I would appreciate it. Thank you."

She dialed the number provided by Lucas White and he answered on the second ring. After the cursory introduction, Kate asked who was the claimant, assuming it was Asa Jaber.

"Mr. White, was it the widow, Asa Jaber? In which case, I can tell you she is definitely not a suspect. We believe the primary suspect is dead." She could hear him shuffling papers.

"Let's see. I didn't have it in front of me. Ahh. Here it is. It was Marwan Ayoub."

"Ayoub?"

"Yes, Detective."

"What was the amount and when was the policy taken out?"

"It was for $500,000 and taken out exactly two months ago. Before we process this claim, I wanted to ask if any actions of Mr. Ayoub would be considered suspicious? If so, I can put it in the pending file and hold off processing the claim for two weeks. I can check back in two weeks to check on any developments."

"I would say not to pay that out. He is still under investigation for his involvement."

"Thank you, Detective. That is all I need to hear for the time being. We can keep this in review for that period and if there's any changes either charging him or eliminating him as a suspect, could you please call me?"

"You can count on it. Mr. White, thank you for checking."

She ended the call and turned to Duffy. "We need to divert. We need to make a quick stop up near Tampa Catholic High School."

"I'm all about coloring outside the lines, but the powers to be will have an aneurysm if I don't get you back."

"Just tell them we need to stop off for some feminine hygiene items. I can guarantee you they will not ask any follow-up questions."

Frank nodded in agreement and in appreciation for an original excuse that would buy them time.

Kate called the lead analyst, John Newman. She asked him to assemble the other analysts for a time sensitive assignment. She asked them to do a deep dive on the history of the assassin's Lumina and the LLC that initially purchased the car at the auto auction and transferred it to the Iranian. Kate also wanted to know the renter or owner of the garage that Firouz had said was where the bomb had been assembled. She also wanted to check on the ownership history for the transit van and analysis on Marwan Ayoub. She told Newman she was on a steep time line.

Newman asked, "I heard what happened. Are you okay?"

"Thanks for asking, John. I am."

"Okay, listen. We are on this. We will gang tackle this like a bunch of beavers chewing through trees. This team has your back, Kate."

"Thank you, John.

Duffy put the car in park around the corner from the residence of Marwan Ayoub, while they waited on the return call from the analysts. Kate continued to scroll through messages and emails. She read a response on the the request for subscriber information and call history for the one 813-area code that Demetri had called prior to counterfeit operation. The call history connected connected with burner phones that she suspected were the Iranian killers.

"How are you holding up, kiddo?" asked Frank

"Alright for now. This is a welcomed detour from my wondering mind space."

"Fleeting thoughts and images bouncing like ping-pong balls."

"You know it."

They discussed everything going on in Kate's life and her relationship with the Professor, as well as Brittney's school. Anything to keep her mind off what had just happened. Kate's phone rang, and she scribbled notes on a pad faster than a stenographer. She was finishing up the call. She motioned to Frank to proceed to Ayoub's house. John Newman and his crew of analysts had come through.

Chapter Eighty-Seven

Walking up to the front door, they saw through the door that Marwan Ayoub was on his phone. He saw them through the glass door and hung up the phone and waved them through. Kate introduced Duffy to Ayoub and said, "That wasn't Tehran you were talking to, was it?"

He scoffed. "Not likely." He played with his prayer beads.

"Really? I thought perhaps you are letting Tehran know their triple assassination plot unraveled like a cheap Persian rug and that all three targets are safe."

One of his eyebrows arched upward, and he had a quizzical, puzzled look. "I do not know what you're talking about."

With her hands on her hips, she smiled coyly. "I just talked to the insurance company about your half-a-million life insurance policy on Reza. Let's just say, I don't think you will see one Iranian rial or genuine U.S. dollar."

He put up a calming hand as he grabbed the oxygen mask. He took a few inhales. After a few coughs, he returned the mask to the cradle.

He continued. "When he was struggling to focus on the productivity of our business, I asked him to ensure the longevity of the business in case anything ever happened to him. I had threatened to call in the outstanding balance unless he provided some assurances. I was concerned when he said that he was working on a plan to free his son. Some characters in that game can be very dangerous and a double-cross is lurking. So, I wanted to make sure that my interests were covered, and of course I will ensure that his widow, Asa, will be well taken care of as well. Sadaqa, as it is known in our culture and in the Qur'an."

Kate listened and smiled, thinking that this man had an answer for everything. It was time to wind up and start throwing fastballs. "I just learned that you were registered as part of Paradise469 LLC. I found the 4:69 passage in the Qur'an." She read from her cellphone. "Whoever obeys God and the messenger–those will be the ones upon God has given favor–of the prophets, the steadfast affirmers of truth, the martyrs and the righteous. And excellent are those companions."

"I know the passage very well. This other nonsense I know nothing of it. I don't know what you are talking about."

"That same LLC rented a garage and paid for the utilities. That same garage was where the assassins stored a Chevrolet Equinox with Texas plates, a transit van where a bomb was assembled and placed inside the van."

"Yes, I was renting it from a friend at a reduced rate and then I was subleasing it for more money to a couple of fellas from Paraguay. They were looking to do auto repairs. If they were doing something illegal, I would have no idea."

"Your LLC was also used to purchase the killer's Equinox, the Lumina and the Transit van from the auto auction in Brandon. Then you sold all three to Alejandro Duarte, the murderer of your friend Reza. Duarte, also known as Ali, is now lying dead in a field. The Secret Service could identify that the paper used in the counterfeiting was the same paper used for Iraqi currency. We know there was a box that cleared customs from the port of New York that was shipped from Turkey to you at this address. On the shipping manifest, it was described as Turkish cigarette rolling paper. So, you were a facilitator in this entire operation. You arranged the paper for the counterfeiting operation. Marwan, you arranged for the suspect's vehicle and rented the garage space that was used as a bomb factory. We are going to check with your neighbor's door cams and security cameras, which will have recorded the meetings between you and your Paraguayan assassins and Demetri, the Russian as well. We're also going to connect you with phone communications as well to the hit team. I already have proof that you spoke with Demetri by phone."

"I am an old man and not in good health. I have many medical bills."

"The FBI will be here soon. Make sure your oxygen tank is filled because, for as long as you are still alive, you will live in a federal penitentiary with no medical bills."

"They can't do this."

"Yes, they can, and they will. The Israelis will demand your incarceration for targeting their attaché. As a result, the U.S. State Department will put pressure on the Department of Justice to prosecute you. If you are lucky in the judicial tug of war, they will reserve a jail cell in the federal medical center in Rochester, Minnesota. Hopefully, you have a nice window view of the frozen tundra and snowdrifts during the winter. It might even bring back warm memories of your youth in Tehran looking at the snowcapped Alborz Mountains."

"I want an attorney."

"Of course, you do. America! What a great country. We will even pay for an attorney. If you had been arrested in Iran, you would already be against the wall in front of the firing squad or hanging from a crane on public display."

He glared. Another coughing fit besieged Ayoub as he reached for his oxygen. Kate gave a goodbye wave like she was on a Gasparilla parade float.

Once outside, Duffy said, "Well done, you. Kick Ass Alexander rides again!"

She nodded and said, "I'll call the FBI. First, I want to call Asa Jaber."

"Hello, Asa, this is Detective Alexander."

"Yes, detective?"

"I wanted to let you know that we have identified you husband's killers. One is dead, one is in custody, and one is soon to be arrested."

"Thank you. I heard from my son. He was released from the jail in Iran and is in Lebanon. I hope to see him soon."

"That is so nice. I am thrilled for you. There is no greater joy than being with your children. I am sorry at the terrible loss of your husband. That is a void that can never be filled."

She ended the call and said to Frank, "One more stop."

"Now, I am worried that you are ignoring or going into denial about what happened."

"Nope. I want to swing by Publix and pickup a pub-sub and dog treats for homeless Pete and Sarge. Brighten their day a bit. Then we can go to the Blue Monster."

"As you command."

The phone rang again. It was Cody, and he asked, "I needed to hear your voice, partner. Are you okay?"

"A little rattled. Yes, I'm good. I'll see you at the Blue Monster."

The end.

Thank you for taking the time to read this book. If you liked this book, I would be extremely grateful if you would be kind enough to leave a brief review on Amazon. This will help to enlighten other readers and spread the word. My Amazon Author page is: https://www.amazon.com/Mike-Roche/e/B00BHEIF78?ref=sr_ntt_srch_lnk_1&qid=1661706928&sr=8-1 I am humbled that you spent your time with Kate and Cody and my fictional tale. Please stop by https://mikeroche.com/and join my email list for a free Kate Alexander short story and upcoming news.

Thank you!

Cheers, Mike

Also By Mike Roche

Fiction:
The Blue Monster
Coins of Death
Backstabbers
Karma! (Young Adult Fiction)

Non Fiction:
Mass Killer: How You can Identify Workplace, School or Public Killers Before They Strike 2nd edition
Face 2 Face: Interviewing and Rapport Building Skills: an Ex-Secret Service Agent's Guide

About the Author

As a teenager inspired by books and television, Mike was attracted to the nobility of the law enforcement profession. Drawing on his experience, he shares the insights of the job and the courageous personalities that hunt evil. Homicide detectives give a voice to the victims and their families. While working as both a local cop and a federal agent, Mike Roche has spent four decades chasing bad guys and conducting behavioral threat assessments of stalkers and assassins. A frequent guest at writers conferences, homicide conferences and podcasts, he was also an adjunct college instructor and law enforcement trainer. Mike enjoys the serenity of his retirement home in Florida, while watching the sunsets and sunrises surrounded by nature.

Printed in Dunstable, United Kingdom